Praise for THE NIKKI BOYD FILES

"A thrill ride from start to finish, the first book in Harris's NIKKI BOYD FILES series is filled with twists and surprises."

—*RT Book Reviews*, Top Pick on *Vendetta*

"The story is fueled with misleading dangers, and the character is so fascinating that fans will be waiting impatiently to see what adventure Nikki Boyd will have next."

—*Suspense Magazine* on *Vendetta*

"Harris draws her readers into the fear and excitement generated by a mission to catch a madman."

—*Booklist* on *Vendetta*

"Lisa Harris has quickly become one of my favorite romantic suspense writers, and she has penned another winner in *Missing*."

—*Radiant Lit blog* on *Missing*

"With *Missing*, Ms. Harris has given us a thriller that becomes more and more exciting and nerve-wracking until you flip the last page and let out a contented sigh of relief."

—*The Suspense Zone* on *Missing*

"Intense. Nail-biting. A real page-turner that is sure to enthrall the discerning romantic suspense aficionado."

—*Fiction Addiction Fix* on *Missing*

"As with everything that Harris writes, this novel is wonderfully plotted and fast-paced, with unexpected twists and turns to keep the reader engaged in the story."

—*RT Book Reviews* on *Pursued*

"Lisa Harris is getting better with each book, and this is probably the best one she has written."

—*Write-Read-Life blog* on *Pursued*

VANISHING POINT

Books by Lisa Harris

SOUTHERN CRIMES

Dangerous Passage
Fatal Exchange
Hidden Agenda

NIKKI BOYD FILES

Vendetta
Missing
Pursued

A NIKKI BOYD NOVEL

Vanishing Point

VANISHING POINT

LISA HARRIS

A NIKKI BOYD NOVEL

Revell

a division of Baker Publishing Group
Grand Rapids, Michigan

Published by Revell
a division of Baker Publishing Group
PO Box 6287, Grand Rapids, MI 49516-6287
www.revellbooks.com

Printed in the United States of America

Library of Congress Cataloging-in-Publication Data
Names: Harris, Lisa, 1969– author.
Title: Vanishing point : a Nikki Boyd novel / Lisa Harris.
Description: Grand Rapids, MI : Revell, a division of Baker Publishing Group,
    [2017] | Series: The Nikki Boyd files
Identifiers: LCCN 2017029618 | ISBN 9780800728489 (softcover)
Subjects: LCSH: Women detectives—Fiction. | Government investigators—Fiction.
    | Serial murder investigation—Fiction. | GSAFD: Christian fiction. | Mystery
    fiction. | Suspense fiction.
Classification: LCC PS3608.A78315 V36 2017 | DDC 813/.6—dc23
LC record available at https://lccn.loc.gov/2017029618

Scripture quotations are from the *Holy Bible*, New Living Translation, copyright © 1996, 2004, 2007 by Tyndale House Foundation. Used by permission of Tyndale House Publishers, Inc., Carol Stream, Illinois 60188. All rights reserved.

Published in association with Joyce Hart of Hartline Literary Agency, LLC.

17 18 19 20 21 22 23   7 6 5 4 3 2 1

To those who have loved and lost.
May you find peace in Him.

Prologue

She could read the satisfaction in her abductor's face. A chilling sense of pleasure that reached from his upturned lips to his piercing gaze, as if he were enjoying contemplating her fate. Even with that knowledge, she was surprised at how calm she was as he motioned her out of the vehicle and onto the soft ground still wet from last night's rain. It was a deep-seated numbness, like when she woke up in the morning, hovering between dreams and reality, and she wasn't sure where she was. Or the feeling when she watched a scary movie and had to keep reminding herself that none of it was real. And no one had really died.

But in real life people died.

And this was no dream.

She looked past the dark figure, who was dressed completely in black, toward the thick, green wooded area located somewhere outside of Nashville. He'd threatened to shoot her if she ran or caused any problems, but for the moment he was busy pulling something out of the car. Was it better to count on the odds that he might miss if he tried to shoot her? Should she try to escape anyway?

She decided to run.

Drawing in a lungful of air, she dashed behind the car and took off into the woods surrounding them. The lingering sunlight was going to disappear soon. And the coming darkness terrified her almost as much as the person who had snatched her. She kept her focus on the ground. There was no path. Only layers of thick underbrush. She stumbled over a rotting log, barely catching her balance on the uneven terrain. He shouted behind her, but she only ran faster. If she could find a road, she might be able to catch a ride leading back to town.

Please, God . . . please help me . . .

She could hear him, crashing through the trees behind her as she tried to maneuver the thick underbrush. Maybe it was simply the terror of the situation beginning to seep through her, but she couldn't get enough air in her lungs. A splash of water from one of the branches above her hit the end of her nose and ran down her chin. She shivered. It was so cold. He'd taken her coat and the gray scarf and beanie she wore weren't enough to keep her warm. She sucked in some air, worried her legs were going to collapse beneath her, both from physical exertion and the mounting fear. To her right there was an opening in the trees. She had run cross-country earlier in the school year. With open ground she might be able to outrun her abductor.

A bullet slammed into a tree beside her. A flock of birds scurried from their perch near the top, the frenzied flapping of wings sending her into a panic. She froze, heart pounding in her chest, unable to stop the escalating fear. She couldn't breathe. Couldn't think, except about how she didn't want to die. Not this way.

"That was a warning," he shouted. "Next time I won't miss."

She started to run again, but it was too late. He grabbed her arm. A sharp pain shot through her elbow. She had no choice now. No one would hear her if she screamed. And more than likely, no one would find her body if he killed her. She walked beside him back through the darkening forest and caught sight of the butt of the gun as he pressed the barrel against the side of her head. He was right. This time he wouldn't miss.

I tried . . .

The last bits of sunlight faded around them as he shoved her shoulder against the bark.

"Stand against the tree. We're running out of time."

Tears welled in her eyes. She didn't know why he was in such a hurry. What did it matter? No one was here to save her. No one was going to stop this monster in front of her.

Her eyes focused on the old Polaroid camera like the one her grandfather had owned where the picture came out.

"Smile."

The machine whirred. She couldn't smile. Instead, she felt the seconds tick by, then a photo slid out of the camera. She knew the picture had caught the terror in her eyes. Any numbness had now completely worn off.

She shifted her gaze from the photo and saw something she hadn't noticed before. A dozen yards in front of her lay a freshly dug grave.

2004

1

January 23
6:17 a.m.
Sumner County, Tennessee

Special Agent Garrett Addison snapped a photo of the freshly dug grave located inside the yellow roped-off crime scene. He would have preferred to avoid looking at the magnified details of the body half buried in the patch of soft earth, but his camera lens wouldn't let him. Instead, it only emphasized the state of the young woman.

She lay in the ground where a couple of hikers had discovered her, posed with her hands on her chest as if she were sleeping. If not for the bullet hole and a single trail of dried blood running across her forehead, he could almost imagine she was simply sleeping. Sixteen, maybe seventeen years old, with long blonde hair pulled back in a ponytail. She wore minimal makeup and there was a smudge of dirt on her left cheek next to a row of freckles. Her faded jeans were ripped at the knee, and the thin black T-shirt she wore wouldn't have been warm enough for the six inches of snow forecast to fall in the next twelve hours.

If she were still alive.

Five years on the force might have made responding to 911 calls routine to him, but even experience couldn't completely prepare him for days like this.

What kind of person does this to another human being, God?

He drew in a deep breath as he snapped another photo. If it had been in the middle of a hot summer, the body would have already started to smell. Instead the cold January weather had prolonged the decaying process. He shook his head, wishing he could shake away the eerie feeling that always came with cases like this. A young life brutally cut short.

He glanced toward the other end of the blocked-off crime scene at the couple who'd called in the discovery. They'd been out hiking the wooded trails when they stumbled across the girl. The woman was crying again, her shoulders shaking, while the man had his arms around her, trying to comfort her. Images like the one they'd just stumbled across didn't simply fade away. They lingered in the back of your mind, resurfacing when you least expected it. He knew that from firsthand experience. Things like this should never happen.

Some first week on the new job working homicide.

He pushed back the growing sense of unease and went back to snapping photos. As a criminal investigator now, he expected to deal with the underbelly of society. That he could handle. It was the innocent loss of life that churned his gut. The heavy consequences of crime had just forever marked this young woman's family. But he couldn't make this scene personal. His only hope was that he'd be able to bring justice to victims like the one lying in front of him. But how could there be justice when it was too late and the scent of death already filled the air? She'd been so young . . . so vulnerable. Someone's daughter. Someone's sister.

Holding back the bile in his throat from the images in his view-finder, he shifted his position and took another shot.

"Hope you didn't have any plans for tonight."

Garrett looked up at Special Agent Sam Bradford, his new boss for the past forty-eight hours. The man was somewhere in his late fifties, balding on top and graying around the edges, but he was still as fit as someone half his age.

"Nothing important," he said, reminding himself he was no longer a seasoned cop on the street but the newbie on Bradford's team.

"Good. Because we need to wrap this case up as soon as we can. The public gets nervous when they find out a young girl's been murdered." Bradford knelt down next to the body, then rubbed the back of his head. "Make sure you get close-ups of her hands and face as well as multiple shots of the perimeter when you're done here. And be careful not to disturb any of the evidence while you're at it."

Garrett started to say something, then decided not to mention that while he might be new on the Tennessee Bureau of Investigation's payroll, he wasn't exactly lacking crime scene experience. "Will do, boss."

A second man, at least a decade younger than Bradford, stepped up beside him. At six foot two, Garrett was used to towering over people, but the ebony-skinned agent had at least an inch or two on him, as well as ten-plus pounds.

"Garrett Addison, I'm guessing," the man said, holding out his hand.

Garrett nodded. "And you must be Special Agent Michaels."

"Welcome to homicide. I've heard a lot about you. You made your way up the ranks pretty fast."

"Not before putting in my time on the streets," Garrett said, brushing off the familiar implications that friends in high places had gotten him his promotion.

One of the patrol officers who'd been first on the scene hollered something at Michaels.

"Excuse me a sec."

Garrett took another step back from the body as Michaels walked off, then flipped back through the photos he'd just taken, ensuring he photographed every angle. They might have the rookie do the grunt work, but he wasn't going to give them any reason to perpetuate the rumor he was here because of his grandfather.

"I met Senator Addison back in '92 when he was running for office," Bradford said. "Heard he went back into law after retiring."

"Yes, he's at the family firm now. Addison, Addison & Green."

"I've heard of it. And I'm guessing you were supposed to be the third Addison?"

Garrett started on the terrain surrounding the body, wishing he could avoid the topic. "Yes."

"So how does an up-and-coming lawyer with a prestigious firm decide to become a criminal investigator with TBI?" Bradford asked.

"I got fed up defending the bad guys."

The older man nodded. "As far as I'm concerned, I'm glad you're on board, no matter who your grandfather is. We could use some new blood around here. Some fresh ideas and perspective. In the meantime, what about an ID? Anything on her before the ME gets here?"

"Nothing's been found so far."

"Keep photographing the scene. Hopefully something will turn up."

Five minutes later, Garrett was still making his way systematically through the crime scene. He took another photo, then paused to check the view screen. Something partially buried beneath a clump of dirt caught his eye. He knelt down in front of the object. It was a Polaroid photo of their victim.

He called out to his boss, who was still studying the body. "I've got something you're going to want to see. It's a photo."

Garrett studied the picture. The girl's expression was haunting. As if she knew exactly what was going to happen to her. His gut clenched. She'd looked her abductor in the eye, and he'd killed her.

Bradford crouched down beside him, picked up the photo with his gloved hands, then brushed off a layer of dirt, his face paling with the action.

"What's wrong?" Garrett asked.

"I worked a case about eighteen months ago, before I transferred to this department's homicide division. A sixteen-year-old girl named Jessica Wright went missing. Her body was found five days later in an unmarked grave about ninety miles from Nashville."

"Did you ever find her killer?"

"No, but a Polaroid photo of the victim was found. Nine months later a second girl, Becky Collier, vanished under similar circumstances. She was supposed to have spent the afternoon at the library. Her body hasn't turned up, but authorities found a photo of her, near where she was taken. A Polaroid."

The sense of unease returned. Garrett snapped a photo of the Polaroid. She'd been terrified. He could see it in her eyes as he tried not to imagine what she'd been thinking at that moment. "I remember hearing about both cases, but I don't remember hearing anything about the Polaroid photos."

"That information was intentionally left out of our reports to the media."

"Any witnesses or a description of the abductor?" Garrett asked.

"We've got a police sketch from a witness in the first case who saw Jessica arguing with someone after school. We never could identify the man and the artist's sketch is pretty generic. Could be anyone. And on top of that, no matchable DNA was found at the crime scene, which means that even after all this time, we still have no idea who the perpetrator is."

"What about trying to track down the buyer of the camera?" Garrett asked. "Polaroids aren't used that much anymore."

"You'd think a vintage camera would be easy to track, but it turns out there are dozens of sellers on eBay alone. We never could narrow it down." Bradford ran his fingers through his thinning hair. "What about the couple who found this body? Did they see anything that might help?"

"Not as far as I know. One of the first officers on the scene took their statements. Apparently they were here watching for eagles."

Bradford frowned. "Eagles?"

"While winter isn't the best time to be out camping and hiking, apparently it's the best time for eagle sightings."

"So they didn't see anyone hanging around this morning?"

"No, but the area's slow this time of year. They said even the parking lot was empty."

Bradford shook his head. "And it's possible she's been here for days."

Garrett turned around as the medical examiner slipped under the yellow tape and headed toward the body with his equipment.

"Sam Bradford." The ME stopped next to them. "I thought I heard you were heading out of town to celebrate your anniversary."

"I was."

"Irene's going to kill you for this. We can handle it, you know."

"And miss breaking in a newbie?" Bradford glanced at Garrett. "This is Special Agent Garrett Addison, by the way. And as for Irene? She's been putting up with me for thirty years. This won't change anything."

"JB Philips," the examiner said, giving Garrett a nod. "Why don't you show me what you've got?"

"You're not going to like this, Philips," Bradford said as the ME crouched beside the victim.

"Another young girl losing her life far too early?"

"It's more than that. Do you remember the Wright case back in '02? A sixteen-year-old was abducted while walking home. Five days later, a couple kids were playing and found her body in a shallow grave."

"Sounds vaguely familiar."

"I was the lead investigator on the case. And here's the clincher. Not only is this body posed exactly the same way—like she's sleeping—but there's also the detail of the Polaroid photo found near her body. We never gave that information to the public. We later found a second Polaroid near the abduction point of another girl who's never been found, Becky Collier." Bradford jutted his chin toward Garrett. "He just found a Polaroid taken of this girl before she was murdered."

Philips straightened up. "I remember those cases. Someone from the local media started calling him the Angel Abductor, proposing we might be dealing with a serial killer, but besides the Polaroid, we didn't have any evidence that tied the cases together."

"Why the Angel Abductor?" Garrett asked.

"Because both girls had long blonde hair." Philips took a step back and frowned. "Like this girl. Do you know what this means, Sam?"

"It means that reporter was on to something. We've now got three girls either murdered or missing in the past eighteen months. All with a similar MO."

"What about suspects?" Philips asked. "Anything pointing toward whoever's behind this?"

"No solid evidence," Bradford said. "Nothing beyond the rough sketch a witness gave us after Jessica Wright went missing. We put out an APB around the time of her murder, hoping to get a hit on our killer's ID, but nothing has ever come of it."

Philips shook his head and started his examination. "Whoever did this to her can't be that good. He had to have left some kind of evidence behind. Who handled the Wright girl's autopsy?"

"Craig Brower from the Nashville ME's office. He was never able to find anything solid pointing to her killer either. Tox screens all came back inconclusive, no fingerprints, no DNA matches . . ."

Philips shoved his thick glasses up the bridge of his nose. "When I'm done here, I'll look over the files. See if something jumps out at me that might have been overlooked."

"I'd appreciate it," Bradford said. "If we'd already caught the psychopath who did this, this girl would still be alive."

"What do you know about her?" Philips asked.

Bradford looked to Garrett for an answer.

"So far there's been no trace of any personal effects, which means we don't even have an ID. We're still waiting to see if we can get a match with Missing Persons."

"I need a time frame of her death," Bradford said.

"I'll know more after the autopsy, but I'd say she's already been here a couple days."

"What else can you tell me?"

Philips frowned. "On the surface, there are no defensive wounds on her hands, no scratches, or indications that her hands were bound. But there's a bruise here on her arm, and another one on her shoulder."

"Implying what?" Garrett said. "He forced her to walk here?"

"I can't answer that yet."

"Then just give us the bottom line at this point," Bradford said. "Should we be looking for another primary crime scene, or is this it?"

Garrett knew what Bradford was looking for. They needed to narrow the focus of the investigation. Which meant they needed to know if she'd been murdered somewhere else and then brought here, or if this was the actual scene of the crime. But until a proper autopsy was done, anything Philips gave them was primarily speculation.

"My best guess is that she was brought here by her assailant, alive." Philips tugged at his collar, then looked up at Bradford. "But like I said, I'll let you know as soon as I finish with my autopsy."

Bradford took a step away from the body. "And I think it's time we put in a call to the FBI."

"Do you really want to get them involved?" Philips asked.

"We're already going to have to explain to the media that we've got a third victim," Bradford countered. "Which is going to cause a panic and blow up in our faces if we're not careful. We need to find this guy."

Garrett felt a shiver brush over him as reality sunk in. "Because we've got a serial killer on our hands."

2

Jordan Lambert felt the burn in her arms as she took another lap in the heated pool and widened her stroke. Classical music from her waterproof MP3 device played in her ears in an attempt to temporarily numb her mind. She pushed through the fatigue, eased up to the wall, then turned around in one seamless motion. Normally the water relaxed her. But not today. Today, her mind wouldn't stop running.

You need to come home, Jordan. Mom and Dad miss you, and I'm worried about Mom.

Jordan filled her lungs with a breathful of air, then skimmed the top of the water, letting her body glide. The email from her sister couldn't have come at a worse time. She went home as often as she could, but she'd missed Christmas last month. And now Clara's email only managed to deepen the guilt and remind her of all the holidays and birthdays she'd missed over the past few years.

She turned around and started another lap. She'd never intended on putting her career above family, but it wasn't as if she really had a choice. She hadn't exactly taken on a nine-to-five job. When she'd chosen to join the FBI, she knew the commitment it was going to take. Which was why when she left Nashville, she was thankful that she was able to leave with her family's blessing.

And because of that, she never looked back. But that didn't mean that now—all these years later—there weren't days when she wondered what it would be like if she'd chosen family over a career. Accepting a marriage proposal over a stint with the FBI, and having two or three grandchildren for her parents instead of spending the majority of her time behind a desk analyzing bad guys.

She pulled herself up against the side of the pool to catch her breath. Christmas with family wasn't the only thing she'd missed. Pushing thirty meant her biological clock was ticking. Not that it was too late. Not yet. But she hated the guilt that came with her busy schedule, even though she loved her work. She loved the research and the chance to bring a fresh perspective to investigations.

She felt a tap on her shoulder, pulled out one of her earbuds, and looked up at her partner hovering over her.

"Ryley?"

"Hey . . . thought I might find you here."

She frowned at the intrusion as she took off her goggles. "The question is, what are you doing here on my day off?"

The only reason she could think of was that a crisis had come up at work.

Ryley squatted on the edge of the pool. "You told me you've been itching to go back to Nashville to see your family."

"So . . ." She bobbed at the edge of the heated pool, breathing in the chlorine and humid air.

"I pulled a few strings, and you've got your wish."

She raised her eyebrow. "What do you mean?"

"I just got a call from the higher-ups. They were going to send just me, but I convinced them to let you go with me. Which gives you about forty-five minutes to dry off, pack your carry-on, and get to the airport so we can make the next flight to Nashville."

"Seriously?"

"Trust me, I wouldn't be here if I wasn't serious."

Jordan glanced at the clock on the wall. Nothing like a bit of heads-up from the FBI. But cases didn't conveniently happen on her schedule. And Ryley was right about one thing. A trip to Nashville meant a chance to see her sister and her parents and maybe find a way to make up for taking so long between visits.

"Grab my towel over there, will you?" She pulled herself out of the water, then wrapped the yellow towel around her. "What's the case?"

"Local authorities just found the body of a teenage girl in Sumner County, an hour or so out of Nashville. Looks like it's a serial killer, and they've asked for some immediate ground support."

She grabbed her bag off the bench, then slipped on her flip-flops. While her job mostly consisted of time spent at a desk doing research, going over case materials, and consulting on both active and cold cases with local law enforcement via telephone conferences, the chance to be on the field always excited her. And getting to see family was the extra bonus she needed.

"They're sending the case file to us now so we can read it over on the plane," Ryley said.

"What's our time frame?"

"Two, three days tops. Just enough time to go over the scene ourselves, review the crime scene photos and reports, and come up with an assessment for them to go forward with. And for you to see your family."

———

At half past three, Jordan stood in the middle of the crime scene in Sumner County, six hundred miles from Quantico, Virginia. They'd driven straight to the scene from the airport in order to grab as many hours of daylight as possible, but so far the past hour of their own investigation of the scene hadn't uncovered anything new. The crime scene itself mirrored the photos they'd received before catching their flight, except for the now-empty grave sitting on the edge of the cordoned-off space.

"Agent Lambert . . . Agent James?"

Jordan turned around at the sound of her name, then immediately felt her stomach drop. She didn't recognize the older agent who was speaking or the taller man with broad shoulders, but there was no mistaking the dark-haired man standing between them.

Garrett Addison.

"Sorry we weren't here when you arrived, but it looks as if you've already jumped into your investigation." The older man waved his hand in apology as he continued. "Our meeting with local law enforcement took longer than I expected, but now that we're here, I'd like to introduce you to our team."

Jordan nodded, but no introduction was needed when it came to Garrett.

"I'm Special Agent Sam Bradford, and these are agents Abram Michaels and Garrett Addison." Agent Bradford nodded at his team. "Special Agents Jordan Lambert and Ryley James will be working the case with us and offering FBI support and resources."

Jordan shook Bradford and Michaels's hands first, then turned to Garrett and tried to force back the unexpected wave of emotion. "Special Agent Addison." She flashed him a smile. "The title sounds good on you. I had no idea you were working this particular case."

Was he just as taken aback as she was, or was it only her imagination?

"It's good to see you," he said. "It's been a long time."

Ryley glanced from Garrett to her, then back to Garrett again. "Wait a minute . . . you two know each other?"

"We were friends at the police academy," Garrett said. "Until eventually she was noticed by someone at the FBI, and she left for Quantico."

He'd supported her decision, even though they both knew their relationship wasn't going to last if she left. Not with their demanding jobs, and the hundreds of miles separating them.

And they'd been right.

There had been emails and phone calls at first, but then their communication eventually began to taper off. And the sad thing was she'd been too busy to notice, until one day she realized she couldn't remember the last time she'd heard from him.

"Nice to meet you." Garrett shook Ryley's hand, and she wondered if she caught a flash of jealousy in Garrett's eyes, or if that, too, had simply been her imagination.

Jordan shook off the feelings. Things had changed from the last time she'd seen Garrett. She was no longer a rookie FBI agent. And Garrett wasn't the man she'd once fallen in love with.

Which was why it was best to get straight to business.

"Before we jump in," she said quickly, "we want to make one thing clear. This is still your case. We're here to assist and give advice. We've dealt with hundreds of cases and interviews, including those connected with serial killers, but you're the ones who are going to solve this."

Garrett caught her gaze as she spoke. She reached up to shove a wayward curl behind her ear, then pulled her hand back down. It was an automatic response she had when she was nervous. Which didn't happen often. Both the academy and the FBI had erased most of her apprehensions and instilled inside her a greater confidence. Still, Garrett had always managed to break through her defenses. But that had been in the past. She was a different person today, and not in love with him. Not anymore.

"We appreciate that," Agent Bradford said. "Have you found anything in your initial investigation?"

"Not yet," Jordan said. "I'd like to see any additional photos you have of the victim, as well as of the Wright girl."

"We should have most of what you need in our van, though we're still waiting on Becky Collier's file," Garrett said.

"Go ahead and get what you need while I poke around here some more," Ryley said.

Jordan nodded, then followed Garrett on the path toward the

van, reminding herself that this was a crime scene, not a place to relive the past. Even if he still looked just as good as he had the last time she'd seen him, with his military-style haircut, dark dreamy eyes, and that hint of five-o'clock shadow along his jawline.

"How many years has it been?" she asked, pulling her long winter coat tighter around her to block the chill. "Five . . . maybe six?"

"If I remember correctly, the last time we saw each other was the night before you left for Quantico."

A narrow branch snapped beneath her boot. She really hadn't forgotten. How could she? He'd come to her apartment, filled with boxes for the move, to ask her to stay. She'd been excited about the FBI's offer, because somewhere in the back of her mind she thought maybe she could find a way to have both the career she wanted as well as the man she was falling in love with. Instead, he'd kissed her goodbye and walked out of her apartment without looking back.

"Any regrets?" he asked, breaking into her thoughts.

"Regrets of joining the FBI? No. But what about you? Any regrets of choosing to leave your father's law firm after all this time?"

"None at all."

Her only regret had been losing him—at least it had been at one time—but she wasn't about to show that card. They'd dated off and on for over a year. She even expected him to eventually ask her to marry him. She liked the idea of coming home to someone who understood her work, and they seemed perfect together. Or so she'd thought. Apparently her decision to pursue a career with the FBI had canceled any plans he'd been entertaining to take their relationship to the next level.

She took another look at his rugged profile. If she were honest with herself, no one had ever reached as deep into her heart as he had. Not that it mattered anymore. She'd promised herself no regrets if she moved to Virginia with the FBI.

No regrets over Garrett. Or the life she'd left behind in Nashville. And she hadn't had either. Most of the time anyway.

"For now, why don't you just give me the photos you have on this crime scene, as well as any crime scene photos you have of Jessica Wright," she said as they approached the van. "We can get the rest of the files before we leave tonight."

"I figured you'd asked for them, so I made sure we had copies."

Jordan nodded. She was back to sounding all business. She could hear it in her own voice. Setting the tone from the beginning was exactly what needed to be done. This wasn't personal. Anything that had been between her and Garrett in the past was long since over.

"Anything else?" he asked.

"No. Thanks."

"Then if you're okay for now, I'm going to see if I can track down Becky Collier's files."

She started back to the crime scene, hating that she suddenly felt like she was back in the academy.

"Jordan?"

She stopped midstride and turned back to him. "Yeah?"

"It's really good to see you."

A loose piece of hair brushed across her cheek. This time she didn't try to stop herself from shoving the wayward curl behind her ear. "It's good to see you too."

She felt a blush rise to her cheeks as she headed back to the yellow tape flapping in the wind.

"So what just happened back there?" Ryley asked, stepping up beside her.

"What do you mean?"

"What do I mean? Seriously? I've known you long enough to be able to read you. The two of you have a history."

Jordan felt her jaw tense. "Like I said, we went to the academy together."

"That's not what I'm talking about and you know it."

"Does it matter?"

"It might to Trey."

She blew out a puff of cold air and watched her breath fog up in front of her. "Trey has nothing to do with this."

Because he didn't, not really. She'd been surprised at how good it was to see Garrett again, but beyond that . . . There would never be anything beyond that. And as for her and Trey, just because they'd gone out on three or four dates didn't mean things were serious between them.

"Are you sure?"

"Ryley, it's nothing. Like I said, it was a long time ago. We went out a few times."

"Okay, but there's still something simmering between the two of you. I can feel it."

"Fine. It was more than a few times. We met at the police academy way back before I ever thought about joining the FBI, and yes, things got pretty serious. I actually thought I might marry him."

"Did he ask?"

She let out a sharp huff of air. "Does it matter?"

"From the look on your face it does—or at least it did."

"I ended up leaving and joining the FBI. We didn't really stay in touch after that."

"Career over commitment. I can see nothing's changed."

Jordan frowned. "So I'm . . . focused."

"That's not the word I was thinking of, but that's okay as long as you're good with how things turned out. And as long as it's not awkward between the two of you while we're working together."

"Why should it be? We're both professionals, and whatever happened between us doesn't play into our current case."

He shot her a grin, clearly unconvinced. "Fine. If you say so."

She tried to focus on the photos of the dead girl's body. Ryley was right about one thing. Her career had always managed to come before commitment to a relationship. That was why she'd left Nashville for the FBI. She could have been a detective by now at some local precinct, but she'd wanted more. And she'd given up a lot to get there.

She loved her own family and respected what her parents had in their own marriage, but she hadn't wanted their life. Their mom-and-pop store had somehow managed to survive the big chain stores coming in over the past decade. But how much longer were they going to be able to compete? They worked long hours and in the end made barely enough money to save for retirement.

She'd always wanted more for herself, even if it had come at a cost. And at this point in her life, she wasn't sure she could even see herself with a family.

But none of that mattered. She'd spend the next couple of days working this case here in Tennessee, and then she'd be gone.

3

4:31 p.m.
Sumner County, Tennessee

Another hour of meticulous combing through the crime scene had turned up little further evidence. They'd systematically widened their search, slowly moving from one section to the next of the grid they'd laid out as they fanned outward from the crime scene. Every item recovered had been carefully packaged and labeled to prevent any damage in its transport from the scene to the lab. But beyond a few pieces of trash and a dozen or so footprints that at this point could belong to anyone, they'd yet to find any concrete evidence that could point to their killer.

Garrett studied the horizon, keenly aware of the fading daylight. An outdoor crime scene was always vulnerable to changes in physical evidence, due to both contamination and environmental conditions. And now with the sun setting in thirty minutes, it was going to be easy to miss or even destroy evidence if they weren't extremely careful.

He kept walking, focused on the terrain in front of him. There was still no word on the results of the autopsy, but that was to be expected. Both the ME's conclusions and the lab results were going to take time. But somewhere out here there had to be a piece of evidence that would lead them to the killer. Because no one committed the perfect crime. And finding whoever did this was the only way of guaranteeing it didn't happen again.

A dozen yards away from where he worked, Jordan was holding a conversation with Sam. He'd forced himself to stay focused since her unexpected arrival, but her presence continued to pull him back to the past, a place he'd rather not go. He'd asked her if she had any regrets, but his question hadn't referred to her joining the FBI. Instead, the meaning behind the question had been far more personal. Had she regretted leaving him and their relationship behind?

He might never hear the answer from her, but if he were honest with himself, he had his own regrets. Not of leaving his father's law firm. He'd never looked back on that decision. But he did wonder what life would have been like if she'd never been recruited by the FBI. If they'd ended up getting married and starting a family.

But all the what-ifs in the world didn't matter at this point. She'd left, closing the door to any further relationship between them. And it wasn't as if he blamed her either. How could he? If he'd been handed the same opportunity she had, he would have jumped at the chance. But instead, he'd been the one who watched her walk away. Maybe he let her go because he thought they'd figure out a way to make their relationship work, but as the weeks and months passed, it became clear—at least to him—that any chance for a relationship between them was over.

And he'd been right.

He'd moved on and so had she. Which was why seeing her again shouldn't matter. She seemed content. Focused on her own work, which was what he wanted for her. His heart had gotten over her leaving. He had his job and his friends, his new position at TBI . . .

He glanced back at the yellow crime-scene barrier, shoving the past aside in the process. The ME had driven away hours ago with the body neatly zipped up in a black bag in the back of his van. All that remained now was a half-dug grave and a dozen law enforcement officers still looking for answers. Someone was in the process of setting up large floodlights around the crime scene so they could continue searching even after dark, but they could only process so much without adequate lighting. And they could only light so much of the thick terrain.

Garrett stopped at the edge of the trail where his grid line ended. They'd divided the crime scene into perimeters, inner and outer, and were using the outer perimeter as a boundary to contain the crime scene. In a situation like this, the decision had to be made—based on resources and personnel—about how far to extend that outer perimeter. It was essential to make sure efforts in the search weren't duplicated and at the same time make sure they didn't miss any essential evidence.

He started walking along the trail, this time in the opposite direction from the crime scene and the parking lot where the search had focused. It was true that the most logical explanation was that the abductor had driven her here. If she'd been conscious, she probably would have been walking, and if she hadn't been conscious, a grown man would be able to carry her the short distance from the parking lot to the site where she'd been found. But what if he hadn't stuck to the trail?

They were going to need to expand their search even farther.

The temperature was beginning to drop again and he could feel a storm brewing, with the wind that was picking up. She'd been out here. Cold. Scared. Somewhere she'd lost her coat, assuming she'd been wearing one when she was abducted. The wind whistled through the trees. He buttoned the top button of his own coat to help block the chill. Two days ago, the temperatures had dropped below freezing. No one would have chosen to be out here dressed in only a thin T-shirt.

Just like their Jane Doe hadn't chosen to be out here with a serial killer.

The gnawing urgency in his gut grew stronger.

Three girls abducted. Two for sure were dead. No solid clues. They needed answers. Something that would point them in the direction of their perpetrator. He peered up at the sky. The sun was already beginning to sink into the horizon, dipping the earth in the bluish-gray shades of twilight.

Within the next few hours, the temperature would drop once again to freezing, with a chance of snow flurries. Which meant if they were going to find anything, it needed to be now.

Garrett kept walking. His shoes crunched against the gravel. Eerie shadows danced through the woods around him. He could almost see her, running through the woods, trying to make her escape, until the killer caught her and ended her life.

A trash can sat partly obscured by overgrown bushes just off the trail. He pulled off the lid, dumped the contents onto the ground, and started sifting through them.

"Got something?" Jordan called out as he dug through the trash with his gloved hands.

"I don't know yet." He pushed aside soda cans, candy wrappers, and water bottles, then stopped.

"What is it?" Jordan crouched down beside him as he pulled out a beaded purse.

"I might be wrong, but if our murderer dumped her personal effects here . . ." Garrett unzipped the bag, quickly sorting through a pile of makeup, gum, and hand sanitizer before finding a fabric and leather wallet. He opened it up and pulled out the driver's license.

Jordan shined her flashlight on the driver's license photo. "That's her."

He studied the photo. Their victim now had a name. "According to the driver's license, her name's Julia Kerrigan. She was born December 15, 1987, she's five foot six, and lives in Nashville." He grabbed his cell phone out of his pocket. "Get Sam over here. I'm going to see if there's an open case file on her."

He ended the call to the bureau headquarters the same time Bradford and Michaels arrived.

"Trying to impress the boss on your first day?" Michaels asked. "If so, you're doing pretty good."

"Just doing my job."

"So who is she?" Bradford asked.

"Her name's Julia Kerrigan. I just got off the phone with Detective Everston, who's been working on the case. Her parents filed a missing persons report four days ago. She was supposed to be on her way home from working at a local coffee shop. When she failed to show up, her family went looking for her. When they couldn't find her, they called the police. She was wearing the same thing she was wearing when we found her, plus a coat."

"A runaway?" Bradford asked.

"Not according to her parents. They insist there was no trouble at home. That she was a bright student, did well in school, and had a lot of friends."

"That's what they all say," Michaels said.

"Maybe, but we know this girl was abducted and murdered," Garrett said.

"What about suspects?" Jordan asked.

"Apparently there were some recent work-related threats against the father in the past few weeks, but nothing they were able to connect to her disappearance."

"For now," Bradford said, "I want every scrap of trash gone through for evidence and DNA."

Jordan shook her head. "I agree, but I don't think you'll find anything here."

Garrett paused. "What do you mean?"

"Everything about this case has been meticulously planned. He wanted her to be found. Wanted her wallet and purse to be found."

"Why do you say that?" Bradford asked.

"First of all, winter isn't the time when most people go camping, but I checked with the park management. There are people in and out of here the entire season. Like the couple that discovered the body, they're bird watching or simply trying to find a quiet place. She was found close to the trail. This time of year, all he had to do was bury her a few more dozen feet into the woods, and she more than likely wouldn't have been found for months. And that's another thing. He could have buried her, but he didn't. Not completely. He wanted her found."

"The same was true with Jessica Wright," Bradford said.

"Normally, you can forget your Hollywood stereotype," Jordan said. "Most serial killers aren't interested in playing games with the authorities, because they have no desire to get caught. But this guy seems to want his work to be discovered."

"What about Becky Collier?" Garrett said, turning to Bradford. "You said her body was never found. How does that fit into the equation?"

"Just because her body wasn't found," Jordan said, "doesn't mean she wasn't intended to be found. An animal could have carried her off, or he might have buried her in a spot he assumed she'd be found, but for whatever reason she wasn't. But so far, at least with this case, it seems as if we're finding what he wants us to find. Nothing more. Nothing less. He poses the bodies and is careful not to unintentionally leave anything behind. He wants to be in control."

"What about her personal effects here?" Michaels said. "Her purse and wallet?"

"I'd say another calculated move," Ryley said. "Think about it. Like every other American, he probably watches crime shows on TV. He knows that every criminal investigation begins with a search of the crime scene and a vigorous search for evidence. He also probably knows that we're going to conduct that search systematically until we find that evidence."

"Which means he knew we'd eventually find her things," Garrett said.

"Exactly."

"Wait a minute," Michaels said. "Why would he want someone

to find her or her personal effects? Seems to me it would be better if they were dumped in another county where they'd never be found. Same with her body. Wouldn't this be a risk? You said most serial killers don't want to get caught."

"Yes, but maybe that's the point," Jordan said.

She was in her element. Garrett could tell by the intensity in her voice and her measured body language. She'd been that way even back at the academy. Always focused. Always centered. Always pushing harder than anyone else. When fitness events required a mile-and-a-half run in under fifteen minutes, she'd shoot to shave off an extra minute or two. And in class, while she might ask twice as many questions as any other student, she also worked twice as hard.

"It's the same reason he leaves a Polaroid," she continued. "It's like a game to him. A *catch me if you can*. That's why he's meticulous to only leave behind the clues he wants to be found. It's more than just his power over the girls. It's his way of standing up to the authorities and maybe even society, believing he will continue to get away with what he's doing."

"Which means he won't stop," Bradford said. "At least not until he's caught."

"So then how do we stop him?" Garrett asked.

"He's got the advantage right now, and he knows it," Jordan said. "We don't know when he'll strike, let alone who he'll strike. He can wait months, even years."

"So you're saying there's a good chance we'll never catch him?" Michaels asked.

"No. I'm saying he's not going to make it easy on us. But I also believe there is no perfect crime. He's going to make mistakes. We just have to find the mistakes."

"And in the meantime," Bradford said, "we need to make a plan. Garrett, I want you to work with Detective Everston. Drive back to Nashville and inform the family that we found their daughter. Special Agent Lambert . . . James . . . I want a complete profile on this guy. Give me everything you've got as soon as you can."

Jordan glanced at Garrett. "I'd like to go speak to the parents with you."

He was surprised at her offer. Most people preferred to avoid having to tell the family their daughter wasn't coming home again, and Jordan wasn't exactly used to dealing directly with victims of the crimes she analyzed.

"Are you sure?" he asked.

"I'd like a chance to speak to the parents. They might not be suspects, but I'd still like to get a feel for their reaction and see what else we can learn from them. If these girls are being taken by someone who knows them, then it's crucial that we find the connection between the cases."

A uniformed officer jogged down the path toward them. "Thought you would want to know that the media's just shown up. A couple news vans, including a local television station. They're asking to speak with someone in charge."

Bradford nodded. "I was hoping to hold them off a bit longer, but it looks as if we've just run out of time. I'll get someone to finish processing the evidence here. Agent Lambert, go ahead and talk to the parents with Addison. If you want to take your car back to Nashville, I'll bring your partner back with me. I'm going to want him to stay here and help me deal with the press. It can't hurt to have the FBI's backing on this one."

"You've got it."

"And let's make sure that there's no leak on the ID of our body until the family's informed," Bradford said. "Or a mention of the Polaroid."

Garrett headed toward the parking lot with Jordan, careful to avoid an encounter with the media. "If you want to follow me back to the bureau, we can drive to the Kerrigans' house together from there."

"Sounds good."

He caught her sober expression. "You ready for this?"

"I might not be used to dealing with cases on such a personal level, but I can still handle myself."

"Never thought you couldn't." Garrett glanced at the news van on the other side of the lot. "And it's a good thing, because we're about to have a firestorm on our hands."

4

6:37 p.m.
Nashville, Tennessee

Jordan pressed her fingertips into the armrest of Garrett's Toyota Camry as he drove the twenty minutes from the bureau's headquarters to their victim's home, wondering—not for the first time—why she'd volunteered to come with him. Not only were they on their way to deliver the devastating news of Julia Kerrigan's murder to her family, but since leaving the bureau, anything in their conversation that had the potential of turning personal had quickly been steered around and avoided.

He'd told her how his brother had gotten married to a girl from Colorado, how they'd celebrated his grandfather's eightieth birthday last month, and how he'd started volunteering as a big brother through a program in his church. She in turn had told him how she'd participated in the Potomac River Run Marathon in November and was planning her first full marathon in March. She told him about her sister transferring to the ER and how her parents were still struggling to keep their mom-and-pop grocery store afloat in a world of chain stores and internet shopping.

"I still miss your mother's *brigadeiros*," he said. "I don't remember the last time I had one."

Jordan couldn't help but smile. It was one of her favorite childhood memories. Watching her mother stir the sweetened milk, cocoa powder, and butter while she waited for one of the resulting chocolate balls with sprinkles. "She still has a hard time making enough to keep her customers happy."

"It's one of the reasons their store has lasted this long. Your parents might not be able to compete with the larger stores in some ways, but no one can beat their customer service."

"You should stop by and see Mom someday," Jordan said. "She's told me more than once that she misses seeing you."

"You're right. I should."

Garrett turned off the highway and headed toward the suburb where the Kerrigan family lived. Jordan stared out the window at the rows of local restaurants, neighborhood businesses, and shops, faced with the uncomfortable realization of how much she'd missed him. And how seeing him again, even after all these years, affected her more than she wanted to admit.

Five minutes later, she let out a sigh as Garrett pulled the vehicle against the curb a couple houses down from the Kerrigans' two-story home. Ahead of them, the driveway was filled with cars, as were the curbs on both sides of the street.

Garrett shut off the engine but didn't make a move to get out of the car. "You ready for this?"

"You've already asked me that at least once."

"I know. You've just been quiet since we turned off the highway. I was wondering if you're having second thoughts."

She'd tried to pin the heavy silence that had developed between them to her wanting to avoid the past. But she knew that wasn't the only thing bothering her. She couldn't shake the haunted images of Julia Kerrigan. "I'm used to sitting behind a desk, giving out advice over the phone to precincts around the country after I've sorted through piles of evidence, interviews, and depositions," she said. "I don't normally have a lot of interaction with the victims' families. Okay, normally I don't have *any* interaction with the victims' families."

It was easier that way. She was never required to show any kind of emotional response to loss or experience it firsthand in the eyes of the victims' families. She didn't have to deal with the tears, anger, and questions. She'd learned to disconnect herself from the photos and crime scene descriptions. All she had to do was analyze the facts.

"You don't have to do any of the talking," Garrett said, grabbing his coat from the backseat. "Just hang back unless someone gets out of control."

"No. I didn't come this far to shy away from what has to be done, but that doesn't mean I feel prepared to do this part of the job. Telling them they've just lost their daughter. How do you even begin to do that?"

"Losing a child is probably the worst thing a parent will experience in their lives, and for me, informing them of their loss is one of the worst parts of my job. The only thing I know to do is try to be as compassionate as possible, because there's no way I can really know what they're going through."

Jordan grabbed her scarf off her lap and looped it around her neck. "I think one of the things that frustrates me the most is that I joined the FBI to help people. To help them find justice and answers. But no matter what I say to this family, they are going to hurt. And honestly, that terrifies me."

"You're a whole lot stronger than you think, Jordan. If I'm remembering correctly, you were always the toughest one in our academy class. In PT you were the one outscoring most of the guys."

"That was the easy part." She hated feeling vulnerable, especially in front of Garrett, but he'd always been able to break through her walls. "And forget what they threw at us at the academy. Quantico's training made the academy look like a walk in the park. And in my job now, I deal with analyzing the carnage left behind by killers like this one every day, but it's never personal. Tell a family they've just lost their daughter, though, and the case is no longer a file on my desk."

"It never is just a file on a desk."

She nodded as she opened her door. "Exactly. Which is why dealing with the fallout can't be something I choose to avoid."

She looped her scarf around her neck a second time in an attempt to block the chilly night air. A vigil was being held outside the Kerrigan home with signs, cards, stuffed animals, and written prayers begging God to help Julia come home. The yellow light of a battery-operated candle flickered in the darkness. Jordan walked past a color photo of Julia, showing her smiling as if she didn't have a care in the world. But now everything her family had hoped and prayed for was about to be shattered, and somehow they'd have to figure out a way for life to go on despite what had happened.

An older woman stood alone on the porch, a trail of smoke from the cigarette in her hand blowing in the wind. Garrett stepped up the stairs with Jordan right behind him.

"I'm Special Agent Addison with the TBI, and this is FBI Special Agent Jordan Lambert."

"I'm Janet Kerrigan, Julia's grandmother. I flew in from Atlanta yesterday."

"I'm so sorry for what you've had to go through these past few days."

"Would you believe it if I told you I haven't had a cigarette in twenty years, and now all of a sudden tonight I couldn't live without one?" She dropped the cigarette onto the porch and ground it out with her shoe. "Do you have news about Julia?"

"We need to speak with her parents."

"Julia's mom—my daughter-in-law—is upstairs in Julia's room. I could take you there, though she's asked to be alone."

"We'd appreciate that," Jordan said.

They followed her into the house, past a room filled with people who were talking quietly in small groups, and up a narrow flight of stairs. No one seemed to acknowledge their presence. At least not outwardly. Clearly, they'd seen their share of the authorities over the past few days. Family photos hung on the white walls of the stairwell and upstairs hallway. Family Christmas portraits . . . Disneyland . . . candid shots of a holiday somewhere in the tropics . . .

Julia's grandmother stopped in front of the open doorway. Jordan stepped into the room behind Garrett, feeling as if she were intruding.

"The police are here," the older woman said from the doorway. "I can stay if you'd like."

"I'm sure she could used the support," Jordan said.

Mrs. Kerrigan shook her head. "I'm fine."

Jordan recognized the woman from photos in Julia Kerrigan's file. Midforties, bleached hair, arched eyebrows, but no trace of makeup. Her eyes were red and glassy, both signs that she'd been crying. But today, Dana Elaine Kerrigan wasn't just another name in a folder, or another file number on Jordan's desktop. Instead, she was a mother who was about to be given the worst news any parent could ever hear.

The woman sat on her daughter's bed, staring at the pink-and-white-striped wall with black accents and Paris theme, including an Eiffel Tower lamp. But the details of the room quickly faded in comparison to the enormity of the situation. It felt cold, as if all the warmth had been sucked out of the room.

"Mrs. Kerrigan," Garrett said. "Is your husband at home? We'd like to speak to both of you if possible."

"That can't be good, wanting to speak with both of us." She pulled a pink throw pillow against her chest and started slowly rocking back and forth. "He went out about an hour ago. Told me he needed to go to the store to buy batteries for the TV remote. Can you believe that? Our daughter's missing, and he's off to the store to buy triple-A batteries."

"We'd be happy to wait downstairs until he gets back."

"She's dead, isn't she?" Mrs. Kerrigan caught Jordan's gaze. "My Julia's dead."

"Mrs. Kerrigan," Jordan said. "I think it would be better to wait—"

"Stop. Please. Why else would you be knocking on my door? If it were simply an update on her whereabouts, the detectives from Missing Persons would be handling things. But she's not missing anymore, is she? My baby's dead."

Jordan turned to Garrett, waiting for his lead, trying to ignore the sick feeling spreading through her stomach. She'd been right. She'd rather be chasing down the bad guys right now than standing here having to tell this woman that her daughter had been murdered.

Garrett's nod was barely visible. "I wish I didn't have to tell you this, but yes. Authorities discovered your daughter's body this morning. Because there was no ID, it took us time to identify her."

"And you're sure it's her?"

"Yes, ma'am. We're sure."

"Clark won't believe you. Not until he sees her. He kept promising me we'd find her. I don't know how, but something told me she wasn't coming home." She clutched the pillow tighter against her chest. Beside her, a pile of makeup spilled across a computer desk. A corkboard on the wall above it held a dozen photos of selfies with friends. "How did she die?"

Garrett hesitated again. "The coroner's report hasn't come in yet."

"But you know, don't you? I can see it in your eyes."

His jaw tensed. "It appears she was shot. More than likely she died instantly."

"Where did you find her?"

Jordan caught the lack of emotion in the woman's voice. She wondered about the wisdom of her hearing all this by herself. She looked toward the hallway, wondering if they should call for Mrs. Kerrigan's mother-in-law to come or someone else from downstairs.

"Please tell me. Where did you find her?"

"In a wooded area a little over an hour from here," Garrett said. "A couple hiking on some of the local trails found her."

"And do you have any idea who did this?"

"Not at this time, but I can assure you that we are doing everything we can to find out."

"Detective Everston kept telling me the same thing. He promised he was doing everything he could to find her. Kept telling me how only a small percentage of kids were actually taken by abductors, and that more than likely she would come home on her own. But I knew he was wrong. We aren't a perfect family, but she never would have run away." She drew in a staggering breath. "And Clark . . . How do I tell him? Julia was always his princess. He would have protected her with his life."

Jordan sat down on the empty desk chair across from the woman and said the only thing she could think of. "Tell me about your daughter. I can see from her picture she was beautiful."

A slight smile registered across Mrs. Kerrigan's lips. She was crying now. Silent tears of grief. Shock had yet to wear off, but when it did, reality was going to hit like a flash flood.

"She loved sports, books, art." She glanced around the room. "We just redecorated her room last month for her sixteenth birthday. She wanted a Paris theme. It's not always easy connecting to a teenager, but I had so much fun helping her. We found this online boutique that sold all kinds of things she liked. I'm not sure how this happened. Three days ago she was begging me to buy this clock she found for the wall, and today . . . today I've got to start planning a funeral."

Mrs. Kerrigan took a photograph off the desk, the tears continuing to flow as she sobbed. "Do you have any children?"

Jordan looked at Garrett, but he had taken a few steps back, leaving her to deal with the grieving mother on her own.

"No," she finally said. "I don't have any children, though I hope to one day."

Julia's mom ran her finger across the glass. "We tried for ten years to have a baby. When I found out I was pregnant with Julia, I didn't believe it. I don't think I really believed it until I felt her kick. And when she was born . . . she was so perfect. I remember looking at her the night we brought her home from the hospital. It was as if I was looking at a clean slate. I knew I was going to be the perfect mother. Attentive. Fun. Not too permissive, but still giving her everything she needed. And now she's not coming home."

"I'm so, so sorry."

Jordan clasped her hands in front of her, wishing she knew what to say. Wishing she didn't feel so awkward. But this wasn't about her or how she felt. It was about a mother who'd just lost her child.

"I don't know how people deal with loss like this. I feel so . . . numb." Mrs. Kerrigan caught Jordan's gaze. "Tell me how I'm supposed to tell those people downstairs. How am I supposed to go to sleep tonight, knowing Julia's dead? How do I wake up tomorrow and function? She has an orthodontist appointment at ten in the morning. They were going to do an evaluation to see if she needed braces. Do I call them and cancel, or just not show up?"

"Right now," Jordan said, "all you have to do is think about yourself and your husband, and let those who are here with you help get you through this."

"But what if I don't know what I need?"

Jordan pressed her lips together. There were no answers. Nothing that could make the horror of what had happened go away. Nothing she could say that could bring Julia back or even offer the slightest bit of hope, for that matter.

"I had a dream last night." Mrs. Kerrigan was staring at the photograph of her daughter again. "Julia was floating face up in a river. She was dead, but she looked so peaceful. So serene. This morning all I've been able to think about is what would have happened if she hadn't gone to work that day. I didn't even have a chance to tell her goodbye."

"Mrs. Kerrigan, there was no way you could have known what was going to happen."

"Maybe." She looked back at Jordan. "Do you believe in God?"

Jordan paused, surprised by the woman's question. "Yes, I do."

Mrs. Kerrigan drew in a deep breath. "I just wish I knew where he was when my girl was dying. Was he watching? And if he was watching, tell me why didn't he stop her from being murdered."

She kept looking at Jordan as if she was waiting for an answer. But Jordan didn't have any answers. She didn't know why God chose to save some people and others he didn't.

Jordan glanced again at Garrett, swallowing the guilt pressing against her chest. Maybe the woman wasn't even looking for answers. Maybe she just needed someone to listen. "Honestly, I don't have all the answers."

The words sounded hollow. Empty.

"But I do know one thing," Jordan said. "When I walked into your house, I saw a roomful of people who love you and your husband and Julia. Let them help you through this."

Mrs. Kerrigan grabbed a tissue from the desk and shook her head. "What about when they tell me that God needed Julia in heaven, how I didn't have enough faith, or that they know how I feel because they lost someone they love?"

"Some of them will say the wrong things," Jordan said, "but all you need to remember is that they're here, right now. They care, and they want to support you."

A man stepped into the room, interrupting their conversation. He stopped short when he saw Mrs. Kerrigan's tearstained face.

"Clark—"

"Dana . . . What's going on?"

There was a slight pause before she spoke. "Julia's dead."

No softening the blow of her words or lessening the effect of what had happened. Not that either was really possible. Jordan watched the reaction of those two words on the man's face as he fought to comprehend what he'd just been told.

"That's not possible. There must be a mistake." He moved in front of Garrett, his body posture tense. His words clipped. "Who are you? Where's Detective Everston?"

"I'm Special Agent Garrett Addison, and this is Special Agent Jordan Lambert with the FBI. Our criminal investigation division has taken over the case."

"I don't understand. Julia can't be dead."

"I'm so sorry. I wish it was a mistake, but your wife is right."

"So have you found him yet?" Mr. Kerrigan asked.

"Found who?" Jordan asked.

He fixated on his wife, the veins pulsing in his temples. "Martin Quinn. The man who murdered our daughter."

5

Garrett took a step back from Mr. Kerrigan at the accusation, knowing he was going to need to proceed extremely carefully. "Mr. Kerrigan, who is Martin Quinn?"

"I just told you. He's the man who killed my daughter." Mr. Kerrigan's loud voice echoed through the room, his fists balled at his sides. "And you didn't stop him."

"I know this is difficult, but why don't you sit down next to your wife and tell me what you are talking about."

"I don't need to sit down. I need to know why you let this happen. Why you let this monster get his hands on my daughter."

"Clark, stop—"

"No, Dana. Julia's dead because these people didn't follow up on the lead I gave them." He turned back to Garrett. "I told those officers who was behind her disappearance. I gave them proof that Martin was behind this and they did nothing."

Garrett glanced at Jordan before speaking again. Grief tended to manifest in numerous ways, both physically and emotionally. Anger and blaming others were perfectly normal. "I remember

51

seeing Mr. Quinn's name in your daughter's case file. He was brought in yesterday as a person of interest, but he had a solid alibi for the time she disappeared. They had to let him go."

"No." Mr. Kerrigan jabbed his finger at Garrett. "I don't care if he said he was singing a solo at the Grand Ole Opry on national television. I know he did this. He wanted us to suffer. And now my daughter is dead. You can't tell me that's a coincidence."

"Then talk to me, because I'm listening. How do you know he wanted you and your family to suffer?"

"You need proof? I gave them proof. He completely lost it at my work in front of half a dozen witnesses, but that's not all." Mr. Kerrigan took his phone out of his pocket. "There are texts. You can read them. There's half a dozen threats he sent to me, starting two weeks ago."

Garrett took the phone and scanned through the string of messages. There were threats against Kerrigan and his business, but none specifically against his daughter.

"You went to the authorities when you started receiving these?" Garrett asked.

"Not at first. In the corporate world there is always someone angry at you. But then a few days ago, my tires were slit. That's when I first went to the police. And when Julia disappeared, he stopped texting me. You can't tell me this is all just some big coincidence."

"Tell me exactly who you spoke to," Garrett said.

"I filed a police report down at the precinct when my tires were slit. Then later, I told Detective Everston—the officer handling Julia's case—about the other texts."

"What did the detective tell you about the threats?" Garrett asked.

"He said they couldn't trace the texts, because they were made on a burner phone, but that they'd do everything they could to find out who'd sent the messages." He was pacing again. "That's what they said about Julia too. That they'd do everything they could to find her. But they didn't do everything they could. I kept telling him they were looking in the wrong place, but no one listened to me."

"I'm going to see if I can get some answers from the detective," Jordan said, slipping out of the room.

Garrett nodded, then turned back to Mr. Kerrigan. "Tell me exactly who Mr. Quinn is, and why you think he would have wanted to harm your daughter?"

"Quinn and I met in college and have been friends for years. Five years ago, we worked together on the ground level of a biotech startup called Ferber Corporation."

"What exactly does Ferber do?"

"We produce medical supplies that treat kidney disease and immune disorders, and provide intravenous therapy. But it's been a tough couple of years. We never quite recovered from falling stock prices and ended up filing for bankruptcy protection. We were forced to downsize last year and had to close one of our factories. Martin had sunk everything he had into the company. With the soft economy and the downturn in stock, he pretty much lost everything, including his retirement. He started drinking heavily, and his wife left him. There was a custody battle, and he lost custody of his daughter because of it. He blames me."

"And you believe, because of the threats he sent you, that he's behind the murder of your daughter."

"He wants me to suffer the way he did. What better way than to force me to lose my daughter like he lost his?"

Jordan stepped back into the room and shoved her phone into her back pocket.

"What did you find out?" Garrett asked.

"I spoke to Detective Everston, and you were right about Quinn. They brought him in twenty-four hours ago as a person of interest, but they weren't able to tie him to Julia's disappearance."

"That's not possible," Kerrigan countered.

"He had an alibi for the afternoon she was abducted."

Mr. Kerrigan's voice rose. "Then you'd better dig deeper, because he was lying to you."

"I've asked that they bring Mr. Quinn in for further questioning," Jordan said.

"Don't you think it's a little too late?" Kerrigan was shouting now, and it was obvious to Garrett that the man was barely holding it together. "You should have been here days ago, putting an end to this before there was a body to be found, but now my daughter's dead. And here's another question. Why is the FBI suddenly involved? You don't normally show up to deal with a homicide, do you?"

Garrett debated how to answer. If it was going to be on the evening news, they didn't deserve to be blindsided.

"While we will dig into the evidence you gave us on Mr. Quinn, we do have another suspect," Jordan said.

"Who?"

"Please understand that it's still too early to know for sure, but I'm here because there is a possibility that your daughter died at the hands of a serial killer."

Mrs. Kerrigan let out a soft shriek, then began sobbing again. Her husband sat down next to her and pulled her against him, but he clearly wasn't done probing for answers.

"You're telling me that not only is my daughter dead, but she was killed by a serial killer? How many girls are dead? Two, three . . . four? More than that? Do you even know? And how many more are going to die because you haven't been able to find who's doing this?"

"Mr. Kerrigan—" Garrett began.

"Please don't try to give me assurances that you're going to find her killer, because it's too late for that. Whether it's Quinn or some serial killer, Julia's gone."

"We know this is an extremely difficult time for your family, but—"

"Difficult? Are you kidding me? My daughter's dead because of you."

"Clark, stop. I want to see her," Mrs. Kerrigan said.

"We can arrange that for you," Jordan said.

"No." Mr. Kerrigan shook his head. "That will only make things worse. It will be better for you to remember her the way she was."

"Clark—"

"What?"

"This isn't their fault—"

"Then whose fault is it? Because last I looked it was the job of the police to stop things like this from happening. They don't even know who killed our daughter."

"Clark . . . Dana . . ." Julia's grandmother rushed into the room. "What's going on? The local news is speculating about a serial killer on the loose and now the FBI shows up at our doorstep. Please don't tell me this is tied to Julia's disappearance."

Mr. Kerrigan rushed out of the room past his mother. Garrett hurried after him. The firestorm had begun.

Detective Kenneth Everston was waiting for them when Garrett and Jordan walked into the TBI headquarters just past eight thirty. The room smelled like pizza, reminding Garrett that they'd yet to eat dinner. Not that it mattered. He didn't have much of an appetite.

"Thanks for coming by at such a late hour," Garrett said, shaking the detective's hand, then introducing him to Jordan.

"I'm happy to help, though I'm not happy about the circumstances. I was counting on bringing this girl home."

"I know," Jordan said. "I can't stop thinking about Julia's mother. They're going to have a dozen reporters on their doorstep before they even have a chance to plan the funeral."

Garrett motioned them to chairs in front of his desk. "I understand that Martin Quinn was just brought in a few minutes ago."

"Yes." Everston sat down next to Jordan. "But I'm not sure you're going to get anything more out of him, and as far as we can tell, his alibi is solid."

"We've only had time to briefly read through the transcript of your interview with him," Jordan said. "What's your gut feeling? Do you think Quinn fits into this scenario?"

Detective Everston leaned forward. "The only thing he's admitted to is being angry at Kerrigan. He says he doesn't know anything about the slashed tires or the threats, and to be honest, we can't tie him to any of it, let alone Julia's abduction."

"He has reason to be angry, according to Clark Kerrigan," Garrett said. "He lost everything, including his wife and daughter."

"Maybe, but turning around and murdering his friend's daughter?" Everston shook his head. "Seems like pretty extreme payback to me."

"What about his alibi?" Garrett asked. "You said it was solid."

"He was working on a project for a new startup company with a friend." Everston pulled a small notebook from his shirt pocket. "Simon Tate. He was able to confirm they were together from just after lunch until about eight thirty Friday night in a string of meetings with investors."

Garrett turned to Jordan. "If that's true, he couldn't have abducted her."

"Double-check his alibi," Jordan said. "We also need to find out where he was when the other two girls disappeared."

"Agreed," Garrett said. "Unless Julia's murder is the work of a copycat—and I don't think it is—this goes much deeper than the collapse of Martin Quinn's life."

Five minutes later, Garrett let Jordan step into the interview room ahead of him, choosing to stand while she took a seat across from Quinn. Their suspect looked to be about fifty, maybe fifty-five, with reddish hair, sallow skin, and bloodshot eyes. Garrett took in his features in one pass. He didn't have to take a second look to know that the man was more than likely an alcoholic, like his own father.

Sweat glistened on Quinn's forehead. "I've been through this already. I answered all the questions they asked me, and nothing's changed."

"We understand that, but the FBI's involved now, Mr. Quinn," Jordan said. "I have a few follow-up questions I need to ask you."

"I won't say anything different. I told them that I was mad, but I didn't do anything to their daughter."

"So you're still insisting that you had nothing to do with the threats against her family?" Garrett asked.

"Yes."

"What about her murder?"

Quinn's face paled. "Her murder? Wait a minute . . . Julia's dead?"

"Her body was found this morning about ninety miles from here, which means we're not just talking about threats and vandalism. We're talking about the death penalty."

"I swear I didn't have anything to do with her disappearance, and I certainly don't have anything to do with her murder. You checked out my alibi. There's no way I could have taken her."

"You threatened Mr. Kerrigan in front of a room full of people," Jordan said. "After that he began receiving threats via texts. That's rather convenient timing, don't you think?"

"I said some things I didn't mean. I was angry, I'll admit that. I lost everything because of him, and he didn't care. But just because I was angry doesn't mean I murdered his daughter."

"You lost your wife and daughter. You wanted him to feel the same way you did. You believed he deserved to lose everything as well."

"They were just threats. I never acted on them."

Garrett pushed a photo of Julia from the crime scene across the table. "So you didn't do this?"

Quinn turned away from the photo.

"Look again, Mr. Quinn," Jordan said. "Because that's not all."

"What do you mean?" The man's chest heaved.

Garrett pushed the photos of the two other girls connected to the case in front of him. "Jessica Wright, abducted and found murdered in June 2002. Becky Collier, abducted April 2003. Her body was never found, but we have evidence that all three abductions are connected."

"Wait a minute." Quinn wiped his upper lip with the back of his hand. "You think I'm somehow connected to their murders? I've never seen these girls before, and I certainly had nothing to do with their deaths."

"Then tell us the truth. Did you send the threatening texts to Kerrigan?" Garrett asked.

"No."

Jordan leaned forward and caught Quinn's gaze. "I believe you're lying to us. And the more you lie, the harder this is going to be on you. This is Mr. Kerrigan's car, three days after you made the threats. We found fingerprints on the tire wall."

Quinn was starting to panic. Garrett could see it in his eyes. "Tell us what happened," he said. "Everything."

"Okay, I threatened Clark, and not just in the office that one day." Quinn wiped his lip again. "I . . . I just wanted to scare him."

"So you did lie," Jordan said. "Which makes it easier to believe that you made good on your threats."

"No. That's all I did. I swear. I slashed a couple tires. Sent a few text messages. But I never hurt anyone. I was mad. That's it."

"Mad enough to kidnap his daughter?" Garrett asked. "Mad enough to kill her?"

"No."

Garrett took the empty chair next to Jordan and leaned forward. "I've read through the texts you sent him. You said you wanted him to suffer like you did."

"I meant financially. I never touched his family."

"Why not? You lost your wife and daughter, something you blame him for. Isn't that true?"

"Yes . . . no." Quinn shook his head. "Kerrigan walked away from the company with money in his pocket. I walked away with nothing. I was angry."

There was a knock on the door. Everston opened the door, then signaled them to step out into the hallway with him.

"We took a deeper look at the alibi Quinn gave us. Simon Tate just confessed that Quinn paid him to lie."

"So they weren't together that day?"

Everston shook his head. "They met in the morning, but not in the afternoon."

"Do you know where he was?"

"No. We only know that he lied."

"He's definitely hiding something," Jordan said, "but I don't think he murdered those girls."

"He just confessed to sending the threatening text messages," Garrett said. "Of slashing Clark Kerrigan's tires, and now we know his alibi is fake—"

"I still don't think it's him."

Garrett let out a huff of air. "Okay. I'm listening."

"I spend all day, every day, analyzing people like him. He's not our serial killer. His shirt was wrinkled, and there was a stain on his sleeve."

"So the man's not a neat freak," Garrett said.

"Our killer is. Everything he does is precise and thought out. From the lack of evidence at the crime scene, to his attention to details like the way the bodies are posed, to the addition of the Polaroid photo." Jordan pressed her lips together. "Give me another five minutes with the man."

"Jordan . . ."

He watched as she stepped back into the room, shutting the door behind her.

"Is she always this tenacious?"

Garrett chuckled. "You don't know the half of it."

Everston flipped on a switch so they could listen to the conversation.

"Your friend, Simon Tate," Jordan began, "just ratted you out, and blew a hole in your alibi. How much did you pay him to lie for you?"

Sweat beaded across Quinn's lip, but he didn't move. "You're lying. Trying to trick me into confessing. I didn't kill those girls."

Jordan laid the photos of the three girls onto the table, without saying a word.

"Fine. I paid him."

"To cover up a murder."

"No. I didn't murder her. I didn't murder any of those girls."

"Then why the false alibi?"

Quinn folded his arms across his chest.

"I'll ask you one more time," Jordan said. "Or I can simply go to the DA and ask to move forward with charges for the murder of Julia Kerrigan, Jessica Wright—"

"Stop. I was in a bar."

"Can you prove it?"

"The waitress there would remember me. I was drinking alone. I arrived around two and didn't leave until five something. I wasn't anywhere near Julia Kerrigan."

"We'll check it out, but again, why the fake alibi? Why didn't you just tell us this in the first place?"

Quinn wiped off the perspiration that had spread to his brow. "My ex-wife will use anything and everything to make sure I lose visitation rights of my daughter. If she finds out I spent the afternoon drinking . . ."

"A judge could have allegations of substance abuse investigated," Jordan said.

"And I might never be able to see Rachel again."

Jordan pushed back her chair, then stepped out of the room, closing the door behind her.

"Looks like you were right, and it wasn't him," Garrett said. "But you don't look happy."

"Because if Quinn's innocent, it means we're no closer to finding out who killed Julia Kerrigan. And more girls are going to die if we don't find out who's behind this."

6

January 24, 2004
12:17 a.m.
TBI Headquarters

Garrett walked out of the glass-encased entrance of the bureau, trying to shake off the heavy wave of fatigue that had settled over him. The day had worn him out both physically and emotionally. And as if dealing with a serial killer wasn't enough, Jordan's appearance back in his life had managed to leave him unsettled and questioning every decision he'd made over the past few years.

The truth was that she wasn't a part of his life. Not anymore. And no lingering feeling he still held was going to change that.

The rain had started again. He popped open his umbrella, then hurried toward his car, avoiding the puddles that had settled into the crevices of the parking lot.

One of the overhead parking lot lights flickered. He looked back at the looming building, then stopped. She was standing just outside the entrance with no umbrella, as if she was trying to decide what to do. He hesitated, then headed back across the lot.

"Jordan . . ."

He took a few seconds to take in her familiar features. Her dark

61

hair was pulled back neatly, but she hadn't been able to quite contain the curls, because of the humidity. Skin the color of caramel, dark-brown eyes, and that smile that had captured him from the first day he'd met her back at the academy. She still looked just as beautiful as she had then.

"You okay?" he asked.

"Yeah, I just forgot my umbrella. I was trying to decide if I should make a run for it, but I really don't want to get soaked."

"I've got mine," he said.

He stepped up next to her, close enough that his umbrella was covering both of them.

"I thought you'd already left," she said as they headed to her rental car.

He tried to ignore the fact that her hair smelled like flowers and still made his head spin. How did she do that? "What about you? Are you headed to your parents' house?"

"Yeah. Though I'm sure they're already asleep. They have to get up pretty early."

Halfway across the lot, the heavens opened. He slipped his arm around her waist in an attempt to keep her under the umbrella's protection as they picked up their pace toward her car.

"This is it." She shivered and pushed back one of the stubborn curls that refused to stay confined.

He'd always loved her hair despite her protests of how challenging it was to manage. And just like when they were dating, he fought the urge to pull all the curls out of their confinement and let them go free.

"You're shaking." Garrett looked down at his keys. "Listen. There's a restaurant down the street that stays open all night. Why don't you let me buy you something to eat? I don't know about you, but even though I'm tired, I'm not sure I can sleep yet. We can warm up, and it would be nice to talk about something other than work for a little while."

He made the suggestion before taking the time to think about the offer. But the truth was, he'd like to catch up with her away from the shadow of the case. It would be nothing more than two colleagues getting together over something to eat. Although the chance to get reacquainted with the FBI agent wasn't such a bad thing either.

She hesitated a moment, then nodded. "I'd like that. I'm not sure I could sleep right now either."

"Great. Do you want to take your car, or do you want me to drive?"

"I'll follow you, so I can drive from there to my parents'."

By the time they got to the restaurant, the rain had almost stopped. A waitress led them to a booth near a crackling fire, and Garrett tried to ignore the familiar sense of being out with her.

She rubbed her hands together. "I didn't think I was hungry, but looking at this menu, I'm suddenly starved."

A couple minutes later, the waitress made her way toward their table, ready to take their orders.

"I'll take a Caesar salad and peanut butter milkshake," Jordan said.

Garrett hid his amusement as he ordered a club sandwich, sweet potato fries, and coffee. He'd almost forgotten her love for sweets, especially milkshakes and pies. But he hadn't forgotten how much he'd always enjoyed spending time with her. He sat back in his chair, listening to B.B. King playing in the background and wondering how he'd ended up here, tonight, with the only woman who'd ever truly stolen his heart and never returned it.

"I've decided I'm impressed with what you do," she said, taking a sip of the lemon water the waiter had just left.

"Why is that?"

"Working these murder cases. I told you before that I'm used to reviewing crimes, analyzing behavior, and coming up with strategies from behind a desk, but going through that crime scene and talking to our victim's parents . . . I don't know. These cases get under your skin and leave you wondering what's happened to our world. Like society's falling apart and nothing makes sense anymore."

"It's because we're supposed to be the good guys. And when the bad guys keep winning, we question if we're really making a difference. At least that's what I tend to do."

"That and spend the day outside in this freezing weather." Jordan nodded toward the fireplace. "I think I've finally almost warmed up."

She pulled off her gray scarf, then peeled off her jacket, revealing the necklace he'd bought her for her birthday when they were still together. It had been one of those impulse buys he wasn't sure at the time if he'd regret or not. Their relationship had still been on uneven ground as they both focused on getting through the academy. But one thing he had been sure of: Jordan was someone he could imagine spending the rest of his life with.

"You're still wearing the necklace I gave you," he said.

She clasped the small silver medallion and slid it across the chain. "I'd forgotten. It's not weird that I still wear it, is it?"

"No. Not at all."

"Because I loved it when you gave it to me, and I still love it. I just . . . I don't know. I never stopped wearing it."

A few seconds of awkward silence went by as the past seemed to hang between them.

"I'm glad you're wearing it," he said. "It was a gift, and just because we're not a couple anymore doesn't mean you should get rid of it. I bought it for you because I knew you'd like it. Not because of any expectations."

And he knew there wasn't some deep psychological reason behind her wearing the necklace. She simply liked it. Nothing more.

The waitress put their orders in front of them, made sure they had everything they needed, then scurried off to another table.

Jordan dipped her straw in her shake, then took a sip. "This was a good idea. I needed to unwind, and I really wasn't in the mood to go sit in my parents' house alone. And . . ." She smiled up at him. "The company's not so bad either. It really has been too long."

"Yes, it has. Tell me more about your family." He wasn't ready to make the conversation too personal. Not yet anyway.

"My parents are good. Like I said in the car, they're still running the store, and managing to keep the doors open."

"And your dad's health?"

"Mom makes him watch his cholesterol and his diet." She let out a soft laugh. "They've always been quite a pair."

She continued talking while he ate. He tried not to notice how the light from the fire brought out the highlights in her dark hair and made her eyes sparkle. She told him about how she and her sister had surprised their parents with a cruise for their fortieth anniversary. Jordan laughed as she explained in detail how her mom had been terrified to get on the boat, almost to the point of refusing to go. He smiled when she told him that in the end she'd loved it so much she'd actually booked another cruise before they even got off the ship.

He'd always loved her family. They were down-to-earth, hard workers who had always treated him like one of their own. His parents, in contrast, had been handed their success on a silver platter and in turn carried certain expectations for Garrett. No matter how many times he'd told them he didn't care about money and prestige, they'd always made it clear that they expected him to marry someone on his own social and economic level. And while it might not have been stated out loud, they also had implied, someone of his own ethnicity. Not a woman with African American and Brazilian roots.

Those expectations had deepened the wedge between him and his parents, and pushed him closer to Jordan. Because none of those things had ever been important to him. They had at times, though, bothered Jordan, and he'd known that her uneasiness wasn't ever going to completely go away. Especially if they ended up getting married.

But of course none of that mattered. Not anymore.

"What about your sister?" he asked, as he struggled to rein in his thoughts. "How has she been?"

"It's hard to believe, but she's been married almost a year now."

"I didn't know you were back in Nashville for a wedding."

"I wasn't, actually." She took another sip of her shake. "They got married in the Caribbean, and I did manage to get away for the wedding. Alex is a great guy and he makes her happy."

"Clara always had good taste in men."

"Because she liked you?" Jordan teased.

He laughed. "Why else?" Suddenly it felt as if it hadn't been that long since he'd seen her. The awkwardness he felt between them when she'd first arrived slipped away, and he began to realize just how much he'd missed her.

"What about your family?" she asked, breaking into his thoughts. "How are they?"

He grabbed a fry and dabbed it in a pool of ketchup. Family had always been a sore spot. "My father's still working seventy-plus hours a week at the firm, while my mother runs from one charity board to the next."

"And your brother?" She stabbed a slice of cucumber with her fork. "How many kids does he have now?"

"He and his wife live in Colorado now with their three boys, which makes me a proud uncle. I try to see them at least once a year."

"How often do you see your parents?"

"Not that often, to be honest, even though they still live in Memphis. My mom will be here in a couple weeks for a charity event if you're still around. I'm sure she'd love to see you."

"Right. Your mother was terrified you'd ask me to marry you, and you know it."

"She wasn't that bad."

Jordan tilted her head and widened her eyes.

"Okay, she was—is—that bad."

"Though she approved of—what was her name—Sabrina?"

"That was only because Sabrina had the right last name and a trust fund. But I decided a long time ago that who I marry will never depend on what my mother thinks. Of course, that doesn't stop her from reminding me every time I see her of how disappointed she is that I didn't marry Sabrina."

"So no girlfriend in your life?" Jordan asked.

"Not presently. It's hard to find time to date, and if it wasn't for my mom's continual attempts to set me up, I'd probably never go out at all. But I've decided that I'm happy being single—for now." He signaled to the waitress for more coffee. "What about you?"

She held up her left hand. "No ring yet, though I have been seeing this guy."

"Oh?" He hid the disappointment in his voice. Not that it should matter. He didn't exactly expect her to stay single after all these years.

"Well, we've gone out more than once. That makes it a record for me, but it's nothing serious. And I suppose for the same reasons. I'm too busy to take the time to really work at a relationship. And I have this feeling that my job intimidates most men."

"Maybe that's not a bad thing. Any man who can't handle who you are doesn't deserve you." The waitress replenished his coffee cup and Garrett took a sip. "What about your partner?"

"Ryley? I trust him with my life, but that's it."

"Just curious. You must spend a lot of time together."

"He's got a girlfriend, actually. Her name's Jill, and she teaches kindergarten."

Garrett took another sip of his coffee, then leaned back, surprised at how good it felt to be with her. How comfortable. But it had always been that way. The connection between them that he couldn't explain. And even after all these years, it was still there. He just wasn't sure he wanted it to be. Because it wasn't as if anything could come of them spending time together.

"You look like you need to get some sleep," he said.

"I've still got a bunch of files I want to read through before tomorrow." She shrugged. "Besides, I've always thought sleep was overrated. In college I stayed up all night and still managed to go to class."

"All I know is that one day you won't be as young as you think you are and those all-nighters aren't going to come quite so easy."

He caught her smile, wishing he didn't have the urge to pull her into his arms and kiss her. He reached for his coffee. It had to be the atmosphere. The music, the crackling fire, and the low-lit chandeliers hanging above them. Maybe this had been a bad idea after all.

"You were good in there with Julia's mom," he said, shifting the conversation. "You were able to relate to her on a personal level, which was exactly what she needed. She'll always remember the moment she heard her daughter was dead, but she's also going to remember how the news was delivered and how you truly cared about her."

"I don't know." Jordan set her fork down and shook her head. "I kept imagining what it would be like if Julia were my sister and my world had just shattered, but the truth is, I honestly can't imagine what she's facing right now."

"I agree. I can't either."

"Thanks for this." Jordan pushed back her salad bowl. "Going out was a good idea. Not only was it one of the best shakes I've had for a long time, the company hasn't been too bad either."

"Thanks . . . I think." He chuckled. "Unless you're comparing me to your shake."

"Seriously. I've enjoyed tonight. It's not often that I take the time to just decompress. Life's gotten too hectic. But I've missed seeing you. The academy seems like a lifetime ago."

"I've enjoyed seeing you too," he said. "A lot. I just wish you were here for other reasons."

"We're going to find this guy, Garrett."

"And if that doesn't happen before another girl vanishes?"

Jordan set her empty glass on the table and shook her head. "We're going to find him first. We have to."

7

Jordan jolted awake at the sound of her alarm the next morning. She grabbed her cell off the bedside table and turned it off. Five forty-five. The scent of coffee and *pão de queijo*—her mom's Brazilian cheese bread—permeated the room as she rolled over in the bed in her childhood home. She hadn't realized how much she missed the ranch-style house her parents had moved into before she and Clara were born, or the room she'd grown up in that looked almost exactly like it had the day she'd left home. It had been the only home she'd known, besides the store.

Pulling back the covers and sitting up, her thoughts shifted unannounced to Garrett. She let out a deep sigh. Even her dreams had been filled with him. And yet she'd promised herself she wasn't going to let her heart go back there. She told herself that the feelings she'd had for Garrett had died out long ago. And yet here she was, still mesmerized by those dark eyes. Glad he'd suggested some casual time together. But that's all it had been. A milk shake and conversation.

She grabbed a sweatshirt and pulled it on over her T-shirt, then

69

headed toward the kitchen. Maybe she was simply being sentimental. Seeing her family again, seeing Garrett. Just because she loved her job didn't mean that sometimes she didn't wish for something more. That sometimes she wished she could escape to some small town, fall in love, raise a family, and grow old without worrying about the world falling apart around her. Maybe the grass wasn't greener on the other side, but sometimes it seemed like it could be.

"Mom?"

"I'm in here!" Her mother's voice sounded from the kitchen.

Seeing her mom made Jordan feel like she was finally home again. They had always been a close family, embracing the cultures from both sides of her heritage. Between her mother's Brazilian roots and her father's African American heritage, she'd been given an appreciation for life outside her small world. She'd learned to appreciate her father's love for jazz and crave her grandmother's ham hocks, collard greens, and sweet potato pie, and at the same time have a decent handle on the Portuguese language and an enthusiastic love for soccer.

"I found your note this morning," her mom said, pulling a pan of the pão de queijo rolls from the oven. "You should have woken me up when you got in last night."

"It was really late. I was afraid I might miss you this morning, though. I know how early you and Daddy leave for work."

"I told your father I was going to be late today." Her mom smiled up at her. "I couldn't exactly concentrate on receipts at the store knowing you were here, now could I?"

Jordan wrapped her arms around her mama's waist and pulled her tight, not missing the fatigue that settled in her mama's eyes, or the fact that she'd lost weight since she'd last seen her. She took a step back and smiled. "I've missed you so much."

"Oh girl, I've missed you too." Her mom stared up at her as if she were taking in all the details of her daughter's appearance. "You look good, but tired."

"This was an unscheduled trip that's come on the heels of a

busy few weeks." Jordan let out a low laugh. "Apparently, criminals don't take time off for the holidays."

"I'd like to say I'll take what I can get, but you're never here long enough."

Jordan dismissed the stab of guilt. "I promise I'll take some vacation time and come for a real visit as soon as I can."

"You're here, and that's all that matters."

"It's nice to be back," Jordan said. "Has Daddy already left?"

"Yes, but you'll see him tonight."

"He works too hard. Both of you do."

"That's the only way we know how to do things," her mom said, covering the bread with a cloth. "The store won't run itself, as you know. Which means long hours."

"I'm sorry about the short notice. We just got the assignment yesterday morning."

"Don't ever be sorry about visiting." Her mom turned off the oven, then hung the potholder on a hook. "How long do you think you'll be here?"

"Not long. A couple days at most."

"It must be something urgent for the FBI to be called in."

"It is." She didn't bring up the case details. She never did. She might spend more time behind a desk than risking her life on the field, but her mom would still worry.

"You look tired, but do you at least have time for a *cafezinhos* and breakfast before you head out again?"

She needed to get to work, but she also needed to be here. "Always."

Her mom started the process of making the Brazilian coffee, adding water to a pan, along with some sugar from a frog canister, then setting it on the gas stove to boil. "Go ahead and eat some bread while it's hot. It tastes better then."

"I will in a minute, but I have something for you." Jordan reached for a box she'd left in the room last night when she got in and set it on the table.

"What in the world is this?" Her mom wiped her hands on her apron and tilted her head.

"Open it. It's just a little present to make up for missing Christmas this year."

"Stop." Her mother started pulling off the wrapping paper. "I never want you to feel guilty because of what you do. We're proud of you, your father and I. Both you and your sister made it further career-wise than we ever dreamed."

"I know you understand, but I missed being here. Skype was great, but not quite the same. And on top of that, I've missed your cooking."

"So now the truth of why you returned comes out." Her mother laughed, then pulled off the last of the wrapping paper before opening the box. "How in the world did you get this in your suitcase?"

Her mom pulled out the frog canister set, then started clearing a space for them on the counter.

"They're from back in the '70s, for your collection."

Her father had bought her mom her first frog on their honeymoon four decades ago, and somehow the theme had stuck. Every birthday her dad would add to the collection. And whenever Jordan came back home, she brought her mom a frog.

"It's wonderful! But your father is threatening to get rid of all my frogs and replace them with NFL paraphernalia."

Jordan laughed. "He'd never do that."

"Maybe not, but he enjoys teasing me."

Her mom added coffee to the boiling water, then strained it before pouring the drink into a tiny espresso cup and handing it to Jordan.

Jordan took a sip. "They don't make coffee like this back East."

"They must not make your favorite dishes, either. I need to fatten you up. You've gotten too thin, like you're not eating enough."

"I'm eating fine, Mama. But I'm not the only person who's lost some weight."

"Trust me, I could use a bit of downsizing." Her mom laughed.

"I'm just a bit worn out along the edges is all. Do you plan on seeing any of your old friends while you're here?"

Jordan didn't miss her mom's deflection. "I don't think I'm going to have a lot of free time, but I have seen Garrett, actually. Turns out we're on this case together. He's working with TBI now."

"Really? I always liked that boy. And what about you? I've always wondered if you were ever sorry for leaving him behind."

Funny how Garrett had asked her pretty much the same thing.

"Things between Garrett and I ended a long time ago." A discussion about Garrett Addison was the last thing she wanted to get into right now. She'd enjoyed catching up with him last night, but that was it.

"Sorry." Her mom put the pan of crispy puffs of cheese bread rolls into a long narrow basket. "But it's hard not to wonder what would have happened if the two of you had married. I'm not sure if I told you, but I always thought you might."

Jordan let out a sharp sigh. "We didn't, so it doesn't matter. And besides, like I just said, anything that was between the two of us was over a long time ago."

Her mom took a sip of her coffee, then added another scoop of sugar. She'd never been able to get it sweet enough. "Any other men in your life?"

"I don't exactly have time for a relationship right now, Mama, and even if I did . . . I don't know. I haven't found anyone who stirs my heart. Not like you always say Daddy does for you."

Not like Garrett once had.

She dismissed the thought as soon as it surfaced. Fatigue and unwanted memories were playing with her emotions.

"It just seems like it's time you thought about marriage and grandbabies."

"One day. I'm not that old."

"I just worry about you and want you to be happy." Her mom reached out and ran her hand down Jordan's cheek. "That's what moms do."

"I am happy. Really. I love my job. I have a circle of good friends. I'm part of a good church—"

"Stop trying to convince me."

"Okay."

Her mom caught her gaze before turning away. "There was a short segment about a serial killer on the loose. The media's calling him the Angel Abductor and the FBI's involved."

"Mom—"

"That's why you're here, isn't it?"

Jordan hesitated. "Yes."

"I worried about you and your sister growing up, but today . . . I can't believe the things that are happening." She pulled Jordan in for a quick, hard embrace before looking at her again. "Will you be here for dinner tonight?"

"I should be. Will you make beans and rice?"

"Your father's favorite meal and both my girls home? You know I could never pass up an offer like that."

"Good, though if it's too much for you, I can always take you out to dinner. I told you you're working too hard."

"Somehow I think you need some home cooking."

"I need to get ready to leave." Jordan downed the rest of her coffee, hoping the extra caffeine would be the boost she needed. "But I'll be back as early as I can."

Thirty minutes later, Jordan had showered and dressed and was almost ready to leave, when she heard someone calling her name.

"Now this room brings back memories." Clara walked into the room, her gaze going directly to the open closet. "I guess I haven't been in here for a while. Do you still have your varsity jacket?"

"Along with the pile of Beanie Babies, my collection of mood rings, and Mariah Carey CDs. Mom refuses to get rid of any of it." Jordan pulled her sister into a hug. "I was hoping I'd get to see you today."

"I just got off my shift and am headed home, but Mom said you were here."

"You look good. Love the hair."

"Thanks. I was afraid to cut it, but I like it a lot, actually."

Her sister plopped down on the end of the bed while Jordan zipped up her suitcase. "And Alex? How's he?"

"Working hard, as usual, but he's happy. Business is great and he spends most of his time under a car, covered with grease, but that's what makes him happy."

"That and coming home to his new wife."

"Marriage has a few challenges, but it's worth it." Clara shot Jordan a smile. "You should try it one day."

"Don't start that." Jordan sat down next to her. "You sound as if you've been talking to Mom."

"Yeah. She used to always bring up the marriage thing with me too, but now it's the baby thing."

"You're making me wish I could just hang out here with all of you for the next week or two, but I've got this case here in town." She always had a case. Always had a pile of paperwork to sort through. How was she supposed to find time to get to the altar with her schedule?

"Mom understands," Clara said. "We all do."

Jordan hesitated. "We need to talk about your email. You said you were worried about Mom."

"I didn't mean to make you worry. It's just that . . . You talked to Mom. Did she tell you what's going on?"

Jordan felt a wave of anxiety spread. "Tell me what?"

Clara's frown deepened. "Mama's sick, Jordan."

Her sister's words felt like a punch to the gut. "Wait a minute. What do you mean? I know she looks tired and she's lost some weight, but—"

"It's more than that. Her doctor's running tests to find out exactly what's wrong. We don't have a diagnosis yet, but I think it's something serious."

Jordan pressed her lips together. It was what she'd always hated about being so far away. "Why didn't you call and tell me something was wrong?"

"I knew you'd worry, and besides . . . we don't know what it is, and it seemed like something you should be told in person. Though if it were up to Mom, she wouldn't tell you at all."

"Why not?"

"You know her. She wants everything to be like it always has been. That's just who she is. The glass is half full, and everything will be okay. But this time . . . this time I'm not sure everything will be okay."

"What aren't you telling me, Clara?"

"We'll know more once all the test results are in, and I promise I'll let you know then."

Jordan felt doubts she rarely struggled with surface like a tidal wave. "Did I make the wrong decision?"

"What do you mean?"

"Let's just say I've been forced to think about regrets lately. I thought I could save the world when I joined the FBI. But instead, I'm rarely home and hardly ever see any of you, and sometimes I wonder just how much of a difference I'm actually making."

"All I know is that Mom and Dad are proud of what you do. They always talk about their daughter who saves lives in the ER every day, and their other daughter who's protecting our country."

Jordan laughed. "That sounds like them."

"They just want you to be happy. And giving them a couple grandchildren—each—wouldn't hurt either."

"So I've been told."

"The only thing is, I'm not ready for kids. Not yet, anyway. We're thinking of a puppy first. Then maybe in a couple years we'll be ready for a baby."

"I'm not ready either." Jordan smiled, but all she could feel was the ache of homesickness she hadn't had since college. "I've missed you."

"I've missed you too." Clara squeezed Jordan's hand. "But I don't want you to feel bad about not being here. We all know you would be if you could." She dropped Jordan's hand and headed for the door. "I'm going to sneak out now and try to get home in time to have breakfast with Alex before he goes to work."

"Sounds as if you meet each other coming and going."

"We're learning to find time for each other. Breakfast dates, late-night movie marathons, pizza nights."

And if Jordan made more of an effort with her family? Could she also squeeze in more special times?

"I've been told we're having a family dinner tonight," Clara continued. "I'll see you then?"

"I'll be there." Jordan caught her sister's gaze. "What if what's wrong with Mom turns out to be something serious?"

"Then we deal with that when—and if—that day comes."

8

6:58 a.m.
TBI Headquarters

Garrett stood in front of the crime board that had been lined with photos of the abducted girls, including the Polaroids that had been left behind. The original police sketch of their abductor hung next to the girls. But the description of the man had been too vague to make an arrest. They had so little to go on.

Detective Everston, who'd run the investigation on Julia's disappearance, had given them the timeline they'd worked up while searching for her. There were still a few holes from the seventy-two hours before her disappearance, but they were now beginning to fill in the gaps. Except this time they were no longer looking for Julia. They were looking for her murderer.

Saturday morning Julia had arrived at the local coffee shop where she worked, clocking out at three thirty. According to a receipt on her normal route, she'd bought a bag of chips and a Coke at a gas station a ten-minute walk from her house. Video surveillance showed her leaving the station with no signs of distress. She'd had plans to spend the rest of the afternoon studying for a biology test with a friend at her house, but had called just

78

before four to say she was running late. When her mom called her thirty minutes later, the call was automatically forwarded to her voice mail.

No one had heard from her since.

Officers had canvassed the ten-minute route she normally took home every day, talking to both shopkeepers and private residents. No one had seen anything unusual. Which meant she'd gone missing somewhere between 3:51 and about 4:20—vanishing without a trace.

Garrett rubbed his neck, trying to relax the tension that had spread from his temples down to his shoulders. The discovery of Julia's body had hit the top of the news last night and would be the first thing people saw this morning when they checked the headlines. Fear was going to creep into the homes of thousands across this part of the country, with the knowledge that a killer was out there who hadn't been caught. The fact that her murder was connected with the disappearance of two other girls—and the murder of one of them—was only going to throw fuel on the fire.

All they needed was a clear piece of evidence. DNA from the autopsy, a witness who could identify Julia's abductor, a connection between the three girls . . . anything that would point them in the right direction.

Garrett reached for his barely lukewarm coffee and took a sip. He'd been restless last night, waking up every couple hours. And when he did sleep, his dreams weren't of the case. Instead they'd been about Jordan. He'd enjoyed spending time with her. Enjoyed reminiscing about the past and catching up on her family.

He tossed the mostly empty cup into the lined trash can and frowned. The last thing he needed right now was a distraction. He sat back down and began working on the list he'd started two hours ago, looking for a connection between the three girls. Each of the families of the girls at the time of their disappearance had provided a detailed list of friends, coworkers, teachers, and favorite hangouts. If there was any overlapping between the three girls, anything that tied them together, he needed to find it. So far, though, the girls had run in completely different circles.

"Morning." Jordan walked into the room and set her bag and a box of donuts on the table, then tugged off her blue scarf. "I'm assuming you still love maple donuts?"

He smiled. "Do you even have to ask? But what about you? I thought you were getting ready to run a marathon?"

"I didn't say I was going to indulge." She shot him a smile, then stepped up to the board. "What time did you get here?"

He shook his head. "You don't want to know. I couldn't sleep, so I decided I might as well get some work done."

"You should have called me. Anything new this morning?"

"I've primarily been going over the notes in Julia Kerrigan's missing persons file as well as going through her social media profiles and looking for a connection to the other two girls. I think you're right about Quinn not being involved. Everything points to our serial killer, including the fact that she'd felt as if someone was following her."

"Where did you find that information?"

"Five days ago she sent a message to one of her friends that she felt like someone was watching her."

"Any descriptions?"

"No." He handed her a highlighted printout of the string of messages he'd found. "But she said there was a man hanging around the coffee shop that made her uncomfortable."

"We need to get their video footage."

"I've already left a message with the manager." Garrett's gaze trailed back to the board.

"But . . ."

He shook his head. "I'm not convinced we'll find anything there."

"Why not?"

He tapped his finger against the sketch. "This is the only composite we have. It could fit the profile of half the men who walked into the coffee shop that day."

She stared at the photo.

"Jordan?"

She turned back to him. "Sorry. Like you, I didn't sleep well. But someone had to have seen something. Because how does someone grab a girl in broad daylight without anyone seeing anything?"

"I don't know." Garrett let out a sharp sigh, feeling the mounting frustration that had kept him restless most of the night. "I've been studying the files of the other two girls believed to be connected. We have confirmation that the gun that killed Julia was the same gun that killed Jessica Wright. But even with our forensics team doing a thorough investigation of the crime scenes, very little evidence was recovered from any of the three cases."

"But maybe that's what's most significant."

"What do you mean?"

She stepped in front of the coffeepot brewing on the countertop and poured herself a cup. "I mentioned it at the crime scene, but I'm still convinced that whoever was behind this is meticulous. This wasn't a crime of passion—it was planned out. From what you just said, we now have evidence that someone may have stalked all three of his victims before they disappeared. Each of them told someone that they felt like they were being followed."

"But what was his motive? Why *this* girl? If you're correct, it wasn't simply because she was at the wrong place at the wrong time. She was targeted. They were all targeted."

"Which is why all of this makes Quinn seem less and less like the guy we're after," she said. "The slashed tires, the threats . . . they were responses to anger, not fastidious planning."

"Agreed. And on top of that, the bartender verified that he was there from just before two until around six thirty the afternoon Julia disappeared. Which means, while it won't help his case for custody of his daughter, it does take him off the hook for murder."

"Okay."

"And there's another thing you're going to want to see," Garrett said, picking up a file. "It will be a while before we get the toxicology report, but here's the initial autopsy report from the ME's office."

"Anything surprising?"

He shook his head. "Her death was pretty straightforward. She was shot in the head at close range. There are no defensive wounds. He probably had a weapon on her the whole time. We'll know more once the rest of the reports are in, but the ME said he's not expecting any surprises."

"Time of death?"

"He's estimating seventy-two hours before her body was found."

"So she was killed the same day she was abducted. What about DNA on her body? Anything that might point to our killer."

"Nothing."

He felt like they were going in circles. They kept coming up with the same empty answers, and they were no closer to finding out the truth than when the search had begun for Jessica Wright eighteen months ago.

Jordan sipped her coffee beside him. "We need to keep searching for a connection between the girls. Their schools, churches, communities, activities—"

"I hope you're making some progress." Sam walked across the room, stopping beside them. "The media's grabbed on to this and isn't going to let up until we give them some answers."

"That's going to be difficult, considering that so far we've got three girls who went missing, two bodies, and zero solid leads," Garrett said, not even attempting to hide his frustration.

"The guy can't be that good," Sam said.

"I don't think he is," Jordan said.

"Meaning?" Garrett asked.

"I was up late working on a profile from the information I have. Without solid leads, we have to look at what we do know. The grave, the Polaroid shots . . ." She held up one of the photos of Julia from the crime scene. "The gunshot wound is up close and personal. He wants to be in control. He's precise. Calculating."

"How is that going to help us find him?" Sam asked.

"It's not easy, but it means that our questions can't just focus on *how*. They have to focus on *why*. When someone commits murder, the reasons behind that murder are usually revenge, or maybe domestic violence, or simply anger. A serial killer's motivation is usually completely different."

"And the profile you've been working on?" Garrett asked.

"For starters, the crime scenes show that he's thorough. He plans ahead, stalks his victims, or at a minimum chooses them ahead of time. He's precise, calculated, and maybe even a bit OCD."

"Here's another thing I want to know," Garrett said, grabbing one of the donuts out of the box. "How does he get these girls to go with him? With all three girls, we never found evidence that he used violence to abduct them except for a couple bruises that may or may not be related. But would any of them get into a car with a total stranger? They're all smart, with no family issues, at least not on the surface."

"So you're saying our guy didn't just drive up and bribe them with a candy bar," Sam said.

"They knew him, or there was something about him that compelled them to go with him." Jordan set her hands on her hips and shook her head. "And he does make mistakes. We just need to find them."

***

Garrett watched Jordan work as she pored over the case files. While the forensics lab worked to process the evidence, they dug for a connection between the cases. If there was a connection between the three girls, as she believed, he had no doubt they would find it.

But the case wasn't the only thing bothering him. He'd yet to put his finger on it, but something was off with Jordan. She seemed distracted, which made him wonder if it was something he'd said or done last night.

He sat down on the edge of her desk. "You doing okay?"

"I'm fine. Why?"

"Even after all these years, I still feel like I can read you. If I said something last night that bothered you or made you uncomfortable—"

"No. It's not you. I enjoyed last night. A lot." She dropped the pen she was holding, then reached up and rubbed her temples. "But you're right. There is something bothering me."

She bit her lip, as if contemplating what or how much to tell him.

"I found out this morning that my mother's sick," she said finally.

"What's wrong?"

"They don't know, other than they believe it's something serious. And I could see it in her eyes, Garrett. She looks so tired and frail. It's like she's aged a decade since I saw her last."

"Wow . . . I'm so sorry, Jordan. Truly I am. I know how close the two of you are."

"I'm just sorry that I'm gone so much. I missed Christmas this year." She looked up and caught his gaze. "I promised I'd make it next December, but what if she's not here?"

"Don't go there," he said, shaking his head. "You don't know that."

"Maybe, but today I realized how much I've missed them. I don't know. Do you ever struggle to balance life? Family, personal, work . . . sometimes it gets so complicated I realize I haven't spoken to my mom in a couple of weeks. Time just keeps slipping by."

"I do feel the struggle, though my family isn't quite as supportive as yours."

"They love you," she said. "They just don't know how to show it."

He wouldn't tell her that he hadn't spoken to his father for six months. Or that the last time he saw his mother, she told him she didn't think their marriage was going to survive another year.

"There is one other thing." She tapped her fingers on the desk. "I know this isn't the most private place, but in case I don't see you again today, I wanted a chance to say goodbye."

"You're leaving already?"

She clasped the necklace he'd given her, making him wonder if keeping it had been a way to hold on to her past. Because for him, he suddenly realized, not running after her was his greatest regret.

"I've been called back to Quantico."

The news took him by surprise. "Already?"

She nodded. "I received a call from my boss a few minutes ago. I have a meeting with the director here in a little bit, I'll have dinner with Mom and Dad and Clara tonight, then leave early in the morning. I'll be able to do any necessary follow-up from there."

"Wow. I guess—I don't know—I guess I thought you'd stay a few more days. Help us find a lead to catch this guy."

"You're going to catch him. I'll be available by phone and will send you a more detailed analysis once I've been able to cross-reference these cases with other crime scenes."

"What time is your plane?" he asked.

"Six thirty."

"If you need a ride, I'd be happy to take you."

"Thanks, but I've got my rental car."

He wanted to stall. Wanted to find a way to spend more time with her. He wasn't ready to watch her walk out of his life again. But that's exactly what was going to happen. She was going to walk out of his life just like she had the last time.

"It's been good to see you," he said. "And if there's ever anything I can do for your parents, please tell them to call me."

"Thank you." She pushed her chair back and stood up. "I've watched you work, Garrett. You're a good addition to the team. And I have no doubt you're going to find this guy."

He wanted to tell her to stay in touch. But their lives rarely intersected. And when she was back home, she needed to be with her family, not digging up old memories. Which was all he really was. Still . . .

She let him wrap his arms around her one last time. He could smell the faint scent of her perfume and feel the softness of her cheek as it brushed against his. Even after all these years she still seemed . . . familiar. He took a step back and brushed away the thought. He didn't have time to be sentimental.

He watched as she said goodbye to Sam and Michaels, then headed out of the office without turning back. It shouldn't matter. He'd stopped loving her years ago. But if that was true, then why was his heart begging her to stay?

2005

9

Garrett pulled the row of photos from the case they'd just wrapped up off the murder board while Sam and Michaels did paperwork. A robbery gone bad had left a widow and three fatherless children. He took one last look at the picture of the victim's three-year-old girl before dropping it into the labeled box. Another investigation closed meant the victim's wife could hopefully find peace, knowing her husband's murderer was behind bars. But it didn't change the fact that more children were going to grow up without their father. It was the reminder he faced every day. There were no guarantees in life. It could end in a moment, whether you were prepared or not.

The special agent in charge, Captain Carly Parks, walked through the doorway, dressed in a dark business suit, with a signature touch of color, this time from a red blouse.

She stopped in the middle of the room and held up a thick file folder. "You're going to have to hold off on any celebrations for the time being," she said. "I know your team's got a stack of cases on your desk to deal with, even with this one off your plate, but we just got a call from the south precinct. Another girl's gone missing."

Garrett looked up at the captain from behind his desk and frowned as she dropped the file in front of Sam.

"The district attorney general has officially assigned your team the lead on this case," Parks continued. "We want this guy caught."

"So no body yet?" Garrett asked.

"I'm hoping we don't find a body. Which is why we need to move fast."

Garrett moved in front of Sam's desk and flipped open the file. He took in the photo of the bright-eyed teen with a broad smile, looking as if she didn't have a care in the world. She fit the profile. Long blonde hair. Fifteen, maybe sixteen years old. "How long ago did she go missing?"

"Her sister was supposed to pick her up after school yesterday, but when she got there, the girl was already gone. She hasn't been seen since." The captain took a sip of the water bottle she always had in her hand. "Without our releasing any kind of official state-ment, the media's already speculating that this case is connected to our Angel Abductor. And you know what that means. They're going to make a circus out of this if we're not careful, and I for one don't want to deal with last year's hysteria again."

Julia Kerrigan's murder had sent the city and surrounding coun-ties into a state of panic. School administrations had reevaluated their open-campus policies, while parents doubled their vigi-lance over their children's whereabouts. And yet despite weeks and months searching for the Angel Abductor and their forensics team combing through the evidence, they were still no closer to finding the killer than they had been three years ago when Jessica Wright's body was found.

Then five months ago, a fourth girl had gone missing. Bailey McKnight's body was found in a shallow grave by a bunch of col-lege kids who were rock climbing north of Nashville. And now it was happening all over again.

Sam turned back to his computer and pulled up the video footage from the local news channel, then swiveled his screen around so they could all see it. A reporter stood in front of a local Nashville school, updating the public on the disappearance.

"According to local law enforcement, another young woman has been abducted in Eastern Tennessee, this time in a Nashville suburb. If this is the work of the so-called Angel Abductor, as the media has dubbed the unknown killer, this will be the fifth girl to be abducted in two and a half years. According to the last statement released by law enforcement, they have yet to find a solid lead related to the case, despite their long-term efforts.

"The Tennessee Bureau of Investigation has raised the status of the missing girl to an AMBER Alert, with authorities asking that the public report anything they might know about the case. There is currently a $5,000 reward for information leading to her safe recovery. As for the victim, Sarah Boyd is fifteen years old, five feet five inches tall, and weighs 120 pounds. She was last seen wearing an 'I Love New York' sweatshirt with jeans and a pair of red sneakers. We are still waiting for news of a press conference by local police, but in the meantime if you have any information on the whereabouts of Sarah Boyd or information on any of the other girls believed to have been abducted by the Angel Abductor, please contact the local authorities immediately."

Sam pushed pause, freezing the video. "So much for avoiding a panic. I'd say it's a bit too late for that."

"We can't exactly stop them from speculating," Garrett said. "And besides, the news coverage is crucial. It means more chance of witnesses coming forward. I guess with no body being found, there also hasn't been a Polaroid shot found?"

"No, but don't forget that so far we've been able to keep the existence of the Polaroid photos out of the media," Parks said. "Something I want to keep that way. But that doesn't dismiss the fact that, as far as I'm concerned, what the press is inferring about the perpetrator being the Angel Abductor could very well be true."

Sam tapped his finger against the file. "The problem is, even now after five girls vanishing, all we've got is a vague sketch of a man who may or may not be involved. We don't even have a list of suspects."

"Maybe, but your team still knows this case better than anyone else. I want this to end. Now. We've got five missing girls, three bodies, and nothing solid that leads us to the person behind this. That's not good enough. I've called a press conference to try and put a lid on the panic, but we need to find this guy and we need to find him fast. I want this girl found alive."

"So what's been done so far to find her?" Michaels asked, leaning forward in his chair.

"Officers are spending a second day canvassing the neighborhoods surrounding the school as well as interviewing students and staff. They're also searching the woods behind the school."

Parks didn't have to say anything else. A wooded area was the perfect place to bury a body.

"Who's the last known person to have seen the girl?" Sam asked.

Parks scanned her notes. "A fellow student, Cassie Stratton. She saw Sarah get into a black car outside the school."

"Willingly?"

"Cassie claims Sarah never appeared to be in any kind of distress. In fact, she didn't even know Sarah was missing until this morning. There's a transcript of the interview in the file. She gave a vague description of the man Sarah got into the car with, but said she didn't really see him that well."

"I'll arrange for our team to interview her, as well as the Boyd family." Sam pushed his chair back. "What about the FBI? Do you recommend we involve them again?"

"I've already contacted them actually," Parks said. "I've requested Special Agent Lambert's input on the case, but she's on leave. Apparently someone in her family is sick."

Garrett's jaw tensed at the news. He hadn't spoken to Jordan since they'd worked together sixteen months ago, but that didn't mean he hadn't thought about her. As soon as he had a few minutes free, he'd call her and find out what was going on. Not for any personal motives. Just as an old friend checking up on another old friend.

"We're going to need to work fast if we're going to find this girl," Parks said. "I've got forensics working overtime looking for evidence, hoping we'll catch a break. Michaels, I want a draft on what we're going to say at the press conference. We go live in an hour."

"I'm on it," Michaels said, moving back to his desk.

"Sam . . . Garrett . . . Pay a visit to the family. I know they've already given a statement, but see if you can come up with some-thing they missed, especially in the light of this connecting to the other girls. In the meantime, I'll make sure you're sent any updates."

Sam grabbed his jacket off the back of his chair and turned to Garrett. "I'll set up a place to meet the family, then we can go."

Garrett nodded and pulled out his phone, deciding to call Jordan on his way out. He was just about to hang up when she answered.

"Jordan? Hey . . . it's Garrett."

"Hey . . . how are you? It's been a long time."

"I'm fine. I was just calling to see if you were okay. Agent Parks said she'd spoken with the FBI about a new case and that you'd taken some leave. I was worried about you and your family."

"I'm here in Nashville actually, and have been meaning to call you, but things have been a bit crazy." There was a long pause on the line. "It's my mom. She's dying. Someone from hospice came to the house three days ago to set things up."

He hated that she'd been right that her mom might not be around for long. "Jordan . . . wow . . . I'm so, so sorry. You should have called me, because if there's anything I can do to help—"

"Honestly, there's nothing anyone can do. We're just taking one day at a time and trying to figure out how to deal with everything. I haven't been able to get my mind wrapped around the fact that she's dying. The good thing is that she's comfortable, and as hard as it is for me to accept it, I think she's ready to go."

He hated hearing the sadness in her voice. They might not be together anymore, but that didn't mean he didn't still care. "How much time does she have?"

"A few days at the most. They're doing everything they can to keep her comfortable, and we're making sure someone is always with her."

As he walked out into the bright sunlight a step behind Sam, he caught the emotion in her words, though she wouldn't want him to know that. She'd always projected strength, but there were still certain vulnerabilities about her, and family was one of them. And while she might not get to see them as much as she wanted, her family would always come first. No matter the pull of her job, she would be there for them.

Man, he missed her.

"I heard there's another girl who disappeared who might be connected to the Angel Abductor," she said.

Her question pulled him out of his thoughts. "They've just given us the case, and we're hopeful she'll turn up alive. But forget about all that, Jordan. You don't need anything else on your plate."

"I know, but I'll be fine, really. I'm planning on taking off a few more days, but at some point I'd like to stop by and help. I need to stay busy and not think too much. I'm going to need the distraction."

"Listen," he said, slowing down as they approached Sam's car. "I'd like to help out. Let me bring your family dinner tonight."

"I appreciate the offer, but you don't have to do that. The ladies from church are keeping us supplied in casseroles. My father won't have to go grocery shopping for weeks."

Garrett chuckled. "I'm not surprised. But let me do something. I'll bring you a coconut custard pie. You probably don't have one of those sitting on your kitchen counter, do you?"

He heard the slight intake of breath in her voice and smiled. She'd never been able to resist pie.

"You remembered," she said.

"I figured pie would be the one remnant of your sweet tooth that you couldn't let go."

Pies had always been their way to celebrate. Peanut butter pie, cherry pie, chocolate pecan pie . . . But her favorite had always been coconut custard pie.

He shoved back the memory and forced his mind into the present. He wasn't going there. Not again. He was calling because he still cared about her and her family's well-being. Nothing more. "And maybe you'll let me get you out of the house for an hour or so," he added. "We could go for a drive. Give you a chance to clear your head."

"I'd like that."

Her answer surprised him. He'd expected her to brush him off.

"Sam and I are heading off to interview the family right now."

"Bring me copies of the case file when you come, will you? I've been staying up pretty late at night with my mother in case she needs something. I could use a diversion."

"I've got to go, but I'll text you when I'm on my way to your house."

"Okay, and Garrett . . . thank you."

Garrett hung up the call as Sam started the car, determined for the time being to put any thoughts of Jordan—and the distraction she brought with them—behind him.

10

Garrett's gut churned as he slipped into the passenger seat of Sam's car. While his conversation with Jordan still hovered in the forefront of his mind, he couldn't shake the reality that they were heading out to meet with yet another family whose lives could be shattered by the so-called Angel Abductor.

"You okay?" Sam asked, pulling out of the parking lot.

"Besides the fact that there's another girl missing?" He blew out a sharp breath. "I just spoke to Jordan Lambert. You remember, the agent who was here from the FBI? She told me that her mom's gone into hospice."

"Hospice . . . wow. I'm sorry to hear that. I've lost both my parents, so I know how hard that is."

"How long ago?"

"My mother died over a decade ago, but I lost my father about eighteen months ago. He'd just turned eighty-nine. And you know what, I still miss him."

"Did he live around here?" Garrett asked.

"They owned a farm outside Nashville. Forty acres of pastureland.

Up until the last six months or so of his life I could show up and still find him out fixing the roof on his house or repairing fences. He always amazed me."

"Sounds like the two of you were close."

"We didn't always see eye to eye, but yeah, we were close." Sam glanced at Garrett as he pulled onto the highway. "What about you? Did your leaving the family firm cause any ripples?"

Garrett laughed. "Ripples? How about tidal waves. Expectations were for me to become a lawyer *and* marry the right southern girl."

"Can I assume that marrying the girl didn't work out either?"

"Nope." Garrett dug into the unwanted memory. "I did get engaged, though, to the right girl. At least according to my parents. And I actually thought she was the one for a while. Problem was, her father was a developer who had a pile of unethical moves in play, and he wanted me to help him skirt the law. When I confronted him, he told me it was the price we paid to get to where we were. Money. Prestige."

He'd tried to justify defending men like Benjamin Hagan, while living out his Christian faith. But in the end, after his confrontation with Hagan, the only option he could live with was walking away from it all.

"And your fiancée?" Sam asked.

"Apparently, she approved of her father's deeds. Six weeks before the wedding, she broke things off."

"I bet that caused a huge stink."

"That's putting it mildly."

"So after that?"

"I decided I'd had enough. I left the firm and joined the police academy, and to be honest, I've never looked back."

"This life isn't so bad. My wife and I have been married thirty-one years, and she puts up with my long hours and obsessive cases. Though I also know that she's waiting for me to retire. But I'm not sure I can. Not yet, anyway. Not when there are cases like this to solve."

"Then you're never going to retire," Garrett said, half serious.

Sam laughed. "I think you're right. She keeps waiting for me to retire so she can travel. Her dream life would be to spend winters in Florida with our oldest son and his family and summers in Colorado with our youngest."

"That's not a bad plan."

"Maybe not," Sam said, pulling off the highway, "but it doesn't give me a lot of motivation to get up in the mornings. This does."

"And you don't feel that it's jaded you after all these years?"

It was a question he'd asked himself more than once over the past year and a half that he'd been working for the department. While he'd never regretted his decision to go into law enforcement, there were days—like today—when he could almost convince himself that defending guys like Sabrina's father would be a whole lot easier than dealing with the aftermath of a serial killer.

"I hope I'm not jaded, but cases like this—the ones we've yet to solve—do grate at me."

"You think she's still alive?"

"The odds say no, but until we have a body in the morgue, there's always a chance."

Garrett knew the statistics. The first forty-eight hours of a missing persons investigation were the most crucial. Technology, public alerts, and cooperation between law enforcement agencies had enabled officers to solve cases more quickly. Especially when a possible abduction was indicated.

He opened the file Parks had given them and started reading through the notes from the officer who had interviewed Sarah's parents after her disappearance.

"Sarah's parents are Rob and Ruth Boyd," Garrett said, giving Sam the highlights as he read through the notes. "They own the BBQ restaurant where we're meeting them. They have four children, Sarah is the youngest. There's another daughter named Nikki who's a teacher and two boys, Matt and Luke. Sarah and Luke are the only two still living at home, but all live here in Nashville."

"Sounds like an all-American family. What about Sarah?"

"According to her teachers, she gets good grades, stays out of trouble, and is well liked."

"So there's no chance that she simply ran away with her boyfriend?"

"I don't think we should rule anything out, but that seems to be the consensus."

Ten minutes later, Sam pulled into the parking lot of Boyds' BBQ restaurant, located in a prime location in downtown Nashville. The restaurant wouldn't open for another couple of hours. The family had asked if they would meet them here where they'd set up a command post to find Sarah.

Garrett breathed in the smell of smoked sausage as he walked into the restaurant, making him wish they were open for breakfast. One of Nashville's up-and-coming artists played over the restaurant's sound system, but he barely heard the catchy tune. He shifted his gaze to the reclaimed wood walls of Boyds' BBQ that displayed dozens of vintage guitars and retro signs, along with sports paraphernalia and photos, primarily of the Tennessee Titans and NASCAR.

Rob and Ruth Boyd met them in the entrance, along with another young woman who, from the resemblance to Sarah, had to be Nikki. Several people bustled around in the background, setting up tables and getting ready to open the restaurant.

"I'm Special Agent Bradford and this is my partner, Special Agent Addison. I spoke with you on the phone a little while ago."

"Of course." Rob Boyd introduced his wife and daughter. "Thanks for agreeing to meet us here. We've decided to use the restaurant as our base to organize the search for Sarah. It seems like the best place for us to get the word out."

"It's not a problem at all," Garrett said. "Our team has taken over your daughter's case, and while we realize this is difficult, we feel it's important to do a follow-up interview to ensure we don't miss anything crucial."

Nikki showed them to a large room in the back of the restaurant where a dozen people were working. "I'm coordinating volunteers. We're putting up flyers, sending updates to the news outlets, and making sure we have a presence on social media."

"That's great. I hope you don't mind my getting straight to the point. Nikki, I understand you were the one who called 911," Sam said, as the five of them sat down at the end of one of the long tables. "Can you tell me what happened?"

Nikki nodded, clearly dealing with a lot of emotion. "I was supposed to pick her up after school. I'd promised to take her out for ice cream to celebrate a good grade on an algebra test. On my way to pick her up, I decided to stop at the mall to buy some shoes I'd had my eye on, figuring I'd have plenty of time to grab them on my way and pick her up on time. I ended up getting to the school fifteen minutes late, and when I got there, I couldn't find her."

Her mom reached out and squeezed Nikki's hand.

"I didn't think much about it at first. I thought she might've caught a ride home with a friend. But when I got home, she wasn't there. That's when I began to worry that something was wrong. Sarah would never have just left school without telling someone where she was going. That's when I called 911.

"The police canvassed the neighborhoods, and we spoke to everyone at the school. They set up roadblocks and put out an AMBER Alert. At that point, no one we spoke to saw her get into a car. None of her friends or her friends' parents. She just . . . vanished." Nikki wiped her cheek. "We finally got an eyewitness statement from Cassie, who saw her get into a black car. To be honest, that's all we know. No one has seen her since. There's been no activity on her MySpace account, and her phone goes straight to voice mail."

Sam leaned forward. "I know it's a hard question to ask, but do you think it's possible Sarah ran away?"

"No. Not Sarah," Mrs. Boyd said. "I know every parent probably says this, but Sarah's got her head on straight. She really does.

Except for math, her grades are high, she has good friends . . . She wouldn't have just run off with some guy."

Sam and Garrett spent the next twenty minutes asking questions and going over a plan before wrapping things up.

"We appreciate your speaking with us," Mr. Boyd said, shaking their hands.

"I'll walk them out," Nikki said.

She didn't say anything until they stepped outside into the empty parking lot. Then she stopped and turned to speak to them. "My parents are frantic, as you can imagine, but I've managed to convince them not to watch the news. I, on the other hand, have watched the reports. They're already guessing that Sarah's disappearance is tied to the Angel Abductor. I need to know if that's more than just guessing."

"I know you're wanting answers," Garrett said, "and we'll give them to you as soon as we have them. For now, I can tell you that, yes, we are looking into the possibility that there is a connection to the Angel Abductor. But we're not ready to jump to any conclusions yet."

Nikki's body stiffened at the remark. "Thanks for telling me. But if it is him, there are things that just don't add up. Like why she'd get into a car with someone she didn't know. Sarah wouldn't do that. Ever."

"And yet we have a witness—one of her close friends—who says she did."

"I know," Nikki said. "And I also know you deal with things like this every day, but this is my family and I need to find my sister. Tell me what to do."

"From what we talked about in there, you're doing all the right things. We'll keep you in the loop as to what we're doing, and we need you to involve us in your plans as well."

As soon as they'd gotten back into the car to leave, Garrett voiced his questions out loud to Sam, "What do you think? Do you think our abductor—whether he's our serial killer or not—is actually brazen enough to simply drive away with her from in front of the school?"

"I admit it doesn't make sense," Sam said. "The problem is that up to this point there hasn't been any witness who's seen him take the girls, but it sure would make more sense if she'd disappeared in some deserted place."

"On the other hand," Garrett said, "if this is our Angel Abductor, he's already proven himself to be both smart and cunning."

Sam pulled out of the parking lot and merged into traffic. "The theory's come up before that he could be someone in law enforcement or someone impersonating an officer. If she thought someone—maybe her sister—had been injured and she thought he was law enforcement, she might have gone with him willingly."

Garrett's cell phone rang and he grabbed it out of his jacket pocket. "Michaels," he said, putting the phone on speaker. "What have you got?"

"We just finished with the press conference, and the media is chomping at the bit for answers. But here's what you need to know. Uniforms canvassing the school grounds just found a Polaroid photo of Sarah."

Garrett let out a low groan. "Which means we're no longer speculating about a connection."

"What about a body?" Sam asked.

"So far all we've got is the photo found about a quarter of a mile from where she got into the car."

"Any fingerprints?" Garrett asked.

"We'll send it to the lab, but it doesn't look like it."

"I want you to make sure the scene is secure," Sam said. "Have the metro police broaden their search to see if we can come up with any more witnesses. Someone had to have seen something."

"We're on our way now." Garrett checked the time. "We'll be there in twenty minutes."

Garrett shivered as he stood in the wooded area where they'd found the photo. Sarah's disappearance was shaping up to mirror that of victim number two, Becky Collier, who had never been found. The other three victims' bodies had been found near the Polaroid photos of them. Which led to a slew of unanswered questions. What had been different about these two girls? Were they still alive? Had they escaped? Or had the authorities, for whatever reason, simply never found their bodies?

Garrett stared at the Polaroid shot of Sarah Boyd. It was a stark contrast from the smiling photo clipped to her file. He'd seen the same look on the other girls' faces in the pictures found near their bodies. The realization of what had probably happened to her turned his stomach. Kids her age should be getting ready for summer vacation, not worrying about being abducted in broad daylight.

"So what do you think happened?" He turned to Sam. "Why leave the photo and not the body?"

"Maybe that wasn't his plan. Maybe something spooked him. Or maybe his MO is evolving. Changing."

"Maybe. What we do know is that he was here."

"Which is why we're going to put this area under a microscope. This guy has to make a mistake at some point, and when he does, we're going to get him."

But they needed to get him before another girl turned up dead.

Garrett walked the grid, circling out from where they'd found the photo. If the perpetrator wanted to bury her, this would be a perfect spot. Isolated. Quiet. If she was dead, why wasn't she here?

Sam picked up a package of weed and slipped it into an evidence bag. "Someone's been out here tokin' up."

"Doesn't really surprise me," Garrett said. "I'm sure all kinds of unsavory things go on in these woods."

"Here's the interesting thing," Sam said. "It rained hard two nights ago and this packaging is dry. The bag is ripped, but there aren't any signs of water damage."

"Which puts whoever had this here in the same time frame as our killer."

"We need to run this for fingerprints."

"How fast can we get it?" Garrett asked.

"I'll pull a couple favors and see if I can't get it to the front of the line. Then we're looking at two, maybe three hours."

Garrett nodded. "And in the meantime, we need to speak to the last person who saw Sarah alive."

11

Garrett walked into the lobby of the bureau headquarters where Mrs. Stratton and her daughter Cassie sat waiting to be interviewed. Cassie looked to be about the same age as Sarah. She sat in a chair, wearing jeans and a shirt with the British flag. Her eyes were red as if she'd been crying. She stared at her phone. Yesterday, she'd been just like Sarah. A young girl with her entire life ahead of her. And now her best friend was gone and everything she knew to be safe and okay had just been shattered.

"Mrs. Stratton . . . Cassie?" Garrett stepped in front of them. "I'm Special Agent Garrett Addison. I appreciate your coming down on such short notice."

Mrs. Stratton glanced at her daughter, then said, "Give us a minute, will you, Cassie."

Her daughter shrugged her shoulders and went back to doing whatever she'd been doing on her phone.

Garrett motioned her mother to the other side of the room. "Is everything all right?"

"I just need you to know that Sarah was Cassie's best friend.

105

She feels incredibly guilty over the fact that she watched someone drive her away without realizing what was happening. To have to relive that again and again . . . I'm just worried about her."

It happened far too often in cases he'd dealt with. Guilt from surviving a tragedy when someone you loved didn't. Guilt from second-guessing how you should have dealt with a situation. But there was no way to turn back the clock. Just like there had been no way for Cassie to have known Sarah's life was in danger.

"I know this is extremely hard on both of you," Garrett said. "But please know that our only interest in speaking with her is finding Sarah."

"I understand, but before you talk to her . . . please keep in mind what I said. I know there's no way to erase what's happened, and I know that what Sarah's family is going through is a hundred times worse than what Cassie's experiencing, but she's still my baby."

A minute later, they met Sam inside the interview room that was supposed to make victims and their families more comfortable, though he doubted it ever did.

"Cassie, this is my partner, Agent Sam Bradford," Garrett said, slipping into the seat across from her. "We appreciate your coming down here to talk with us. I know this has been a rough couple days for you."

"So you haven't found Sarah yet?" There was a hint of expectation in Cassie's voice. Like she'd been secretly hoping they'd really called her in to tell her that they'd found Sarah. Instead, they were going to have to disappoint her.

"I'm sorry," Sam said, "but we're doing everything we can to make sure she comes home safe. And one of those things we need to do is verify what you said in your statement to ensure we don't miss anything."

"Okay." Cassie sniffled, and her mom handed her a tissue from her purse. "I just . . . I just can't stop crying." She blew her nose, then wadded the tissue between her fingers. "If I would've waited with Sarah instead of walking off, this might never have happened."

"Before we start, there is something I want you to know," Garrett said, leaning forward. "It's easy to blame yourself. But you had no way of knowing what was happening. You have nothing to be sorry about or to feel guilty about, for that matter. This isn't your fault. Do you understand that?"

"I don't know. Maybe." Cassie tilted her chair back and tapped her black painted nails against the table. "I'm just so scared. I watched the news this morning. They said a serial killer took her. They called him the Angel Abductor. Is that true?"

Garrett glanced at Sam before responding. "That is a possibility we're looking into, but right now we don't know who took her. And since you're the last person who saw her yesterday, we're hoping that there might be something you saw that will help us find her."

"I wish I could give you more, but I already told the other officers everything I know."

"I understand, which is why this won't take long. I'd just like to ask you a few more questions, if that's okay. Sometimes there are little details that end up helping us that you didn't even know were important."

"Are you sure you're okay?" her mom asked.

Cassie nodded. "If I'd been the one who disappeared, Sarah would be doing anything she could to find me. I have to do the same thing."

Garrett picked up his pen. "Let's start with you and Sarah. How long have the two of you been friends?"

"We've been in school together since, like . . . the second grade, I guess. We've been best friends ever since."

"So you would know if she was unhappy or not feeling well."

"Of course."

"Had Sarah been acting differently lately? Moody, withdrawn, anything that might have had you worried about her?"

"No. Not that I can think of."

Garrett caught the hesitation in Cassie's voice while he waited for her to answer. While the number one suspect on their list might be the Angel Abductor, they still had to verify that Sarah hadn't simply run away.

"Are you sure?" Sam asked.

Cassie nodded. "Sarah was hardly ever moody. You know, she's one of those people who are always happy. She always sees the good in everything."

"So you don't know of anything she might have been upset about?"

"No. She was excited about her birthday. She was planning a big party. She seemed fine, and if something had been wrong, she would have told me. We tell each other everything."

"And you don't think it's possible that she was hiding anything from you?" Sam asked.

"Sarah couldn't keep a secret if her life depended on it. Especially not from me."

Sam eyed the file in front of him. "I understand that you and Sarah were in a car wreck a few weeks ago?"

Mrs. Stratton leaned forward and shook her head. "What does this have to do with Sarah's disappearance?"

"We need to look at what Sarah's frame of mind might have been when she got into the abductor's car," Sam said.

"It's okay, Mom."

"Listen." Garrett caught Cassie's gaze. "I know these questions are hard, but here's the truth about missing teens. Most teens who go missing aren't abducted. They run away because of boyfriend issues or problems with their families, so we have to look into every angle and hope that in the process we can come up with a solid lead to follow that brings her home."

Cassie shifted her gaze away from his and stared at the table. "Sarah and I were in a car wreck with a couple of boys about six weeks ago . . . it was pretty bad, but we weren't drinking. None of us were."

"I read that in the report. Can you tell us what happened?"

"Ricky, this guy we were out with, was driving too fast and

missed a curve. It was stupid, I know, and scared me so bad I'll never go with anybody like that again. They had a hard time getting me out of the car." She held up her arm to show them the almost-healed wound running from her elbow to her wrist. "The doctor said I was lucky that this was the worst of it. It took them over an hour to get me out."

"What about Sarah's parents? Were they upset?"

"All our parents were upset." Cassie avoided her mom's gaze. "We were supposed to be studying. Sarah got in trouble, we all did. But she wouldn't run away just because she was grounded."

"What about boys?" Sam asked. "Did she have a boyfriend or someone she was interested in? The guys from the wreck?"

"No, Ricky and Hayden were just friends of ours. She liked this one boy, Brice Mitchell, but it wasn't serious or anything. She didn't even know for sure if he liked her."

"So there wasn't anyone she was involved with that her parents would disapprove of? Or maybe someone they didn't know about?" Garrett asked.

"No . . . not Sarah. I love the girl, but she's way too much of a Goody Two-shoes to do something like that."

"So she got along with her parents?"

"Sarah got along pretty well with everyone. Her parents, teachers, coaches, the kids at school. I'm not saying her life was perfect. I mean, everybody gets mad at their parents, but Sarah was lucky. Her mom and dad are pretty cool. They invite me over to eat at their restaurant sometimes, and I hang out at their house a lot."

"Was there anything that she might have been upset with her parents about?"

"Dumb things. Like she wanted a new dress for her party, but her dad didn't think she needed one. She's into clothes and makeup. Her sister was going to talk her dad into getting the dress. But you don't run away over a dress, either. At least Sarah wouldn't."

"Let's move on to what happened yesterday after school."

Cassie pressed her lips together and nodded. "It was just like any other day. Our last class was over, so we left together."

"What were you talking about?"

"How glad we were that we were done with our biology test and how she couldn't wait for her party. She was really excited about it."

"What happened next?"

"She was meeting Nikki, and I needed to go and talk to another friend of ours about this project we were working on for English, so I left her. Told her I'd see her tomorrow."

"But you still saw her get into the car?"

"Someone's car alarm went off, and when I turned around to see whose it was, Sarah was getting into this black car. I thought it was weird, because she'd told me she was waiting for her sister and I knew it wasn't Nikki's car. But that's all I know. I watched her get in and then she was gone."

"And yet she didn't seem upset. Meaning no one was forcing her into the car."

"No. Not from what I could see."

"I understand you gave a description of the man to the officers who spoke with you yesterday."

"I didn't see him well, but I know it was a man. I didn't recognize him."

"Could this be him?" Sam pushed the artist's sketch across the table in front of Cassie and waited for her to study it.

"I don't know. Maybe. It kind of looks like him, though I don't think he had a beard. But like I said, all I got was a quick look. Who is he?"

"A possible suspect." They'd have to leave it at that, though Garrett had no doubt that the media was already spewing out every conjecture they could come up with. But there was nothing he could do about that right now.

"Let's move on to the car she got into. Can you remember anything about the vehicle that stood out to you?"

Cassie shrugged. "I don't really pay much attention to cars."

"That's okay. Just try to remember. Any bumper stickers? Un-usual lights? Anything that that would help us recognize it?"

"The hubcaps were shiny, but it was just another car to me." Cassie spread her fingers out on the table in front of her, palms down. "If it wasn't this Angel Abductor who took her, then where is she?"

Garrett caught the panic in her voice. Things like this always happened to other people. And teenagers in particular believed themselves to be invincible. Except they weren't.

"We can't answer that," Garrett said. "But our job is to go through the evidence and then keep digging until we find out what happened."

Cassie leaned forward. "I might not know what happened to Sarah, but she didn't run away. I spoke with her right after school. She wasn't upset at all. She was getting ready to meet her sister for ice cream, not some guy she was planning to run away with. And Sarah would never get into a car with someone she didn't know."

"So you're saying that she had to have known the person she got into the car with."

Garrett looked at Sam. They'd come to the conclusion that either there had been some kind of contact with the abductor ahead of time, or that he'd stalked each girl, waiting for the right moment to take them. But they'd yet to come up with a connection between the abductor and all the girls. With the past four victims, they'd investigated everyone from teachers, to school janitors, to church connections and extracurricular activities, but still hadn't found the link they were looking for.

Garrett slid his business card across the table to Cassie. "If you think of anything that might help us find her, please don't hesitate to call. Day or night."

Garrett waited for one of the officers to escort the Strattons to the exit, then turned to Sam. "What do you think? Just like Sarah's family, Cassie is insisting that Sarah wouldn't have just got into a car with a stranger. But we know she *did* get in the car with someone."

Michaels met them outside their offices. "We might have a lead. We found fingerprints on the bag of marijuana that was found near the Polaroid and matched them to a man by the name of Matthew Banks. He's been arrested twice for possession."

"So who is he?" Garrett asked.

"He works at a place called Rob's Gym as one of their personal trainers. He's also a marathon runner, which could explain the marijuana."

Sam shook his head. "Why marijuana?"

"Legal or not, a lot of runners use it in sports," Michaels said. "Especially extreme sports like long-distance running."

Garrett frowned. He'd heard of the practice from more than one person he ran with, but had never had any desire to try it. As far as he was concerned, the high he got from running was enough for him. But if it connected them to Sarah . . .

"We need to pay Mr. Banks a visit and see if we can connect him. I'm pretty sure he isn't going to come forward himself with information regarding what he saw. Not if he had weed on him."

"Did you get an address for him?"

"I called the gym where he works. He's there now. And here's the clincher. He owns a black Crown Victoria that matches Cassie Stratton's description of the car that drove away with Sarah."

Garrett took the address and plate number Michaels had written down and nodded at Sam. "We might have just found our killer."

12

Rob's Gym was located on the end of a busy strip mall less than two miles from Sarah Boyd's school, the location where she'd last been seen. Garrett strode across the parking lot toward the entrance with Sam, surprised at how many cars were in the parking lot in the middle of the day. He preferred to do his workouts early in the morning—often before the sun was even up—rather than deal with the hassle of trying to find time during the day to fit it in. But apparently not everyone felt that way.

Halfway to the front door of the gym, he stopped in front of a black sedan and pulled out his phone to double-check the license plate number they'd been given.

"This is Banks's car," Garrett said, dropping his phone back into his pocket.

"An interesting choice of vehicle for our suspect."

"You can say that again. What are the odds that the man drives a Crown Victoria?" The most widely used automobile in law enforcement.

113

"It could be the answer as to why they were willing to get into the car."

Garrett walked around the vehicle and stopped at the driver's side. "There are marks under this window and above the door handle. And the frame is slightly bent. Looks like someone tried to jack it recently."

"Now that's definitely odd. Your average car thief doesn't usually go for this model." Sam stepped up next to Garrett. "But this looks familiar. When I was in college, my father and I restored a '51 Packard. Someone tried to steal it one night and did this same kind of damage in the process. My father was fit to be tied."

Garrett scanned the interior through the window but didn't see anything of significance. "I didn't know you were into cars?"

"I've rebuilt a couple engines since then," Sam said as they started back for the entrance of the gym. "A '65 Ford Mustang and a '62 Pontiac Grand Prix."

Inside the two-story building was row after row of state-of-the-art fitness equipment. To the left on the main floor, cardio equipment lined up beneath flat-screen TVs playing the news and reality TV. To the right was a separate glassed-in swimming pool where an instructor was teaching a class.

Garrett flashed his badge at the receptionist, who didn't look a day over eighteen. "We're looking for one of your employees. Matthew Banks."

She nodded toward the wide staircase beside them. "Last time I saw him he was headed up to the weight room on the second floor."

"Thanks."

Garrett and Sam hurried up the stairs to the large room that held even more rows of equipment with mirrored walls that opened to the floor below. They searched for their suspect among the couple dozen members working out.

"There he is," Sam said, heading for the far side of the room. "Matthew Banks?"

Banks looked up. "Yes."

"I'm Special Agent Bradford and this is Special Agent Addison with the Tennessee Bureau of Investigation. We'd like to have a word with you about your car."

"My car?" Banks peered behind him, then started running.

"You've got to be kidding me," Garrett said.

He headed after Banks with Sam right behind him, weaving his way between weight machines and a group of bodybuilders who stood gawking at the chase.

Where in the world did he think he was going?

Banks kicked a barbell on the ground and rolled it toward them. Anticipating the move, Garrett jumped over the obstacle and kept running. Banks scurried down a side staircase that led directly to the pool and swung open a glass door. Garrett managed to catch it before it swung shut and breathed in the chlorine and high humidity in the air as he ran into the pool area where a group of middle-aged women were participating in a class. A large sign hanging on the wall said No RUNNING. Right. At the far end of the room was an exit sign over the door leading, he presumed, back out to the parking lot. That was where Banks was headed. But not if he stopped him first.

Garrett pulled a round life preserver off the wall, aimed, then threw it like a Frisbee as hard as he could at the man, hitting him square on the back of his legs. Banks lost his footing and took a nosedive into the pool.

A scurry of movement erupted as the women scrambled to get out of the pool and their instructor shouted at Garrett and Banks for disturbing their class.

Banks bobbed in the water like an apple at a carnival.

Garrett held up his badge to the women, then turned back to Banks and folded his arms across his chest. "It's over. Get out of the pool."

Banks pulled himself onto the tiled deck, then followed orders to lie on his stomach in order for Garrett to handcuff him.

"Sorry for the interruption, ladies," Sam said, shooting the women his best smile.

"Maybe we should start over outside," Garrett said to Banks as they walked toward the exit.

Garrett led the man out the side door, with Sam following right behind, then headed across the parking lot, stopping at the man's car.

"Like my partner said before you decided to bolt," Garrett said, "I'm Special Agent Addison and he's Special Agent Bradford with the Tennessee Bureau of Investigation. Why'd you run?"

Water dripped from the man's gym clothes, forming a puddle on the ground beneath him. "I owe some money to a couple of rough guys. Thought you were them."

"Is this your car?" Garrett asked.

"Why?"

Garrett raised his brow, waiting for an answer.

"Yes, it's my car."

"Good, because we need to take a look inside," Garrett said. "Do you happen to have the keys on you?"

Banks frowned. "You can't just search my car."

"A bag of marijuana with your fingerprints on it was found near a crime scene. I'd say that gives us probable cause."

"What crime scene?"

"Where are your keys?" Garrett repeated.

Banks hesitated, then shrugged. "They're in the zippered pocket in my shorts."

Garrett fished out the key and opened the driver's door, then stepped aside for Sam to take a look.

"It's been temporarily fixed," Sam said, "but someone definitely pried out the ignition switch so they could get to the wires." He stepped away from the car. "But you already knew that, didn't you? And I'm guessing that you didn't report it, because you were afraid your secret might be discovered."

"What secret?" Banks asked.

Sam popped open the trunk, then walked to the back of the car.

"You can't search my car—"

"Actually he can," Garrett said.

"Is this what you're worried about?" Sam asked, nodding to a small stash of weed. "These pick-me-ups in the back of your car?"

"Ouch," Garrett said. "Did you know that a third offense of possession of marijuana is a felony and, according to our records, you've already been arrested twice for possession?"

Sam closed the trunk and nodded at Banks. "I think it's time we have a long talk. About murder."

Matthew Banks stared at the table in the interrogation room, looking terrified. "I don't understand what you're talking about. I didn't murder anyone."

"First things first. We understand you were out running last night," Sam said, sitting down beside Garrett.

"I run most nights, and last I checked, there's nothing illegal about running at night. I'm training for a marathon."

"What time did you go running?" Garrett asked.

"I don't know. I got off work at five thirty and met a friend shortly after that to go running for a couple hours. I'm training for a marathon and usually do a long run on Tuesdays."

"Where'd you run?"

"Percy Warner Park."

"Are you sure?"

"Of course I'm sure. It's one of my regular routes."

"What about the trail that backs up to the high school? Do you ever run there?"

"Why would I run there? It's private property."

"We're asking because you left something there." Garrett slid the photo of the marijuana they'd found near the school across the table. "This matched those we found in your car."

Banks's gaze shifted. "I said I wasn't there, and even if I was, there's no way you can prove that's mine."

"I wouldn't be so sure about that." Garrett frowned. The guy was either innocent or incredibly stupid. "It has your fingerprints all over it."

"Whatever." Banks's jaw tensed. He was clearly feeling defeated. "But it's not like it hurts anyone. People believe that if you use marijuana you're some . . . druggy . . . but the truth is that more runners use it than you think. It helps with fatigue and anxiety, and helps to control pain."

"And it also happens to be illegal," Sam said. "Did you know that in Tennessee, possession of more than half an ounce of marijuana is a felony? And if you're caught cultivating even just one plant, it's also automatically a felony. You're looking at a felony with your third arrest of possession." Garrett leaned forward, pausing for emphasis. "You're looking at jail time no matter how this goes down. And if you're cultivating or distributing, there's a lot more jail time involved."

"No . . . no. I'm not selling. I swear, it's all for personal use. I figured I'd have less of a chance of getting caught if I grew it myself. I didn't have to deal with a seller. And I was hoping to not have to deal with the likes of you."

"Now back to the question of murder," Garrett said. "Do you recognize this girl?"

He slid a photo of Sarah across the table.

"No. Who is she?"

"She went missing yesterday, and we have evidence that puts you on the scene. We believe it's very possible you abducted her."

"Whoa . . . wait a minute." Banks shoved the photo back across the table and held up his hands.

"I need you to think, Banks, because the evidence is stacking up against you. Your car was seen outside the school where Sarah Boyd disappeared. Your fingerprints were found on a bag of weed right next to where we found evidence of her abduction. And it's not just this girl. You've heard of the Angel Abductor, haven't you?"

Garrett laid out the photos of the missing and murdered girls, one at a time.

"No." Banks shook his head. "This wasn't me."

"Then where were you around three thirty yesterday?"

"At the gym. Like I said, I worked till five thirty. I didn't even leave the parking lot until I got off work."

"And you have people who can vouch for you?"

"Of course. The gym is full of people who saw me there." He gripped the edge of the table, realizing perhaps for the first time how serious the situation really was.

"Okay, but if you knew your car was jacked, why didn't you file a police report?"

"Would you have gone to the police if your car had traces of weed in the trunk? But forget the weed. I wasn't near the school, and I didn't kill those girls. Whoever took my car had to have. He jacked the car, then brought it back and tried to frame me." He folded his arms. "I want a lawyer. I'm done talking about this."

"What do you think?" Sam asked after they'd stepped out into the hallway and shut the door behind them.

"I think we need to confirm his alibis with his coworkers and his running partner, but I think he's being set up."

"I tend to agree with you. I'll have Michaels do the follow-up." They started back toward their offices.

"What about cameras at the gym?" Garrett asked.

"Already checked. They have fake cameras up. No recordings. They're just supposed to help deter crimes."

"Well, whoever jacked Banks's car didn't bother to try and hide the crime," Garrett said.

"Which is why I think he wanted us to find Banks." Sam stopped in front of Garrett's desk. "He wanted to send us on a wild-goose chase and keep us distracted. He's playing games."

They were going in circles again, but this wasn't a game. Not when girls' lives hung in the balance.

Sam glanced at the pile of files sitting on Garrett's desk.

"How late were you here last night?" Sam asked.

"Most of the night," Garrett said. "I went through the notes we have on the five victims, then did a search of abductions over the past three years, trying to find any similarities."

"I thought Jordan already did an expanded search of crimes across the state, matching our killer's MO."

"She did. But I keep going back to this case we looked at last winter. It comes close to matching the parameters, but not close enough that we gave it priority."

He had his boss's attention. "Which case?"

"Amanda Love."

They both knew the case well. Amanda Love had been kidnapped one afternoon six months ago on her way home from school, but she'd managed to escape from the location her abductor had taken her. She never saw his face, because when he captured her, he'd grabbed her from behind and blindfolded her.

"Did you find something else?" Sam asked. "Because nothing else about the case fit with our abductor's MO. Our guy is precise, and this guy—whoever took her—fumbled from the get-go."

"True, but she does fit the physical profile of the other victims."

Sam leaned against the edge of the desk. "What else?"

"I've been going over the transcript of Amanda's interview." Garrett said, sitting back down at his desk. "We have a witness that has Sarah Boyd getting into a car with a man."

"Okay."

"Until now, we haven't had any evidence of how our abductor takes the girls," Garrett said. "Does he grab them off the street when no one's looking? Does he lure them into a vehicle? We just haven't known. We only have a sketch of the man because a witness in Wright's case saw her talking to someone. We have evidence that our abductor watches the girls, looking for an opportunity to take them, but we've never known exactly how he takes them. We always assumed that he grabs them when no one is looking. Sarah's case, though, shows us something different.

At least in her abduction. We have a witness who saw her get into the vehicle of our abductor. We just don't know why she would go with him.

"In the interview with Amanda," he continued, "she talked about feeling as if she were being followed—just like most of the other girls. She mentioned an incident that happened when she was walking home from school by herself, three days before her abduction. A car pulled up alongside her and a man rolled down his window. When three boys rode past on bikes, the car drove away. When she was shown the sketch of Julia Wright's abductor, she said it looked like him."

Sam shook his head. "There are still far more discrepancies than similarities. The main one is that Amanda didn't just get into a car when she was taken, she was grabbed from behind, bound, and blindfolded. There were no signs of the other girls being bound or blindfolded."

"I agree, but while there have been basic similarities to each abduction, I also see him evolving in his methods. Changing them to fit the situation. It makes sense."

"Or like I said, it has the fingerprints of a copycat. Because if it was a copycat who took Amanda, he wouldn't have known about the photos. And he wouldn't have known what we know now—that maybe the girls went with him willingly, like Sarah did."

"Or maybe something just went wrong and he didn't get the chance to take her photo. I'd like to bring her in and speak with her again," Garrett said.

"I'm not sure it's worth the trauma on her end of bringing her in and making her relive her experience again. She's had it rough. Her parents weren't too keen on her being interviewed the first time. You remember the interview. She talked about her ongoing nightmares. Her fear of strangers and dark places. And I'm not sure how speaking to her again is going to help."

"We dismissed any connection she could have had to the Angel Abductor, which means there might be things we missed. What if we met outside the department? Somewhere neutral that she chose so she wouldn't feel intimidated."

"You think it's that important?'

"It's possible she's the best eyewitness we have. And we're running out of time to find Sarah Boyd. I think it's worth a second look."

"Okay." Sam nodded. "Go ahead and make the arrangements."

13

Jordan walked beside Garrett as they started across the iconic pedestrian bridge that crossed the Cumberland River. She finally felt her entire body begin to relax. While they were dating, he'd always seemed to be able to read her mind and anticipate her needs. It was one of the things she'd loved about him. And tonight, once again, he'd anticipated exactly what she needed. As much as she loved her family and wanted to be near her mother, she needed an hour away to catch her breath and refocus. And she could tell he'd needed it as well. The case to find the latest girl who'd been abducted was grueling.

The outlook from the bridge seemed to stretch for miles, giving them a stunning view of both the football stadium and the familiar skyline of the city she'd always consider home. Soon the sun would set across the river, followed by a display from the night lights of the city. Part of her missed the leisurely southern pace, live music, and the open green spaces. But what she missed the most was family, friends . . . and Garrett.

"That was the best pie I've had in months," she said, breaking

123

the comfortable silence between them. "Okay, the only piece of pie I've had, but definitely the best."

"Somehow I had a feeling you'd enjoy it." Garrett laughed as they fell into a comfortable stride.

He'd always been good at remembering what she liked. They'd created dozens of memories together. Hiking in Percy Warner Park, canoeing on the Cumberland, music at the Bluebird Café . . . Their relationship hadn't been perfect, but if she closed her eyes, she could almost imagine everything from when they were back in the police academy. Rookie officers out to save the world. They'd been young and invincible. And yet for some reason she'd chosen to walk away from him.

"Any changes with your mom?" he asked.

She pulled her thoughts back to the present. "She sleeps most of the time now. The nurse says it won't be long. One of us tries to be with her all of the time, but today, when she did wake up, she didn't know who we were. Kept asking for her sister Kitty, who's been gone for years."

"How are you holding up?"

"Honestly, I suppose it depends on the hour." She drew in a deep breath. "What's struck me most is that beneath the grief is this sense of peace I never would have anticipated. We've cried as we've talked to her, given permission for her to leave when she's ready, promised her we'd take care of each other. And while I can't be sure, I think she hears us. It's like God has allowed us to create sweet memories of our time together, despite the grief we all feel."

"I know it's hard, but you're right. This time you've been given with her is a gift."

"It's also made me think about the girls who were murdered." She slowed down, catching the fading sunlight sparkling against the water. "Their families never had the chance to say goodbye. I don't think I ever realized how important it is emotionally to say goodbye, but not everyone gets to do that."

"I've never thought about that, but you're right."

"I heard Special Agent Parks called my boss." She studied his solid profile. "What do you know about the missing girl?"

"Her name's Sarah Boyd. Her parents own a restaurant. She vanished outside her school." Garrett shoved his hands into his pockets, the frustration clear on his face.

"Have you confirmed she was taken by the Angel Abductor?"

"So far no body has shown up, but we have found a Polaroid. Beyond that, we haven't been able to find a solid lead. I even dug through a bunch of missing persons cases to see if I could find something we've missed."

"And did you find something?"

"A young woman was abducted about six months ago, but was able to escape her captor. Her case hit just outside the parameters we're looking at, but I think it merits taking another look."

"I think it's a good idea, though personally I'll never be able to wrap my mind around just how many kids go missing. And the sad thing is that I see hundreds of cases behind the scenes that never stay on the radar with the media, because they want the sensational ones like what we see here with these girls." She felt the tension start to seep back into her muscles as she spoke. "No matter their social status or their color, every missing child needs an advocate to ensure they're found." She nudged him with her elbow. "I'm sorry. I'll get off my soapbox now. It's just that I've seen too much in my job. It's impossible not to let it affect me."

"Sometimes I think you actually have the harder job," he said.

"But you're the one who has to face the families. I still find that the toughest."

She stopped and stared out across the water. Even though thousands of cases were never reported, there were still over eight hundred thousand missing persons in the country's NCIC database. Of those who were under eighteen, most were categorized as endangered runaways. A much smaller percentage were family abductions, and only around 1 percent were non-family abductions.

But when taken by a stranger—like their Angel Abductor—the odds of finding them alive were frighteningly slim, with only a quarter of the victims surviving the first few hours.

Downtown Nashville rose up along the horizon. She didn't want to think about death and sorrow. She'd seen enough of that lately. The last rays of sunlight burned across the horizon, casting shadows across the buildings. There was always something mesmerizing about the scene, and it made her wonder once again why she'd left this city.

"Do you remember when we first came here, to this spot?" she asked, changing the subject.

"How could I forget?" he said. "It was just a few weeks before we graduated from the academy. Sometimes it seems like a lifetime ago. At other times it seems like yesterday."

It had been the first time she'd realized she was falling in love with him. The feelings had been unexpected, but then everything had changed with her decision to go with the FBI. She'd never found out what could have happened between them. And now, after all these years, it seemed that too much time had slipped away from them.

"What about the guy you were dating?" he asked, as they started walking again. "I figured you'd have a ring on your finger."

She shook her head. Trey wasn't exactly someone she wanted to think about. Not right now.

"Too personal?" he asked when she didn't answer.

"No . . . sorry. Let's just say Trey didn't end up being the kind of guy I wanted to spend the rest of my life with. We broke up shortly after I returned home last year."

"You thought he might be the one?"

"Maybe I just wanted him to be. My mom used to always remind me that I hadn't given her any grandchildren."

Garrett laughed. "My mom kept pulling that card on my sister. Thankfully, she doesn't bug me about it, but that might just be because she's given up."

"So what about you?" she asked, flipping the subject back to him. "Any women in your life?"

"Besides my mom? No."

The glowing sunset lit up the city in a closing grand finale, leaving shades of yellow and orange splashed across the water.

"I always envied how close your family was," he continued. "I show up for our family dinners on holidays, and everyone pretends like we're one big happy family. But we're not."

"Your parents love you."

"Yes, but they've always been so focused on building their careers that they never bothered to see who I really am. They only saw who they wanted me to be. And unfortunately, I never met their expectations."

"If you ask me, that's not a bad thing. You've followed your heart and done extremely well."

"And I wouldn't do any of it over, though I wish . . ."

She looked up at him as his voice trailed off. "You wish what?"

"You told me once that you didn't regret joining the FBI. Do you ever think about what might have happened between us if they hadn't come calling?"

Unable to tell if he was serious or just reminiscing, she decided to take the easy way out. "I'm not sure, but we'd probably both be married and have a couple of kids by now."

"Married to each other, or someone else?"

"I guess we'll never know, will we?"

She'd dated on and off while living back East, but she'd never found that one person she wanted to spend the rest of her life with. There had always been some reason why it wouldn't work. If she were completely honest with herself, Garrett had been the only person she'd ever thought about marrying.

They turned around and started walking back across the bridge. Garrett wouldn't let the subject drop. "If we had married, what about our careers? Where do you think we'd be? I've heard that two cops married to each other can be tough."

"But there has to be advantages of being married to someone who understands the long hours and the dynamics of our jobs. I guess I thought that marriage would just happen. The whole family, kids, and a picket fence, but then . . . I don't know. Then it didn't, and I wonder now if it ever will. It's sad, because I'm realizing that if it does happen, my mom will never see the grandkids she wanted to hold so bad."

The process of losing her mom was so hard. Knowing that soon she wouldn't be able to pick up the phone and call her. That she'd never again sit at the kitchen table eating her pão de queijo and drinking Brazilian coffee. All the things she'd taken for granted over the years. The emails and text messages her mom had sent, making sure she was okay and knew she was loved.

Garrett's arm brushed against hers, and he took her hand, lacing their fingers together as they walked the expanse of the bridge on the way back to his car. The sun was making its final curtain call of the day as it slipped out of sight, leaving behind subtle hues of twilight. Her heart stirred at his touch. Being with him seemed so . . . natural. As if all the years that had separated them were gone.

But she didn't want to feel anything for him. Not anymore. Things might have been different if she'd stayed around, but she hadn't. She'd left Nashville and never looked back. And being here now, with her mother dying and her heart broken . . . none of it was going to change the past or give the two of them a future.

So if all of that were true, then why did the thought of leaving him again seem to magnify her loneliness? It must be the emotion of losing her mother that had her feeling so vulnerable. The lack of sleep from staying up with her night after night so her father could get some rest, and in a way, maybe trying to make up for all of the time she hadn't been here.

She pulled her hand away as they neared the parking lot. In spite of her confusion, in spite of her indecision, she knew the truth. She'd let Trey go because he wasn't Garrett.

"How's your father doing?" Garrett asked. "I can't imagine how tough this must be for him."

"He told me his heart is broken. After forty years of marriage, they were still so in love."

She studied Garrett's profile. His strong jaw and confident stride. Her parents' marriage was the kind she'd always wanted. Passionate, deep, and dedicated, even when things got tough. There seemed to be fewer and fewer couples who stuck it out for the long haul, but that was what she'd always dreamed of. Maybe that was the reason she'd avoided settling down. Because if she couldn't find what her parents had, she wasn't sure she wanted to settle for anything less.

Could she and Garrett have had the same thing? Who knew? Too much time had passed, and their lives had run separate courses.

"What about your father?" she asked. "Are things still as strained as they used to be?"

"Yes. Nothing's really changed, though I found out from my mom that he's here in the city working with a client. Not that I'm expecting to hear from him."

"You should go see him," she said. "Spend some time with him. Double your efforts, even when it's hard. He's your father."

"You remember what it's like with him. If I show up, he'll pick a fight."

"I know he isn't easy to get along with, but with all that's happened in our family over the last few months, I'm beginning to realize what's really important."

He was quiet for a few moments, then nodded. "I'll think about it."

"Good."

Twenty minutes later, Jordan stopped at the front porch of her parents' house and fingered the key in the palm of her hand. "Thanks for tonight. I needed to get out for a while."

"Anytime. Just promise me you won't push yourself. You need time to grieve and let go through this process. You need to take care of yourself."

"I know."

He looked down at her in the yellow glow of the porch light. Feelings she'd purposely buried years ago flooded through her. She breathed in the familiar scent of his cologne, and felt her heart tremble.

He caught her gaze and held it. "Jordan . . . I know this isn't the best timing, but seeing you again . . . I can't stop thinking about you. After being with you tonight, I don't know how to get rid of the feelings I have for you. Because as much as I keep shoving them away, they keep coming back, just as strong as they were before."

She wanted to pull away. To tell him none of that was true. That whatever they were feeling was sentimental and completely impractical. Instead, she didn't move while he leaned toward her and brushed his lips against hers. He paused for a moment, as if he expected her to pull away. But she didn't. Instead she returned the kiss, with a fervor she hadn't known was still simmering inside her.

A moment later, she stepped back breathless, then pressed her fingers against her lips where she could still feel his touch. "What just happened?"

"I don't know." He shot her an apologetic smile. "You always were irresistible."

But this wasn't a place she could go. Not when she was feeling completely vulnerable. Because the timing couldn't be worse. Even if they could somehow figure out a way to make a relationship work, they'd tried it before. They lived two separate lives. As much as she wanted to, she couldn't turn back the clock for their relationship. She needed to move forward.

"Jordan—"

"I need to go inside," she said. She couldn't deal with this. Not now. Maybe not ever.

"Okay." He squeezed her fingers before letting go and turning around.

She didn't move as he looked back at her one last time before slipping into his car and driving away.

14

May 18
7:29 a.m.
River Hollow Stables

Amanda Love was brushing a chestnut-colored mare early Thursday morning when Garrett pulled into the gravel driveway that curled around the corral. Her mother had made it clear on the phone that she wasn't happy about his request. Garrett in turn had explained that their questions had to do with another missing girl, but he wasn't sure even that was going to be enough to get Amanda to talk.

"She's a beautiful mare." Garrett approached the fenced corral that was attached to a red barn with a green roof. "I always wanted a horse growing up, but my mom wouldn't let me. She got me a hamster instead."

Amanda ran the brush across the horse's belly and let out a timid smile.

"Is she yours?" Garrett asked.

"My father got her for me for my fourteenth birthday."

"I'm Special Agent Addison," Garrett said, holding up his badge.

"I know who you are. My mother told me you were coming."

131

"I appreciate your letting me talk with you."

She shrugged, ignoring eye contact as she kept brushing the horse.

Garrett searched for a way to connect. "I know this isn't easy for you. I have a cousin your age, and I can't imagine how she'd react after going through what you did. I want you to know that we are doing everything we can to find out who abducted you. That's why I asked to talk with you again."

Amanda didn't say anything, so he decided to keep talking.

"Your mother told me you were going to a trauma counselor."

"Yeah."

"Has it helped you?"

"Some days."

"She also told me you ride horses."

"Yeah . . . I compete. I started when I was nine. It's the one place I can feel free."

"I bet you're good at it."

"She is good." A woman walked out of the barn, dressed to ride, in a pair of gray breeches and tall boots. "She's already looking at competing in a world equestrian championship. But that's not why you're here. I told you I wasn't happy about letting you come back and talk with Amanda. The only reason I'm letting you is because she thinks it's important."

"I won't be long. I promise." Garrett turned back to Amanda. "I know you've told your story, but I need to know if there are any details you might have remembered since you last spoke with the police."

"You think it could help the other girl who's missing?" Amanda asked.

"It might. We're trying to find any detail that might connect the girls who went missing."

Amanda's face fell and tears came to her eyes. "I know I should be able to do this, but I'm sorry. I just can't."

"Can't what, Amanda?" he asked.

"Every time I try to talk about what happened, I freeze. I'm sorry. I just . . . I can't."

"Amanda, I want you to go on back to the house," her mom said, stepping in front of her daughter.

"I understand." Garrett reached into his pocket and handed Amanda a business card with his number on it. "Another girl was taken, Amanda. Her name's Sarah Boyd. She was just a few months older than you are. We don't know if she's alive or not, but I believe it's possible that the man who tried to take you might have taken the other girls. If you remember anything . . . anything at all that you haven't told the police, please call me."

Amanda started to walk away, then stopped and turned back around. "Her name is Sarah?"

"Amanda—"

"It's okay, Mom."

"Sarah Boyd," Garrett said.

"What happened to her?"

"Her sister was supposed to pick her up from school, but when she got there, Sarah was gone."

"And you haven't found her?" she asked, stepping up to the fence.

"No. Not yet."

"But you think it was the same man who took me?"

"It's possible, though we don't know for sure. We thought if there was something new you remembered, anything at all that could give us a lead, it might help us find her."

She pressed her hand against the bristles of the brush. "I go over it in my head. That day. It never stops. Everything I thought and felt. The same thing repeating over and over. I can't get it out of my head, but there are so many details I can't remember.

"Something came up in my therapy the other day. Remember the man I saw in the car? I saw him before that too."

"What do you mean?" Garrett asked, taking a step forward.

"Four, maybe five days before he kidnapped me. I was leaving the library with a pile of books for a research paper. I dropped them on the way down the front stairs and this guy stopped to help me pick them up. He said he was a teacher and was going to start teaching math at the middle school. He asked me if I had any advice for a new teacher."

"What did you say to him?"

"I told him I couldn't think of anything. It was awkward, even though he was nice. Then he asked me if I like horses. I thought that was weird. Like he knew stuff about me. Then I realized I was wearing a T-shirt from one of my competitions. And then he left."

All of this fit the profile that she'd been followed. Stalked.

"Do you remember what he looked like?" Garrett asked.

"I know I should remember what he looked like, but when I try to picture him, I can't see his face. I think he was wearing a suit jacket. Something . . . dark. No tie."

Garrett could see remnants of fear still lingering in her eyes and tried to imagine the horror she'd gone through. Abducted. Blindfolded. Terrified.

"But I remember something else," she said.

Her mom wrapped her arm around her daughter's shoulders.

Amanda took in a deep breath. "He had the same voice as the man who took me."

"Are you sure?" Garrett asked.

Amanda nodded.

"I know this is extremely hard for you, but this will help. I promise."

She looked up and caught his gaze for the first time. "Please find whoever did this to me."

He nodded. "I promise I'll do everything in my power to do just that."

Garrett pulled out his phone as he slipped back into his car, called Sam, and put it on speaker.

"Did you find out anything?" Sam asked.

Garrett started the car and backed out of the driveway. "I'm leaving the Love residence now, and while I can't prove it, I think we might have missed one of our abductor's victims. I need you to find the number for the middle school Amanda attends and find out if they hired any new math teachers this past year, then call me back."

Two minutes later, Sam was back on the line with an answer. "The secretary just confirmed that they didn't hire any new math teachers this year."

"There might be a connection here," Garrett said, quickly filling in the blanks for Sam. "I think we need to keep digging."

"I agree."

Garrett noted the time as he headed toward the freeway. "I'm heading back now, but I need to make one stop on the way."

He hung up the call, fervently praying that Sarah could somehow escape her captor the same way Amanda had. Because if that didn't happen, she was quickly running out of time.

Ten minutes later, Garrett parked along the street in the middle of Music City, paid the metered parking, then started walking to the hotel where his mom had told him his dad was staying. As he walked, he replayed the conversation he'd had with his mom on the phone. She told him that his father had been drinking more. That he'd been coming home late most nights and had a tendency to miss appointments. On top of that, she was worried about the people he'd gotten the law firm involved with.

His father had always known how to get around the law. He'd hover just enough on the right side of the fence that he'd never get caught. But that was what was scary. Never getting caught made him feel invincible. And according to Garrett's mother, the people his father was involved with were the kind of people that if you cross them, they wouldn't hesitate to kill you.

Garrett nodded at the doorman, strode across the five-star lobby, and pressed the button on the elevator for the fifth floor. Trying to pretend like he belonged. Which he didn't. He never had.

Two minutes later, he stopped outside the door to room 548, wondering if he'd made a mistake in coming. Talking to Jordan had made him realize that his father wasn't the only one who had never tried to improve their relationship. Garrett hadn't tried either. Which meant maybe he was partly to blame for the fact that any relationship he'd had with his father had died years ago.

The elevator opened at the end of the hallway. He watched a couple step out and head to their room. He turned back to the door and knocked before he chickened out.

His father opened the door, holding a drink in his hand. He leaned against the doorframe. "Garrett. I wasn't expecting to see you today."

"It's been a long time." Garrett stood in the hallway, deciding not to ask his father why he was already drinking so early in the morning. "I tried to call, but never got through. Mom said you were in town, so I thought I'd stop by and see how you're doing. I thought we could go out to dinner or something."

"Yeah . . . that would be great. I was planning to call you while I was here—maybe tomorrow—but I have a new client who's kept me on the phone or in meetings ever since I arrived. You know how some clients are. They think they're paying you for more than just handling their case."

"That's okay." Garrett forced a smile. "I didn't expect you to have a lot of free time, knowing you were here on business."

He tried to smother his disappointment. Nothing had changed in thirty years. It had always been something. Sixty-hour weeks meant missing basketball games and camping trips. There were always plenty of excuses to explain his absence.

"Do you mind if I come in, or do you need to head out to another meeting?" Garrett asked.

His father hesitated, then stepped aside to let him come in. "You caught me at a good time, actually. I've got a few minutes until I have to be somewhere." He swung the door closed.

Garrett frowned as he walked into the suite. He knew how his father played the game. He knew that the five-hundred-dollar-a-night room, the dinners in the hotel lounge, and all the liquor he wanted would be billed to his client.

Funny. He'd been headed in that direction and he didn't miss any of it.

He walked across the carpet to the floor-to-ceiling window that overlooked downtown Nashville, suddenly wishing he'd never come.

"Would you like a drink?" his father asked.

"No thanks. I'm fine."

He turned around to study his father. His mom had been right. He looked terrible. He'd gained ten pounds, making him look bloated and puffy. His hair had grayed, and his skin seemed paler than normal, but the worst part was that it wasn't even lunchtime and he was half drunk.

"Working a case, I guess?" his father said, joining him at the window. "How is your job going? You're with TBI, right?"

Garrett nodded, surprised his father remembered. "I don't regret my decision to leave the practice, if that's what you're asking." He stopped. He wasn't here to fight. He was here to make peace.

"I've always wondered about your job," his father continued. "What are they paying you? Forty . . . fifty thousand a year before taxes?"

Money was the last thing he wanted to talk about. "It never was about the money."

"Maybe not, but it takes money to make this world go round. And it buys a better bottle of Scotch." His father held up his half-empty glass and laughed before setting it down on the coffee table. "I'd insist you try some, but I'm afraid it might be a bit too rich for your blood."

He swallowed the insult without reacting. His father knew how to throw an illegal punch with his passive-aggressive spin on things. It was the way he'd always taken out his hostilities. And in turn Garrett had always taken the brunt of them. But not today. His words bounced off of him, because he wasn't that nine-year-old desperate to win his father's approval.

This time it was his father who needed his help.

"How's your case coming?" Garrett asked.

"You know that's privileged information."

Garrett shook his head, feeling any control on his temper slipping away. "What happened to you?"

"What do you mean, what happened to me? You're the one who left, not me. I gave you every reason to stay."

"I never wanted the things you gave me. But I'm your son. I guess I thought you'd accept me no matter what career I chose to follow."

"It was never about you choosing your own way," his father said. "It was about family and tradition, and you gave all of that up, for what? The chance to wear a cheap suit and tie and carry a badge?"

Garrett fought to control his anger. It was happening again. No matter how many times he promised himself he wouldn't sink to his father's level, he found himself wanting to jump into the ring and fight. All these years later, and they were still dealing with resentments neither one could let go of.

"But what if the tradition you're talking about wasn't what I wanted?" Garrett said. "I guess I thought that maybe what I wanted might matter to you."

"We don't always get what we want."

"When have you not gotten what you want?"

"Have you seen your mother recently?"

"I spoke with her yesterday," Garrett said.

"Did she tell you she walked out on me?"

"What?"

"I guess she forgot to mention that little detail. It's been a month now. She filed for a divorce. Thought she would have already told you by now."

Garrett felt a sickness wash through him. No matter how frustrated his parents made him, this wasn't what he wanted for them. "Is that why you're drinking again?"

"A Scotch now and then doesn't mean I've fallen off the wagon. Have you ever wondered where that expression came from?" He let out a low laugh. "During Prohibition back in the '20s, men used to climb up on water wagons that were used to sprinkle water on the ground in order to keep the dust down, and they'd take an oath that they'd give up alcohol and drink nothing more than water. Can you believe that? When they started drinking again, it was said that they fell off the wagon."

"Dad, stop. She's worried about you."

"Sorry." His father nodded toward the door. "I really should get ready. I'm supposed to meet with a client soon."

"Who are you meeting with today?" Garrett asked.

"Like I already said, it's no one you need concern yourself with. Nothing your mother needs to worry about."

Meaning, none of your business. "I've heard rumors that one of the higher-ups of the Albanian Mafia is in town. If that's who you're planning to meet with—"

"Wait a minute. So is this what it's come to? You're now some hotshot in law enforcement, and you think you can come after me and accuse me of being in bed with the Mafia?"

"I'm not accusing you of anything. But if you're working for the wrong kind of people . . ."

His dad headed for the door. "You're just jealous. Your mother could never handle my success and you . . . you can't either."

Garrett gave up. He'd never cared about success the way his father had. All he'd really wanted was to be a part of his father's life and be accepted for his choices. That was never going to happen.

His father opened the door. "That is why you shouldn't have come."

Garrett froze at the words, his arms at his sides in defeat. Silence hung between them. Seconds passed, then he crossed the room and walked out the door.

15

May 21
2:37 p.m.
Spring Hollow Cemetery

Jordan stood on the cemetery's freshly mowed lawn, her black maxi-dress blowing in the afternoon breeze as the minister said the final prayer in front of her mother's casket. She pulled the dark-gray cardigan tighter around her shoulders, cold despite the warm breeze. She'd known this day was coming for weeks, and yet it still seemed so unexpected. So raw. Somehow she thought she'd have more time. Barely sixteen months had passed since finding out about her mother's cancer. Sixteen months hadn't been enough time to say her goodbyes.

She stood with her father, Clara, and Alex. A row of gravestones lined up in front of them, making the significance of today seem even more real. Not long ago, her mom had still been fairly alert. She'd spent her time reminiscing about the past. She'd told stories of her own childhood, of how she'd met their father, then listened while Jordan and Clara told their own favorite memories from their childhood.

And now today they were burying her.

Jordan gnawed on her lip, trying to stop the flow of tears. She knew she needed to let go, but even the knowledge that her mother was no longer suffering on this earth wasn't enough to erase the physical pain of missing her.

She grabbed her father's hand and leaned against his shoulder at the final amens from the small group gathered around the gravesite. It was over, and she wasn't sure how to move on.

Her father squeezed her hand, then wrapped his arms around her. "Thank you for being here. I can't tell you how much it's meant to me. To your mother as well."

"You know I wouldn't have been anywhere else. I just wish so badly I could take away the pain you're feeling. I know you miss her so much."

He pulled her hand up to his chest. "You always were my fixer, but there are some things that even you can't undo."

"I know. And I knew it would be hard, but today . . ."

She couldn't quite find the words to say goodbye. Part of her still believed she'd turn around and see her mother walking toward them, across the manicured lawns of the cemetery, to tell them it had all been a mistake.

"She's with her Jesus, Jordan. A far better place than this world. She was ready."

"My head knows that, but even that knowledge only barely scrapes away the pain of how much I miss her."

"I know." Her father squeezed her hand. "But we'll get through this together. What are your plans for the rest of the day?"

"I don't have any besides being with you."

She couldn't tell him that she longed for a distraction, like looking through emails and reports that had piled up since she'd come home. But today wasn't the day for that.

"Good, because there's enough food at the house from the women at the church to feed an army. Once we're done here, I thought we could go through some of the pictures of your mom.

I'd like to put together some kind of photo album, but you know I'm not good at that."

Jordan nodded at the suggestion. "I'd like that. Clara's driving you home, and I'll be right behind you."

She glanced behind her. Several people waited to speak to her father, including Clara. And there was someone Jordan needed to talk to as well.

She hugged Clara, then turned around. Garrett stood near the edges of the dispersing crowd, watching her. She made her way across the grass, past the freshly turned dirt where they'd just buried her mother. She'd seen him arrive right before the funeral started and had hoped she'd get the chance to speak with him before he left.

"Thank you for coming." She tried not to think about how handsome he looked in his charcoal-gray suit and white-collared shirt. Or that the last time she'd seen him he'd kissed her. And she'd kissed him back. No matter what her head kept telling her, she knew her heart had never completely let go.

"I wish there was something I could do," he said. "I know how close the two of you were."

"I'm still trying to grasp the idea that she's gone. I don't think I expected to miss her this much. I picked up the phone to tell her something yesterday before I remembered she was gone."

"I'm so sorry."

"Me too."

"How's your father?"

"Strong on the outside. Concerned about me, like he's been my entire life, but I know how much he's hurting."

"The grieving process takes time, and everyone goes through it differently. He's lucky that he has the best two daughters a father could ask for. Does he know what he's going to do now?"

"We told him he shouldn't make any decisions right away, but he's already thinking about selling the store. Actually, I think he's been thinking about it ever since we found out my mom was sick.

But while I can't imagine him going into work by himself every day, I also know that he loves that store. Still, it was his and mom's store. Something they worked at together."

"Good advice, but you're right. It can't be easy for him."

"Clara's offered for him to move in with her and Alex, thinking he won't be as lonely living there. They have a basement with a guest room and bathroom, but I don't know if that's going to be enough. Especially if he sells the store. He'll need a purpose."

"Your family needs time to grieve. And while it won't always be easy, he'll figure out what his new role is."

"I just don't want him to sell the store and then regret it later. I think he needs something to keep him going. Mama and the store were his life, and without those two things . . . I'm not sure what he's going to do."

"He's got you."

She reached up to tuck her hair behind her ear, but the wind was playing with her untamable curls. They felt out of control, just like her life seemed at the moment. She knew God was right here in the middle of their loss, but sometimes . . . sometimes it was hard to feel him there.

"What are you thinking?" Garrett asked.

"My mother lived a hard but full life, and while I miss her like crazy, I know my father's right about one thing. She was ready to go at the end. And I didn't want to see her suffer any longer. I guess that's the one thing that makes all of this okay and gives me some peace."

"That's what I've always loved about your family. The way you help and love each other."

"Did you see your father while he was in town?"

He started walking again, then sat down on a wooden bench overlooking the endless lawn. "I went to see him Wednesday morning."

"You did?" She tried to read his expression, but couldn't.

"You were right about one thing. I haven't really made an effort to spend time with him. But I'm not sure that matters anymore."

"I just didn't want you to regret your relationship with him. I might have been close to my mom, but that doesn't mean I did everything I should have for her. And I've realized now that, once they're gone, it's too late." She looked up at him. "How did he respond?"

"I guess I had these high hopes that everything would somehow work out between us."

"You don't look like that happened."

"It didn't. He told me I shouldn't have come."

"He didn't mean that."

"I think he did. But I'm realizing that sometimes you can't fix people or relationships. Sometimes all you can fix is yourself. You have to forgive them, love them, and then move on. It's what I'm going to have to do."

She started to take his hand, then stopped. Like the kiss they'd shared, it suddenly seemed too . . . intimate. Instead, she told him how sorry she was.

"Me too," Garrett said. "Especially because he seemed so alone. Hard, and yet tired. Honestly, I felt sorry for him. He's pushed everyone away. Everyone who doesn't do what he expects them to do. But enough about my family saga. Today's about your family, not mine. Do you know how long you're planning to stay?"

"I'll leave in a few days. I've been on bereavement leave, but I have plenty of unused vacation days, so I'm already planning to come back as soon as I can."

"Have you ever thought about moving closer?"

She hesitated with her answer, wondering for a moment if he was asking for her family's sake or for his own. What she did know was that she still thought about him. Missed his smile and the way he made her laugh. The way he listened to her and always knew what to say.

And now she was leaving again.

"I have thought about transferring, actually. Especially recently. There are several FBI posts here in Tennessee that would put me a whole lot closer to my family."

"What about your family?" Garrett said. "Can I do anything for your dad?"

"Maybe call from time to time, or come see him? He's got a pretty good support group at his church, but I know he'd love to see you."

"I can do that."

"Do you have an update on the case?" she asked, changing the subject.

She didn't mention that every few months over the past year and a half she'd gone over the Angel Abductor case files to see if she could find anything they'd missed. Because not finding him meant that there was a chance he was going to kill someone else.

Like Sarah.

"What's the latest about Sarah? I haven't watched the news the past couple days. Has she been found?"

"There's still no sign of her. It's like we're spinning our wheels, not making any traction. We've got the public and media involved, but so far every lead turns out to be a dead end. In the meantime, he's still out there—along with Sarah—and the case is growing cold."

"I'm sorry." Jordan caught the frustration in his voice. "I've gone over the files you brought me the other night. And while I can give you analysis after analysis, in the end, that's all it is. There just isn't enough evidence for me to go on."

"Forget about that for now. You need to be with your family."

"I know, but another girl might be dead. We have to find a way to stop this guy."

"We will. But you need to promise you'll take off as much time as you need," Garrett said.

"Okay, I promise, but I need to do something to keep my mind off things. And as for you, I don't think it will hurt for you to have an extra pair of eyes."

"Your input is always welcome, you know that."

"It's one of those cases I haven't been able to shake." She'd dreamed about them at night. Jessica, Julia, Sarah, and the others. She tried to save them over and over, but she was never able to get to them in time. Instead she'd stumble across their half-buried bodies. Too late to save them.

"I just can't help but think . . ." She paused, not sure she wanted to verbalize her question. One of the things that had drawn her to Garrett when they first met was his faith. They'd had many discussions about how their faith could impact the careers they'd chosen. Hearing him talk about his faith was something she missed.

"Think what, Jordan?" he probed.

"Dana Kerrigan asked a question that day we were in her daughter's room. She asked where God was when Julia was abducted, then murdered."

"I couldn't hear everything you talked about. What did you say?"

"I should have been able to answer, but I didn't know what to say. I analyze cases every day. Tragic cases, where I have to put aside my feelings because the details are so horrible, that if I don't, I wouldn't be able to get up in the morning and go back to work. But I still didn't know what to say to her."

"I think you're being too hard on yourself. It's a question people have been asking for centuries. Think about how many of the psalms are cries to God for help."

He might be right, but Mrs. Kerrigan's question had haunted Jordan. She wanted to believe that her faith was stronger than this. That she could have said something that would have made a difference.

"Do you ever ask yourself that question?" she asked.

"Yeah. I do." He caught her gaze. "My sister-in-law lost a baby last year. She was five months along and it devastated her and my brother. It was a little girl they named Anna Grace."

"I'm so sorry."

"Me too. My brother told me that everyone had answers for them, but they just ended up making him angry. Like everything happens for a reason. Heaven needed their baby. Even that she shouldn't worry, because they could have another child."

"Except another child would never be Anna Grace."

"Exactly."

"They didn't lose Anna because they didn't pray enough, or because they didn't say the right things, no matter what people said."

"No. But sometimes it's easier to spout off pat answers than dig deeper and ask the questions that aren't so easily answered."

Jordan drew in a deep breath, wishing she could simply skip over this day . . . this part of life. "I'm supposed to know how to deal with this, Garrett. I was trained for this, and yet I feel so powerless. We can't stop this guy. We have no idea who he is or when he's going to strike again. Dana's question is one I can't answer. Where was God when these girls were abducted and terrified? I joined law enforcement to stop people like this."

Garrett leaned forward and rested his elbows against his thighs. "I'm not sure I have the answer. I know that we live in a fallen world, but even that seems like too pat an answer."

Sometimes she felt God's presence, but other times, she felt as if her faith was hanging on by a thread.

"You need to go," he said, nodding toward the group of mourners leaving for their cars. "Your father needs you."

"I know," she said. "But you need to find this guy, Garrett. You need to find him before he kills Sarah. We can't let it happen. Not again. Because how can you tell another family that their daughter isn't coming home?"

2006

16

January 19
9:34 a.m.
Nashville International Airport

Jordan stepped out of the passenger pickup area in front of the Nashville Airport to find Garrett waiting for her.

"Thanks for picking me up, stranger," she said, dropping her carry-on onto the backseat before sliding into the passenger seat beside him. "Though I'm second-guessing my agreeing to come. It's freezing here."

"And unfortunately, the temperature's predicted to drop another few degrees by the end of the day," he said, turning up the heater a notch. "But it's good to see you. It's been a long time."

Eight months to be exact, since Sarah Boyd vanished without a trace. And while Jordan had continued as a consultant on the case via regular conference calls, it had taken a sixth missing girl to bring her back to Nashville.

"It's good to see you too," she said.

"What about your partner?"

"Ryley's working for NSA now. It ended up being a move that made sense for him."

"And you?" he asked, easing his way back into the traffic leaving the airport. "How are you doing?"

"I'm good, actually." She leaned back in the seat and let out a soft sigh, glad to be back on the ground again. "Besides the fact that I'm here because another girl's gone missing."

"I bet your father's looking forward to seeing you."

"He is. It's been a tough year for him, but I've been able to see him more since transferring to Memphis. He even drove the three and a half hours last month and took me out to lunch."

Garrett glanced at her before changing lanes. "I'm glad you came."

"The FBI wants this case closed as much as you do."

She didn't miss the implication that his comment had less to do with their job ahead and more to do with the fact that he'd missed her. And if she were honest, she'd missed him too. But while visits to her father since her mother's death had been frequent, she'd always found an excuse not to drop by to see Garrett. Her father needed her. Or at least that's what she told herself. Today, though, the only thing that really mattered was finding Marissa Dillinger.

Twenty minutes later, Jordan stepped through the open doorway of the Dillinger home in front of Garrett and felt a sense of déjà vu sweep over her. Another girl. Another family.

How had they not found a way to stop this?

Past the entryway, the living room opened up to the kitchen area, where half a dozen women were bustling around food that was spread out over the counter. Another fifteen or so sat working around a long table that had been set up in the middle of the living room. The murmur of low voices filled the room. A photo of Marissa smiling at the camera sat in the middle of the dining room table, ensuring that no one forgot the real reason they were there.

A woman with dark hair and even darker brown eyes approached them from the kitchen. "You must be the officers I spoke with this morning."

"Yes. I'm Special Agent Garrett Addison with TBI," Garrett

said, holding up his badge. "And this is Special Agent Jordan Lambert with the FBI. We're here to speak with Marissa's parents."

"Candice Martin," she said, shaking their hands. "I'm Marissa's aunt. We've set up our own command post, as we're calling it here."

"I'm impressed," Jordan said. "What all are you working on?"

"Initially, we started gathering photographs and video, which wasn't difficult coming from a teen. We've got DNA samples together, search teams are recanvassing the area she was last seen, people are answering telephone calls, keeping up a MySpace page, and making sure she gets media attention. Contacting hospitals . . ." She shook her head. "Honestly, the list of things that needs to be done seems endless, but we're determined to be here for the family."

"I hope you know that what you're doing could be a big part of bringing Marissa home," Jordan said.

"I hope so." The woman pressed her lips together. "I know you deal with things like this every day, but for us it's like trying to maneuver our way through a nightmare."

"We know this is extremely hard for you, and we want you to know that we are doing everything we can to find your niece."

"Of course. Why don't you follow me into the den. You'll have more privacy in there."

Jordan recognized Marissa's parents from the briefing she'd been given before catching her flight. Nathaniel Dillinger worked as a computer programmer. Bethany Dillinger was an office manager for a group of dentists. The couple sat on the couch across from a flat-screen TV and a stack of Disney movies, looking as if they had no idea what had just hit them. No idea how to deal with what was playing out in front of them. Jordan knew they were feeling that any sense of control had been suddenly jerked from their grasp and there was no way they could guess the enemy's next move.

"Mr. and Mrs. Dillinger. Thank you for seeing us," Garrett said, urging them to stay seated after they introduced themselves. "I know this is an extremely difficult and emotional time for you both, and we promise not to take much of your time. We just have a few questions to ask you."

Mr. Dillinger nodded. "Of course."

Jordan studied the photos hung on the wall behind the couch. "Are your other children here?" she asked.

Mrs. Dillinger shook her head. "They're a lot younger than Marissa, so we haven't told them what's going on. They're at their grandparents' house an hour from here."

"When Candice told us you called," Mr. Dillinger said, "we were praying you were coming with some good news. It's already been over twenty-four hours. And like we've said over and over, Marissa would never run away. She does well in school, volunteers at a local preschool . . ."

"We do have some news," Jordan said, moving forward carefully. "There was a witness that just came forward. She saw your daughter in the parking lot of the library last night."

"That's the last place we know she was," Mr. Dillinger said. "She'd gone there to do some research."

"Our witness saw Marissa exit the library ahead of her, but she was on the phone with her husband, so she wasn't paying close attention. What she did notice was your daughter getting into a car in the parking lot."

"Do you know whose car it was?"

"No. She didn't see the driver. And in fact, she didn't think anything about the situation until later when she saw the news story."

Mrs. Dillinger pressed her hand against her mouth and shook her head. "I just can't believe that. Marissa would never get into a car with someone she didn't know. And she had no reason not to come straight home in her own car."

Jordan felt their frustration. The evidence showed that the abductor had somehow convinced these girls to get into the car with him. But they still didn't know how.

She held out the police sketch of the Angel Abductor. "We need to know if you recognize this man."

154

"Is that the man she left with?"

"He is a suspect," Garrett said.

Mr. Dillinger shook his head. "He doesn't look familiar. I'm sorry."

"What do we do now?" Mrs. Dillinger dabbed her eyes with a tissue, clearly fighting to hold back the tears. "We were given a list of things to do to help, but I still feel as if I'm just sitting here waiting for her to walk through the door."

"I know this is extremely hard," Jordan said again. "What you need to do is make sure you take care of yourselves and your family. The stress and exhaustion makes decision making harder. Rely on the people who are out there right now. And in the meantime, we'll keep you updated on any developments."

Jordan knew her words rang hollow. Any hope the couple had held that she and Garrett had come with good news had vanished when they arrived.

They headed back through the house toward the front door, feeling the tension that filled the room. Parents weren't supposed to have to worry about their daughters getting home safely from studying at the library.

Garrett hesitated halfway across the living room. Jordan followed his gaze to a man standing in the corner of the room talking to one of the women.

"Garrett?" Jordan's hand pressed against his elbow. "You okay?"

He pulled his car keys out of his pocket and nodded. "Yeah. I just thought I saw someone I knew."

She followed Garrett out the front door, wishing she could melt some of the tension that had built up in her muscles. Even the couple of pain pills she'd downed an hour ago had done little to take away the throbbing at the base of her skull. She couldn't shake the heavy weight of this case. Another girl gone. Nothing but a handful of flimsy leads at best. They couldn't find another dead body. Not this time.

Jordan walked through the open-office floor plan of the TBI headquarters, surprised it was already half past two. And surprised that Garrett was still sitting in front of the computer where she'd left him over an hour ago. After comparing notes with the officers who'd canvassed the neighborhood where Marissa had gone missing, Sam and Michaels had left to go speak with the woman who'd witnessed Marissa leaving the library. Jordan had spoken briefly with her boss, then decided to go pick up lunch for the two of them.

She stopped in front of his desk. Garrett looked up from his computer screen to the takeout bags she was carrying.

"Thought you might like a late lunch. I was craving a spinach veggie wrap," she said.

He wrinkled his nose.

"Don't worry." She set a bag down next to him, along with two bottles of water. "I got you the Reuben sandwich. Half a pound of corned beef, Swiss, and sauerkraut, and fries."

"Ah . . . you're the best," he said, pulling the sandwich from the sack and breathing in the aroma.

She laughed. "I know. I figured that would make you happy."

She didn't even try to stop the memories that surfaced. The deli two blocks from the police station had always been a favorite hangout of theirs. Sometimes they'd eat in. Other times they'd grab takeout and watch a movie at her apartment. She always ordered the spinach veggie wrap. He always ordered the Reuben.

"I didn't think I was hungry," he said, "but I'm just smelling this and my stomach's already starting to growl. You're a lifesaver."

"You look exhausted."

He leaned back in his chair. "I didn't sleep much last night. I want this guy caught, but it's the same old problem." He unwrapped his sandwich and took a handful of fries. "Everything so far leads us to a dead end. The security cameras at the library weren't working, our witness didn't get a close look at the guy . . ."

"There's got to be something we're missing," Jordan said. "Nobody's this smart. He had to have made some kind of mistake. And hopefully the witness will end up remembering something that will help."

"In the meantime," he said, "I think we need to consider reinterviewing the families of the other girls. We need to find a common denominator that connects them, beside the fact that they're all teen girls with long blonde hair."

"I agree, but Sam called me as I pulled into the parking lot," Jordan said, taking a sip of her water. "He needs us to follow up on another lead that just got called in."

"What is it?"

"A woman was watching the news this morning and said she saw Marissa. No license plate, but she can give a description of the vehicle."

Another photo popped up on Garrett's computer screen. He was clearly not listening to what she was saying.

"Garrett? You've been sitting here for hours, like you're on to something. What's up?"

"I'm not sure yet."

"But you think it might be something. I know that look of yours. What'd you find?"

He looked up from his desk that was covered with the piles of evidence and testimonies they'd been going through. "Something's been nagging me ever since we were at the Dillinger home. There was a man in a suit, talking with a woman in the living room. I've seen him somewhere before."

"Where?"

He leaned back and caught her gaze, his sandwich forgotten. "Remember a couple years ago, when we had to tell the Kerrigans that we'd found their daughter's body?"

"I've never been able to forget it."

"There was a large group of friends and family at their house as well. They were all sitting around. People were coming and going to give their condolences to the family. That's where I saw him. He didn't have the goatee and his hair was a bit lighter, but it was him."

"That was two years ago," Jordan said. "Are you sure?"

"I know it's been a long time, but there's more."

"What do you mean?"

"He was at the vigil for Sarah Boyd."

"Wait a minute." Jordan set her wrap down on his desk and stared at his computer screen. "Are you sure?"

He scrolled down to the news brief he'd dug up from the archives. "Watch this."

He clicked on the arrow and replayed the video. A reporter was standing outside the school where Sarah Boyd had disappeared.

"Authorities with the Tennessee Bureau of Investigation have asked for the public's assistance in finding a missing sixteen-year-old. Sarah Boyd was last seen getting into a black sedan after school yesterday afternoon. Many believe that this case could be tied to the notorious Angel Abductor, who continues to terrorize Eastern Tennessee. But according to the latest reports, authorities are still no closer to finding the person behind these horrible abductions and murders."

"This is a candlelight vigil that was held for Sarah back in May of 2005, four days after she disappeared."

"Okay . . . I'm still not sure what you're looking at. I've seen this footage before. We never found anything significant."

He paused the video, then tapped on the screen. "That's him, at Sarah Boyd's vigil. And I saw him at both the Kerrigan home and today, at Marissa Dillinger's home. Tell me the odds that he just happened to know the three families whose daughters have vanished, and that he was simply there to give his condolences."

"The odds aren't high, granted, but it's not impossible." Jordan leaned closer to the screen and frowned. "And while this guy looks a bit like the man we saw today, the video's too grainy to make a positive ID. Do you have a name?"

"Not yet."

"And you honestly think he could be our kidnapper?"

"Think about it, Jordan. It's not unusual at all for the perpetrator to return to show up at something like this."

She shook her head and frowned. "I still think you're pulling at straws. I see the resemblance, but I'm still not convinced that this is the guy we saw today. It seems too much like a—"

"Like a coincidence? I thought you didn't believe in coincidences."

Jordan frowned. "I don't, but—"

"I can find out who he is, bring him in, and see what he has to say."

"On what charges?"

"No charges. Just as a person of interest."

"What about this other lead? Sam wants us to move on it now."

Garrett was back to staring at the screen.

"Fine. I'll go follow up on the witness Sam gave us," Jordan said. "You go with your gut."

"Are you sure? You don't normally do fieldwork."

"Thanks for the reminder," she said, picking up her wrap and taking a bite. "I think I can handle an interview."

"Okay."

"How are you going to find him?" she asked.

"I'm going back to the Dillinger home. Someone there should know who he is."

"You think Sam and Parks will go for this?"

"They don't have to know," Garrett said, grabbing his coat and the rest of his sandwich. "Let me find out who he is, and then I'll tell them."

17

Garrett headed out of the bureau headquarters lobby toward his car, thankful that the predictions for snow had been cancelled. The last thing they needed right now was a string of dreary wet weather. It was only January, and he was already anticipating spring.

"Chasing a lead on our killer?"

Garrett stopped at the familiar face. "Nikki Boyd. I heard through the grapevine that congratulations are in order on your graduation from the academy."

The disappearance of her sister had been all the motivation Nikki had needed to turn in both her resignation to her principal and an application to the police department. Not long after that, she'd entered the police academy training program.

"I'm now officially a rookie, but thanks," she said, stopping in front of him. "That's not why I'm here, though. I heard that another girl's gone missing. Do you have a minute to talk?"

"I'm on my way out," Garrett said, "but you can walk with me to my car. I'm on my way now to follow up a lead."

"Do you think he took her?"

He knew all too well who *he* was. And he wished he had something to give her. "We don't know at this point what happened to Marissa Dillinger."

Nikki followed him across the parking lot. "I left everything I knew to join the police academy because I had this crazy idea that it would put me in a better position to find my sister. I spend every free moment going over phone calls and leads that have come in, trying to find something—anything—that might have been overlooked, all while trying to keep my sister's face in front of the media and the public. I've been researching every abductor and serial killer case across the state, trying to see if there might be a connection. I just need you to understand that I'll do anything to find Sarah. Whatever it takes. But it's been eight months, and we're no closer to finding out who took her than we were the day she disappeared."

"I understand you're frustrated that we haven't found your sister, because I'm just as frustrated. We're doing everything in our power to find Sarah and the guy who took her, so we can bring closure to the other families."

"But now it's happened again," she said. "Another girl is missing. When is this going to end?"

"I understand—"

"I don't think you do understand," she said. "You don't have children. My mother's not sleeping at night. My parents are struggling with their marriage and wondering if they should shut down the restaurant. It's like a nightmare that you never wake up from. It's been eight months, and you haven't found anything. No solid leads. You can't even tell me if my sister's dead or alive."

Garrett rubbed the back of his neck. He had no idea what to say. She was right. He didn't understand. And saying he was sorry didn't do anything to help her find her sister.

"Were there any witnesses to Marissa's abduction?" she asked.

"A woman leaving the library saw Marissa get into the car that wasn't her own. She didn't think about it until she saw on the news that the girl was missing."

"Did she get a description of the driver?"

Garrett shook his head and started walking again to the end of the row of cars. "It was too dark, and she never saw his face."

"What about the vehicle?"

"A dark-colored SUV. It's not much to go on, but we've got people checking video surveillance in the area to see if we can come up with any hits around the time frame she left."

"It's the same thing that happened with Sarah. He did something to lure them into his vehicle," she said. "And I think I might have found something."

He stopped next to his car and pulled his keys out of his pocket. He needed to leave, but he also knew her well enough not to dismiss her. She'd probably spent as much or more time as he and Sam had, looking for her sister over the past few months. "What have you got?"

"I think I know the reason the girls got into the car—or at least why Sarah got into the car. We know for certain that she'd never just get into the car of a stranger. It had to be someone she knew or trusted."

"We came to the same conclusion."

"I talked to the librarian this morning, where Marissa went missing," Nikki continued. "She told me something she forgot to tell the police. Just before eight thirty, the time Marissa left the library, she saw a blue strobe light reflecting on the wall of the library. She went to the window to see what had happened, thinking there was a wreck or maybe someone had been pulled over. But by that time the light had stopped, and she didn't see anything, so she forgot about it."

"I'm not sure I understand," Garrett said. "It could have been a squad car passing, or an ambulance—"

"I don't think so." Nikki shook her head. "I think there was a squad car outside. Or at least someone who wanted Marissa to think he was in a squad car."

She pulled a folder out of the bag she was carrying and set it down on the hood of Garrett's car.

"These are photos of the Crown Victoria believed to have abducted Sarah. I've looked at them a thousand times, but for some reason up until now I never noticed this. If you look carefully, you can see suction cup marks on the windshield. Anybody can buy a police strobe on eBay that fits onto your windshield with suction cups."

"I don't know. I see where you're going, but it still seems like a stretch."

"I don't think so. I called and talked with the owner of the car, Matthew Banks. He told me he'd noticed those marks after his car was jacked. He said he never sticks things to his windshield because he knows how hard it can be to get the marks off. You think it might be a stretch, but if we knew we were looking for someone posing as a police officer, it might help."

He couldn't argue with her reasoning. "That was always one of our theories, but we haven't been able to prove it. Your sister's case was the only one where someone actually saw one of the girls get into the car. But even if you're right about this, I'm not sure how it's going to help us track him down."

"Let the public know you think he might be gaining the girls' trust by impersonating a police officer. That information might not save Sarah, but it might save someone else."

"He'll just find another tactic." Garrett hesitated, wishing immediately he could take back his harsh words. But they were true. This guy was like a chameleon, and they needed to find a way to stop him. "I really do need to go, but if you leave me what you have, I promise I'll follow up on this."

"Thank you."

"And Nikki . . . ," he said as she handed him the file. "We are going to find her."

Nikki nodded. "I just hope that when we do find her, she's still alive."

Garrett was still thinking of what Nikki had shown him when he arrived at the Dillinger home twenty minutes later.

Marissa's aunt met him on the porch. "Special Agent . . ."

"Addison."

"Sorry . . . Please tell me you have some news about Marissa. We're doing everything we can to put out the word about her disappearance, but so far we just seem to be running into brick walls."

"Not yet, ma'am, but we're following every possible lead. Which is why I'm here. I'm looking for a man who was here this morning." Garrett described the man to her.

"I think I know who you're talking about. He stopped by for a few minutes to express his condolences to the family."

"Do you know what his name is?"

She shook her head. "No, I can't remember, but I can find out for you. I'm keeping a logbook of everyone who comes by. It helps keep things organized, so we know who's volunteering, who's brought food, flowers. Just give me a second."

She came back with a notebook, flipped it open, then tapped her finger on the page. "This has to be him. His name is Jason Fisher. I'm not a hundred percent sure, but I believe he's a financial adviser who has worked with Nathaniel's company. He came with some flowers just before you got here. He didn't stay long, after giving his condolences to the family."

"Thank you," Garrett said. "I'll be in touch."

Garrett dialed Jordan's number as he slid into his car. "Hi, Jordan. Where are you?"

"I got delayed, but I'm getting ready to leave the bureau in the next couple minutes to meet our witness. Any luck on your end?"

"I was able to ID the man I saw at the Dillinger house. His name is Jason Fisher."

"Who is he?"

"Marissa's aunt wasn't sure exactly, but she thought he was a business associate of Mr. Dillinger's. He didn't stay long. He just came to express his condolences, then left."

"Give me a second to look him up . . . Okay, I've got something. Jason Fisher works for Raynott International Group."

"What is that?"

"Looks like it's a financial service company that's located not too far from here. From the description on their website, he's a financial analyst who helps clients know when they should buy and sell investments, among other things."

"Sounds like he fits the profile you gave us. He's educated, detail-oriented, works well with people. And the financial angle could be our missing connection. He's got dozens of clients, and over the years he'd come to know them and their families. Though it seems like if he knew their financial situations, he'd be asking them for money."

"Obviously, it's not about money for him," Jordan said. "We've always thought it's about power and control."

"Before you go interview your witness, get a team looking into this guy. I want to know everything there is about him."

"I thought he wasn't a suspect?"

Garrett ignored the comment. "Have them find out if he has connections with any of the other families. And in the meantime, I'm going to call him and ask him to come in."

"And you think he'll just agree?"

"I can be very persuasive."

"Funny," Jordan said.

"Seriously, I just want to see how he reacts. Then once we get some more information about him, we can see where things go from there. Does the company's website give you a phone number for him?"

"I'll send it to you now," she said. "And by the way, I spoke with Nikki Boyd. She said she ran into you in the parking lot."

"Did she tell you her theory?"

"Briefly. I told her that I can pull up cases of people impersonating law enforcement, but the problem is that there's hundreds of them. Still, if she's right, it makes sense. From a behavioral point of view, it's a gutsy move to pull off something like this. But you'd be amazed at how effectively it eases people's suspicions, because they think they're dealing with a legitimate officer."

The thought was terrifying. "Making them willing to get into the car of a serial killer."

"Exactly."

"Okay, then, I'll meet you back at the bureau when you're done with your interview. And in the meantime, I'm going to give Fisher a call."

After being transferred three times, Garrett finally had Fisher on the line.

"Thanks for taking my call. I'm Special Agent Garrett Addison with TBI's Criminal Investigation Unit. I'm calling in regards to the disappearance of Marissa Dillinger. I believe you know the family and visited the house earlier today?"

"Marissa Dillinger . . . of course. It's so horrible that she just vanished, but I'm not sure why you're calling me?"

Garrett chose his words carefully. "In a missing persons case like this it's essential to follow every lead, and we've discovered that important information can come out when we interview people who knew the family."

"Of course. I understand, but I was just there offering my condolences to the family. I'm not sure how I could help. I'm an acquaintance of her father, but I've never even met their daughter. I just stopped by on behalf of our firm to express our condolences. Dillinger has been a client for years."

Garrett felt like he was playing a game of chess. Push too hard, the guy would scare. But if he could convince him he was simply a person of interest—like every other person who'd walked into the Dillinger home—that the department was looking for information and nothing more, Fisher might bite.

"Would it be possible for you to come down to the TBI headquarters to answer some basic questions for us?"

"I suppose I could. How long would it take?"

"Shouldn't take more than twenty minutes."

There was a pause on the line. "I suppose I could come down. I just had a client cancel an appointment, so I could be there about four thirty."

Garrett hung up, wondering if he'd gotten sucked into following the wrong lead. There had been no anxiety in Jason Fisher's voice. No hint that he was nervous. A bit irritated, perhaps, that he had to fit a trip to TBI into his day, but there was nothing that indicated that Fisher might be their serial killer. Of course that was going to be true for whoever *had* killed the girls. He wasn't someone who would be tripped up by a mere phone call. He wouldn't come to the bureau wearing a shirt that said *I'm a serial killer*. Most serial killers weren't the dysfunctional loners Hollywood made them out to be.

Maybe it was just a coincidence, but he couldn't shake the urgency in his gut to follow up on the guy.

His phone rang as he started the engine.

"Garrett . . . hey. It's Sabrina."

Garrett stopped. He'd expected Jordan's voice again. Not his ex-fiancée. "Sabrina. It's been a long time."

"I know, and I'm in town, believe it or not. I thought it might be nice to see you. Maybe have dinner together."

"You know, I'm sorry, but I'm in the middle of a case, and I can't get away right now, but it's nice to hear from you."

"I figured you'd be busy, but I promise I don't need long. Just ten minutes of your time. Seriously. I won't keep you. Surely you can give me that much. I need to talk to you about something."

Garrett glanced at his watch. With Fisher not coming for another hour he had a few minutes, but still, her timing couldn't be worse. The last thing he wanted to do today was deal with some of Sabrina's drama.

"Please, Garrett . . . it's personal."

Being personal definitely made him want to run the other direction. Which was probably exactly what he should do. Run.

Sabrina had always had a knack for trouble, and he didn't want to get involved.

"Please?"

"Where are you?"

"Not far from your work." She gave him the address of a hotel. "I can meet you in the restaurant, whenever you have a free minute."

He let out a sigh. "I can't stay long, but I can be there in fifteen minutes."

18

3:40 PM
Vanderbilt University Medical Center

Jordan stepped off the elevator onto the third floor of the hospital, trying to squelch the irritability that had mushroomed since leaving the bureau. Maybe Garrett was right on target to follow his instincts. He had a legitimate—albeit weak—lead. There was a chance it might pan out and this guy he'd seen today was actually the Angel Abductor. But it was a long shot. She felt he was focused on looking in the wrong direction.

But no matter what route she believed the investigation should go, there was something she had to remember. Garrett had been involved with the search for these girls and their abductor for two years, and she knew he'd taken their inability to close the case extremely hard. She couldn't really blame him for going after every possible lead. Knowing that another girl had been taken was a devastating blow to the investigation. And for Garrett, that blow had been personal.

She walked toward the nurses' station, engulfed with a sudden feeling of loss as she walked down the hall. She slowed her steps to look into one of the rooms. Several bouquets of flowers sat on a countertop surrounded by a handful of cards. A woman her age sat beside the bed, holding the hand of an elderly woman who was hooked up to an IV and an assortment of monitors. Familiar waves of grief washed over Jordan as she watched the all-too-familiar scene.

She took in a deep breath as she approached the nurses' station, forcing back the emotion. Something she'd become all too good at doing.

"I'm Special Agent Lambert with the FBI," she said to the woman going through a stack of files behind the desk. "I was told I could find Gloria Mather here."

"Of course. I'll let her know you're here." The woman placed a call, then looked back up at Jordan. "She's on her way."

A minute later, a petite woman wearing penguin scrubs walked up to the nurses' station. "You must be the FBI agent I spoke with on the phone. I've been so upset ever since I saw the news this morning. I can't imagine what that family is going through."

"As you can imagine, they're having a hard time. You said you saw Marissa Dillinger early this morning?" Jordan held out her phone and showed the woman a photo of Marissa. "Is this the girl you saw?"

"Yes." Gloria nodded. "That's definitely her. She was in the vehicle next to me when I stopped at the red light on Blakemore and 21st. I could see her because the streetlight was shining into the car she was in."

"What time was this?"

"Let's see." Gloria gnawed on her lip. "I was on my way home early this morning. I got off late, around twelve thirty, so this was probably about twelve forty-five . . . maybe as late as twelve fifty."

"Did she look scared or seem as if anything was wrong?"

"No, not particularly. I didn't notice anything unusual about her behavior at all. She just stared out the window. If I'd thought she was in danger, I would have reported it immediately. I didn't realize there was another girl missing until I watched the news this morning. But I do remember that she was wearing a bright red sweater, just like the news reported. That's what made me realize it had to have been her."

Jordan mentally went through the timeline of Marissa's disappearance. She'd been snatched around eight thirty from the library parking lot. And now, according to their witness, Marissa had been seen less than ten miles away four hours later. If they could pinpoint the car on city surveillance cameras, they might be able to backtrack where she'd been as well as where she was going.

"And the driver," Jordan asked. "Did you get a look at him?"

"Unfortunately, no." Gloria leaned against the counter. "I could only see her from where I was sitting."

"What about the vehicle she was in. Can you describe it?"

"I'm actually surprised I remember, but it was a gold-colored Honda Accord. My husband and I used to have one, so I recognized the make and model. Unfortunately, I didn't get a license plate number."

"Anything else you can tell me that might help track them down?"

"I wish there was, but no. Not that I can think of anyway."

"I appreciate your calling this in." Jordan handed her a business card. "If you think of something else, please call me."

"You bet."

A minute later, Jordan was heading back down the elevator toward the parking garage. As soon as the doors opened, she started to call Garrett, then decided to call Sam instead.

"I think we might finally have a solid lead," she said, once Sam picked up.

"I hope so, because I need some good news. Couldn't get anything new from the woman who saw Marissa leave the library, and the library doesn't have any video surveillance. I feel like we're moving blind here. All we really have is confirmation on the time she left the library and Nikki Boyd's interview with the librarian and her theory that we've got someone posing as law enforcement."

"I spoke to the woman who called in about seeing Marissa early this morning," she said, filling him in on the details.

"That means she could be anywhere at this point, but I'll make sure her AMBER Alert is updated to include the vehicle and that the information goes out to every law enforcement across the state. Someone has to have seen something."

"We can only hope." Jordan walked toward her rental car, her footsteps echoing against the cement floor.

"Have you heard from Garrett?"

Jordan hesitated at the question. "He's following up on a lead of his own."

The sound of breaking glass punctuated the quietness of the garage as she turned the corner.

"I need to go."

Jordan dropped her phone into her pocket, then pulled out her gun, aiming it toward her car, where the noise had come from. There was no sign of anyone, but the back window of her rental car was shattered. Adrenaline surged through her as she walked back toward the car.

"FBI!" she shouted into the dimly lit garage. "Who's out there?"

An eerie stillness greeted her, but someone had been here. A note lay on the rear dash attached to a brick. Jordan stared at the handwritten words.

You'll never find her alive

The elevator door slid open behind her, jerking her attention away from the car. Jordan turned around as a man wearing scrubs stepped out, then stopped. She lowered her weapon to her side and showed him her badge.

"What's going on?" he asked.

"Get back in the elevator."

The man backed up into the elevator and the doors slid shut.

Something clattered behind her. She spun around and started walking forward. Shadows danced along the edges of the wall, but no one emerged. She had to find whoever was out there.

172

Jordan ran toward one of the emergency call boxes located throughout the garage, quickly calling Sam back at the same time.

"Sam—"

"What's going on? We got cut off."

"Where are you?" she said.

"Heading back to the bureau. Why? What's going on?"

"I'm in the parking garage outside the hospital. I just had a brick thrown through my car window. It's him, Sam. He left a note telling me I wouldn't find her alive. The Angel Abductor. He's here."

"What? Are you okay?"

"I'm fine, but I haven't been able to find him yet."

"Stay where you are. I can be there in five . . . maybe ten minutes."

"He'll be long gone by then, if he's not gone already. I'm headed for the emergency call box to get the garage locked down, then I'm going to start looking for him myself. You have to get uniforms here to secure the hospital."

"I'll take care of all that, but Jordan, you need to be careful."

"I will. I promise. I've got to go."

Jordan shoved her phone into her back pocket just as she reached the emergency call box. She pushed the button.

"This is Special Agent Jordan Lambert with the FBI," she said as soon as security answered. "We've got a possible murder suspect in the garage. I need the entire parking garage shut down, including the elevators. I've got backup on its way to commence a systematic search of the entire facility."

"Wait a minute. Who are you?"

"You can argue with me, but in the meantime there's a serial killer in your garage. You can either be a hero or let a killer escape."

"Whoa . . . okay. I'm shutting down all exits now."

Jordan hung up and started back toward her car. Chances are, whoever had thrown the brick was already long gone. But if he was still here, she was going to find him.

She slowed down every few feet, checking under each car she passed. She hadn't heard a car leave this level after the brick was thrown, which meant he was probably on foot. That significantly lowered the chances of catching him. She eyed one of the surveillance camera's red light. If they couldn't find him, maybe they'd get lucky and have video footage of him.

Three minutes later, metro police swarmed the building and began a systematic search of the hospital and parking garage. When Sam and Michaels showed up fifteen minutes later, the garage had been cleared, with no sign of their suspect.

"Jordan?" Sam strode across the parking area with Michaels to where she was talking to one of the officers. "You okay?"

"I'm fine," she said, excusing herself from the conversation. "The guy's long gone, but the Crime Scene Unit's seeing if they can get any fingerprints from my car. They're also analyzing the note, and we've got a team going over the garage's video footage. I'm hoping we can get something from that."

But she knew there would be no fingerprints on the brick or the note. There would be no evidence that would lead to their killer. Not if it really had been him. He was too smart for that.

"What are you thinking?" Sam asked.

"That none of this makes sense," she said. "I'm wondering why he would do something so juvenile, like throwing a brick through my car window. Why take the risk of getting caught? If I'd left a few seconds sooner, I would have seen him, or if another car had come along . . . it just doesn't make sense."

"But he's not normal," Michaels said. "You've got to have profiles on people like this. If he was normal, he wouldn't be out killing young girls. You said a while back he was becoming bolder. Maybe it's not enough for him anymore that he just gets away with what he's doing."

"Maybe he's rubbing our noses in the fact that he's winning," she replied. "That would fit his psych profile."

Miles Duncan, the TBI intelligence analyst she'd asked to check the video footage, came up to them. "Sorry to interrupt, but you told me to let you know as soon as we found something."

"What have you got?" she asked.

"We found your guy on the hospital security cameras, but the footage isn't going to help us identify him. He wore a hood, and he knew how to avoid the cameras."

"Figures," Sam said.

Jordan didn't even try to mask her disappointment. She was afraid that if there was any chance of saving Marissa, they'd just missed it.

"But we were able to clip together his movements," the agent said, holding up her laptop. "Here's where he entered the garage on foot through the south entrance. Seven minutes later he hit your car. Another minute, and he was gone from the building."

Jordan groaned. A lot of good that did them now.

"We're tapping into city surveillance," Duncan said, "but it isn't going to be easy to find him."

"Expand your search and look for a gold-colored Honda Accord," Jordan said, "and let me know as soon as you find something."

19

Garrett parked the car outside the ritzy hotel, wondering for the umpteenth time if he'd made the right decision by showing up. But just like when they'd been dating, Sabrina had always been persuasive. Today, though, he wasn't sure why she'd called—or even why she was in Nashville, for that matter—but he did know he wasn't in the mood for one of her antics.

Modern country music pulsed through the speaker system as he walked into the hotel lounge adjacent to the lobby. She was sitting in one of the cozy chairs in the corner, wearing a form-fitting gray dress with tall black boots and perfectly matched accessories. Perfectly manicured nails, perfect brows, flawless makeup . . . Most people had thought he was crazy when he quit the firm, but that world—and it included Sabrina—was what he'd tried to escape five years ago.

Funny how he couldn't remember that last time he'd seen her. Probably some formal gathering at his parents' upscale home outside Memphis. It seemed like a lifetime ago that he'd asked her to marry him. Looking back, he wasn't sure what he'd seen in her.

176

Thankfully they hadn't gone through with the marriage. That would have ruined him in the end.

"Sabrina . . ." He walked up to the table and forced a smile. "My mom didn't mention you were coming to Nashville."

"I didn't realize she kept track of me."

"She always had a soft spot for you. She updates me on how you're doing every once in a while."

"It's been a long time." She motioned to the empty seat next to her. "Can I order you a drink?"

"No." Garrett hesitated, then slid into the chair. "You're not drinking again, are you?"

She shrugged her shoulders and stared at the glass she was holding. "Nothing I can't handle."

Except she'd never been able to handle her liquor, and he was sure nothing had changed.

"You always were a bit dull." Sabrina waved at the bartender. "Can we have a coffee here? Black."

"I'm fine," he countered, then decided not to make a big deal of the gesture. "I meant it when I said I couldn't stay. You said it was urgent."

"It is." She shot him one of her smiles and grabbed his hand, lacing their fingers together. "I can't believe how much I've missed you."

"Sabrina—" He pulled his hand back, immediately regretting his decision to come. What had he thought would come of this? Because be knew her far too well. Knew she was used to getting her way.

But not this time.

This time the only thing he was going to do was hear her out and leave. And he really shouldn't have given her that much.

"I knew you'd get all up in a huff if I said that," she said, "but it's true."

"Just tell me what's wrong."

"Does it always have to be straight to the point? Why can't we spend some time catching up first? It's been so long—"

"Because I haven't slept, I'm on a case, and I'm tired."

"And grouchy."

He frowned. She was right, but that didn't change how he felt.

"So what is it that's got you so tense?" she asked. "Another case?"

"I'm sorry, Sabrina. I can't talk about my work."

"Funny. You couldn't talk about your cases when you were a lawyer with all that client privilege stuff, and now as a detective, or agent, or whatever you are, you still can't talk about them."

"Sabrina—"

"It doesn't matter. It's still good to see you. We should have met and caught up a long time ago." She looked up at him. "Sometimes I regret our not going through with the wedding. I still think we could have been good together."

"If I remember correctly, you're the one who broke things off with me."

"Only because I was hoping it would shock you into realizing what you were about to lose." She took a drink, then laughed as she sat back in her chair. "But don't worry, Garrett. I didn't call you to try and get you back. I'm engaged." She held up her hand, displaying what had to be at least a carat-and-a-half diamond. How had he missed that?

"Really?"

"You sound surprised. To a lot of people I'm the perfect catch, in case you didn't know."

"I didn't mean it that way. Congratulations."

The bartender slid a cup of coffee in front of him, then walked away.

"It has been five years, Garrett. You didn't expect me to join a nunnery, did you?"

"Of course not." He took a sip of the coffee and burned the tip of his tongue. "I'm just surprised my mother didn't tell me the good news."

"She doesn't know. Charles just asked me last night. We haven't

178

made the announcement yet. In fact, you're the first person I've told."

"And the next day you're asking to meet with your ex-fiancé. What is Charles going to think about that?"

"He knows all about you, Garrett, and thankfully he isn't the jealous type. But what about you? You're not wearing a ring, but I'm going to assume you're seeing someone else?"

"No."

"Hmm . . ." She stared at him until he wanted to crawl under the chair he was sitting on. "I could always tell when you were lying."

"I'm not lying."

"Then if you're not seeing her yet, you wish you were. Who is she?"

Jordan wasn't someone he was ready to tell anyone about. Especially his ex-fiancée.

"Listen, Sabrina, I'm working a case, and while it's nice to see you, I don't have time for an interrogation. You told me there was a problem. If I can help, I will, but that's it. Nothing more."

"And it certainly shouldn't be about something personal, right?"

Garrett ignored the comment and took another sip of his coffee.

"Fine. Charles is here on business and brought me with him. But I came to see you."

"I still don't understand."

"It's Brandon."

"Your brother?"

Sabrina nodded.

That hadn't been what he was expecting. The last time he'd seen Brandon, her brother had been sixteen, maybe seventeen. He'd spent high school in and out of trouble, getting away with far too much, and never taking responsibility.

"What kind of mess did he get himself into this time?" he asked.

Sabrina let out a pout. "Don't just assume he's in trouble."

"I might be an investigator, but trust me, it doesn't take much to deduce that one."

"Fine. He made a few dumb choices."

"And . . ."

"He needs a good lawyer."

"In case you forgot, I'm not a lawyer anymore, Sabrina."

"I know, but I thought maybe you could put in a good word with your father, so he'd take on his case. I can't get past his secretary, who keeps telling me he's not taking on new clients, but I don't believe her. And it's obviously not a matter of money. My family can pay."

"I'm not sure I'm the one you should be talking to. If you've forgotten," Garrett said, "I've never exactly been on good terms with my father. He's still convinced I threw my life away when I left the firm."

"You can understand why, can't you? You had everything. A prestigious job on the fast track to being a partner. A half-million-dollar house in East Memphis . . . and me."

Garrett frowned. Somehow she always steered the conversation back to herself. "None of that was enough."

"Including the deal your father wanted to make with my father?" she asked.

"What they wanted to do was illegal."

"Not technically."

"That shouldn't matter. It was wrong."

"Garrett, please. Forget all of that. I'm serious. I need your help. You're father has a track record with difficult cases. I need him."

"You could talk to my mother." Garrett thought about asking what her brother had done, then decided he had no desire to hear the details of the case. "She has a lot of pull with my father."

"Maybe I will. I haven't seen her for a while. But I need you to call her first. Give her a heads up. Will you at least do that for me?"

He nodded, hoping he didn't regret getting involved. Sabrina had always been hard to say no to.

"One last thing before I go." She swallowed the rest of her drink, then set the glass back down on the table. "I just want you to know that I really am sorry for what happened between us."

He brushed away the comment. She wasn't the only one. They both had things they regretted. "It was a long time ago, Sabrina. Forget it."

"No . . . because I mean it. I said a lot of things I shouldn't have."

He'd put the past behind him and had no interest in dredging it up.

"Okay . . . just so you know." She stood up, then bent down and kissed him on the cheek. "See you around, Garrett."

Then she walked away.

Garrett swallowed the last of his coffee, paid the bill, then walked out of the hotel. He glanced at his watch as he walked to his car. He had about twenty minutes to get back to the bureau for his interview with Jason Fisher. Twenty minutes to get his mind back on his job. Because Sabrina had been right about one thing.

Jordan.

He'd been a fool all these years. No matter how many times he told himself he wasn't in love with her anymore, he knew it wasn't true.

He wanted them to be together. For them to pick up where they'd left off. Her living so far away made pursuing a relationship with her complicated, but if he were honest, he didn't care. He never should have let her walk out of his life.

He had no idea how she was going to respond, but before she left this time, he was going to tell her the truth. When he'd kissed her after their walk on the bridge, he'd convinced himself they'd been caught up in the emotions of her losing her mom. Nothing more.

But he'd never know how she felt unless he spoke with her. He might regret making himself vulnerable, but he'd regret it more if he didn't say anything.

He pulled his phone from his pocket. Now might not be the

time for a discussion about their relationship, but he did need to update her on Fisher.

"Jordan," Garrett said once she'd answered. He put his keys into the ignition but didn't start the car. "Fisher agreed to come in. I'm meeting him back at headquarters in twenty minutes."

Her response was barely audible against the background noise on the line.

"Jordan . . . I can barely hear you." He upped the volume on his phone. "You sound like you're underwater."

"Just a second . . . Sorry. Is this better?"

"Yeah, I can hear you now. What's going on?"

"I'm in a parking garage, and not only is the reception spotty, but noise echoes like crazy."

He rested his hand against the steering wheel. "Sounds as if you're having a convention there. Is everything okay?"

"Yes." A full five seconds passed before she continued. "But I just got a message from Marissa's abductor."

"What do you mean, a message?"

She gave him the CliffsNotes version about what had just happened and Garrett felt his gut clench. This guy had already killed three girls, maybe more. Why would he all of a sudden threaten Jordan? This situation could have ended a whole lot worse than a brick shattering her car window.

"Listen," he said, "I can be there in about ten minutes—"

"Forget it. There's nothing you can do here. Nothing either of us can do, unfortunately."

Maybe she was right, but another question loomed in the forefront.

"What if Fisher is our guy? Is it a coincidence that I just called him about coming in for questioning? I'm not sure how he would have known where you are, but if it is him, he would have time to hit your car before meeting me."

"It's possible," she said.

"But you still think Fisher's not our guy."

"I honestly don't know. But maybe I should be there with you when you talk to him. I'd like to see how he reacts to being questioned."

"Are you sure?"

"I'm sure. Sam and Michaels can finish up here. I'll get a ride back to headquarters and meet you there."

20

4:28 PM
Tennessee Bureau of Investigation

Jordan stood outside the small interview room where Jason Fisher sat waiting for them. She took a sip of her coffee, surprised the man had agreed to come in without demanding to see a lawyer. He'd seemed perfectly willing to speak with them, even though their reason to bring him in was flimsy at best.

She studied his face while she waited for Garrett to show up. The man's features matched those in the sketch they had of the abductor, but so did hundreds of other people in the city. There was simply no way they were ever going to make a positive ID based on that sketch. But what else did they have?

Garrett hurried down the hall, right at four thirty. "Sorry. Last-minute phone call."

"You're fine. I just got here and so did Fisher."

He stopped in front of her. "You're sure you're okay?"

"My rental car's window isn't, but I am." She brushed off his concern. "I just read the background check you had run on Fisher."

"And?"

"There isn't much, as I'm sure you saw. Two speeding tickets over the last decade. Nothing that pointed to him being a serial killer."

"I didn't think there would be," Garrett said. "What about the connection between Raynott International Group and our victims' families? Have they found anything there yet?"

"They're still tracking that information down." Jordan hesitated, taking the last sip of her coffee, then dumping the empty cup into a nearby trash can. "I just spoke with Sam. Not that you don't already know this, but he reminded me that we need to be careful. We don't have any solid evidence that this man is involved. And just because he showed up at a couple vigils for missing girls doesn't exactly make him guilty."

"I know that. That's why he's simply a person of interest. All I want to do is talk to him about what he might know."

"The problem is that the only thing we do know about this guy is that he was at the house of two of the victims, but that isn't exactly a crime. And the fact that he agreed to come in freely makes me tend to believe he's not involved."

"We don't know that. Not yet."

Jordan frowned. She understood the reasoning behind Garrett wanting to bring this man in, but she also wanted to make sure that they weren't on another wild-goose chase. Marissa had already been missing twenty hours. If they focused on the wrong man, it could very well cost her her life.

She swallowed her frustration. She knew that Garrett had been agonizing over their powerlessness in this case ever since his first week on the job with TBI when they'd found the body of Jessica Wright. It was understandable that he was dogged about pursuing every possible lead, no matter how tenuous.

Garrett caught her gaze. "I just need you to trust me."

"You know I trust you completely, but that really isn't the issue here. I'm worried we're not focusing on the right lead."

"I'm not dismissing Gloria Mather's statement. That's why we've got the entire state looking for a gold Honda Accord. Agents are scouring camera footage of the area. We've even solicited help from the public. But I can't just dismiss this as a coincidence."

She held his gaze. Her job was to highlight pertinent facts and put them into a logical order to help him and his team solve the case. It wasn't to make judgment calls.

"Okay," she said. "So, do you have a plan?"

"Yes."

Jordan frowned. "And do you plan on telling me what that plan is?"

"Just play along."

"Garrett . . ."

Garrett turned and walked into the room. "Mr. Fisher. We appreciate your taking the time to come and speak with us. I promise this won't take long."

They quickly introduced themselves, then sat down across the table from the man.

"I don't mind coming down," Fisher said. "Especially with a girl's life on the line, though I'm not sure how I can help."

Jordan sat down next to Garrett across from Fisher, determined to let Garrett take the lead on the interview.

"On the phone you said you were aware of the recent disappearance of Marissa Dillinger?"

"Of course. I think everyone in the city's aware of what's going on. It's horrible." He looked from Garrett to Jordan, then back to Garrett again. "I just realized why you both look familiar. You were there earlier today. At the Dillinger home."

Jordan glanced at Garrett. She was surprised at the man's answer, though it wasn't as if he could deny being there.

"How well to you know the Dillinger family?" Garrett asked.

"Not extremely well. At least not on a personal level. I work for a financial service company, and I've had some interaction with Nathaniel Dillinger. He's one of our clients. And when I heard about what had happened . . . I don't know . . . I don't have children, but I just wanted to drop by and show my support. So I did."

"I'm sure they appreciate that. We noticed the family has an incredible support network."

"I wish I could volunteer in some way, but my workload is pretty heavy right now, and I simply can't commit to the time. Stopping by seemed to be the least I could do."

"And we don't want to take too much of your time," Garrett said, "but we're currently interviewing those who knew the Dillinger family and could tell us what Marissa's relationship with her parents was like."

Jordan watched Garrett pause, as if waiting for the implications of what he was saying to sink in.

"Wait a minute." Fisher leaned forward. "You think they're somehow involved in their daughter's disappearance?"

"I'm not implying that. All I can say is that there has been some new evidence that has come to light, and we're simply trying to follow up on all leads. Often people have information without even knowing it."

Jordan sat back in her chair, wondering if she should pull Garrett out of the room or simply go along with his plan. She wasn't sure how his line of questioning was going to get them anywhere. They were already on thin ice just having him come in for questioning.

"From your interactions with him, what can you tell me about Nathaniel Dillinger?" Garrett asked.

"Like I said, I didn't know them well, but I always had the impression that they were a solid family. He was active in choosing his investments and did well."

"Did he ever speak of his daughter?"

"I think I saw a picture of her in his office. And he might have mentioned her once or twice, but when we met, it was to go over his financials. It was never a social call."

"I understand. We just have to ensure we're not missing anything. You probably know how teens can be," Garrett said. "And unfortunately, accidents happen. There are things people have to cover up. Secrets to hide."

"I guess I'm just surprised at the angle of the investigation, but even if there was something going on, I wouldn't know. I thought the case was somehow supposed to be connected to the Angel Abductor."

"The media has picked up on that, but at the present we aren't eliminating any suspects. Did you know any of the other victims allegedly taken by the Angel Abductor?"

Fisher paused a few seconds before answering. "I know the Boyd family, actually, though again, not well. Rob Boyd has done some investments with our company. And like with the Dillinger family, I thought it was appropriate to stop by and express my condolences. Again, such a tragedy."

"What about any of the other Angel Abductor victims?" Garrett asked.

"No . . . I'm sorry. I've heard the news reports over the past couple of years but don't remember recognizing any of the other girls."

"Last question. Can you tell me where you were yesterday evening between seven and nine?"

Fisher sat back in his chair, clearly not happy with the sudden shift in the conversation. "I'm not sure why you're asking me that question."

Garrett shook his head as if to wave off the importance. "It's nothing more than a routine question. We're asking everyone who comes in here."

"I don't know . . . the past couple days have been pretty hectic. I was in and out of meetings most of the day, including a dinner meeting. I didn't get home until after eleven. My secretary can give you the details if you'd like."

"I'm sure that won't be necessary." Jordan stood up. "We appreciate your taking the time, Mr. Fisher."

"Jordan—"

But she was already walking toward the door. "An officer will be here in just a minute to escort you out."

"Thank you."

Jordan waited until Fisher had left before she spoke to Garrett. "He was supposed to be a person of interest. Not a suspect."

"I wanted to see his reaction, but we have his alibi. We can check it out and—"

"We have nothing, Garrett."

"He lied. He was at the Kerrigan house. I saw him."

"You think you saw him. That was two years ago." Jordan clenched her hands, then slowly released them. "Listen. We'll check out his alibi, but we need to move on. Every moment counts—"

"You think I don't know that?" His voice rose. "You might be the behavioral expert, but he's playing us, Jordan. He walked in here knowing the answers. It was all too smooth. Too rehearsed."

"Not everybody reacts the same way when they're interrogated."

"He never flinched. Never asked to see a lawyer—"

"So because he wasn't anxious, he was lying?"

Garrett rubbed the back of his neck. "If he's the Angel Abductor, he's getting away with murder. Again."

"He just gave you an alibi, he answered all of your questions. He doesn't exactly act like a man who's guilty of murder."

"That's what he wants. He's playing us. This is a game. Why else would he show up at three different vigils?"

"You're pulling at straws, Garrett."

"Maybe, but I don't think so. We should check out his alibi."

"We shouldn't waste time chasing an unsure lead when we have a solid one."

Garrett pulled his phone out of his pocket and studied the screen. "I missed a call from Sam," he said.

Jordan watched his expression as he talked to Sam and felt her stomach clench. Something was wrong.

"What is it?"

Garrett wouldn't meet her eyes. "They just found Marissa Dillinger's body."

21

5:24 p.m.
Highway east of Nashville

Garrett pressed on the accelerator as he maneuvered his way through traffic toward the forested trail just outside the city where Marissa's body had been found. The thirty-minute ride had been completely silent so far, with neither he nor Jordan in the mood to talk.

"The note said I wouldn't find her alive." Jordan's sudden statement broke into his thoughts.

He glanced at her. "Because he knew she was already dead."

He'd run through the timeline over and over since leaving the bureau. Fisher, or whoever was behind this, could have brought her out here and killed her at any time over the past twenty-four hours. He would then have had plenty of time to leave Jordan the chilling message, before disappearing again. But why the games? Why the note?

"Have you ever had to deal with a case that keeps you up at night and haunts your dreams?" he asked, thankful the traffic had finally lightened up.

Jordan nodded. "Four years ago, the FBI was hunting for a man who killed his three stepchildren. I still can't shake the images of

190

the crime scene. Or forget their mother's pleas to find him as she spoke to the press."

The Angel Abductor case was the one that kept him up at night. The one that motivated him to study case files and scrutinize details as he searched for answers. Applying logic didn't help, because there was nothing rational about their abductor's motives. Only a vague pattern that moved from girl to girl, leaving in its wake a trail of destruction.

Jordan glanced at the GPS and motioned for him to take the next left off the road into a paved lot that led to a popular hiking trail. He pulled into a parking spot and turned off the engine.

The parking lot was a flurry of activity. The ME's van was already in there, along with half a dozen other vehicles.

Jordan opened her door, pausing when he didn't move. "Garrett?"

He sighed. "Let's go."

They made their way up the winding trail that had been blocked off to hikers, and approached the cordoned-off crime scene. The medical examiner and his technician were conducting the external examination of the body. A dagger of anger pierced through Garrett as he slipped under the yellow tape flapping in the wind.

He'd been here before. Another crime scene. Another girl. But the results were the same. He moved a few steps closer, to where Marissa's lifeless eyes stared up at him. He recognized her from the photographs he'd seen at her house, and the photos the family had given them that were supposed to have been used to help find her. He took all of it in. The mole on her chin, the birthmark above her left eyebrow, and the lifeless expression on her face. Except for the bullet hole in the center of her forehead, like the other girls he could almost imagine she was simply sleeping.

"Can you tell me how long she's been dead?" he asked Philips.

"You can talk to the officer that took their statement, but according to the witnesses who found her body, they heard a gunshot about four twenty-five."

Garrett looked at Jordan. "Wait a minute. Are you sure?"

Philips stood up and nodded. "That timeline matches my findings. Her complexion is extremely pale from the lack of blood flow, something that becomes apparent pretty immediately after death, plus rigor hasn't set in, and there isn't any discoloration from settling blood."

Garrett stepped back from the body. Someone was bagging a Polaroid photo of Marissa, taking away with it any doubts as to who the killer had been. And who it hadn't been. Fisher had been with them at the police station from four thirty to five o'clock. Which meant if Philips was right, and Marissa was killed at four fifteen, there was no way Fisher could have killed Marissa. He had the most airtight alibi possible.

Garrett turned back to the ME. "And they're sure about the time?"

"Like I said, check with the officer that interviewed them, but that's the information I was given."

Jordan grabbed his arm and pulled him back a few steps. "Garrett, give it up. Fisher didn't do this. He's not our man."

"He could have had an accomplice."

"We'll check out his alibis, but it's not him, Garrett."

The truth began to settle over him, followed by an even more disturbing realization. This was his fault. Marissa shouldn't be dead. If he hadn't used up precious resources and time running down false clues, she might still be alive. The personnel he'd had investigating Fisher could have been looking for a gold Honda Accord. But instead his bad judgment had led to another girl's death.

"What else do we know from the witnesses?" Garrett asked, as Sam walked up to them.

"They're pretty shaken up," Sam said. "They were out walking their dogs when they heard a gunshot. A few minutes later, they found the body."

"And they didn't see anyone in the area?"

"Unfortunately, no. But they did see a gold-colored Honda Accord in the parking lot when they arrived."

Gloria Mathers had been right. The gold Honda. He'd followed the wrong lead.

"What do we do next?" he asked, turning to Jordan. "You know we're not going to find anything here that tells us who he is. We never do. Instead it's this game he keeps playing, and every time we lose, someone dies. He's probably out there laughing right now because I chased after the wrong clues."

"Honestly, the only thing I know to do is dig deeper until we can find a way to stop him," Jordan said.

"But how?" Garrett asked. "When Julia went missing, you told us that he wanted us to find her, because this is all nothing more than a game to him. But he's getting more and more daring. This time we have witnesses who heard him shoot her. We didn't even have to search for her body."

Garrett started back toward the car. He was done with all of this. Done with the games and the wild-goose chase whoever was behind this kept sending them on. Gravel crunched under his feet as he walked. The temperature had continued to drop, but he barely felt the cold. He was already numb. What was he supposed to tell Marissa's parents? That he made the wrong decision and because of that their daughter wasn't coming home? He should have been searching for that car. Following up the legitimate leads they had. They were supposed to stop the bad guys. That was his job. And he'd failed.

"Garrett?"

He kept walking. He didn't want to talk to Jordan. Didn't want to talk to anyone.

"Garrett, listen to me. You've got to shake this off."

"You know what this means?" He turned around to face her. "It means Fisher's innocent. It means I made the wrong call and wasted hours working on a false lead." He shoved his hands into his pockets. "I pulled agents away from the one viable tip we had, and had them chasing ghosts instead of doing something that might have saved her. He won again, Jordan. Just like he always does. Every. Single. Time."

"There was nothing wrong with your lead." She reached out to touch him, then pulled her arm back. "We don't know that doing things any different would have made a difference. Garrett, we had the entire state looking for her. The photos on the news, the picture of her in her red sweater, the lead about the car . . . None of those were enough, because we didn't have enough information to find her."

"I'm sorry, Jordan." He turned back around and started for his car again.

"Where are you going?" she asked, following after him.

"Walking away from this." He waved his hands in the air. "I can't do this anymore."

He'd seen the same anger he felt right now in his father's eyes growing up. An anger that had blinded him to everything around him. He'd always promised himself he'd never be like his dad. Never lose his temper. Never let circumstances push him in a direction he didn't want to go. But he was being sucked into that place.

He unlocked his car and pulled open the driver's door.

"Garrett?" Sam stopped next to Jordan.

"I really don't need a lecture from you too right now, Sam. I made a bad call and now a girl is dead."

"Maybe you're right. Maybe you should have followed the lead I gave you, but then again, maybe you were on to something with Fisher. There was no way to know until you followed that lead."

Garrett looked up at his boss. Conjecture wasn't going to take away the all-consuming guilt spreading through him. "I spent years working on the streets, and I learned to cope with what I saw. I could go to a crime scene and shrug off the emotional side, but this case . . . these girls. This is different."

"Trust me, I understand. We all have cases like this. The death calls that cut right through your emotional Achilles heel. I've been there, Garrett, and there's no way to just brush it off. Just like there was no way for you to know which lead to follow. The case against Jason Fisher had merit. It just turns out it wasn't true."

"And somehow that excuses the fact that we didn't do our jobs and find Marissa's killer *before* he murdered her? All these girls . . . none of them deserved to die the way they did."

"You're right. We all want to stop things like this before they happen, but it doesn't always work that way."

"Then tell me, how do you do this?" Garrett yelled, not caring any longer that his anger was seeping into his words. "Because I'm not sure I can anymore. For seven years, I've come to work every day. I've dealt with families in the middle of trauma. Seen things on the streets that most people can't even imagine. I thought I could come here and make a difference, and I walked away from everything I knew to do just that. But this case . . . this job . . . I can't do this anymore."

"You are making a difference. What about the cases we do close? The criminals we do catch and take off the streets?"

"Half the time we bring justice *after* someone is dead by making sure that person pays for his crime. But I don't want to do that anymore. I want to stop things before they happen."

"Sometimes you can't do that, no matter what you do. But here's what I can promise you. We're going to find this guy. No matter what it takes, no matter how long it takes, we will find him. We'll process the scene, see if we can find some witnesses. We're going to put an end to this."

"When?" Garrett shook his head. "Because I've reexamined every piece of evidence we have, every witness testimony and lead, and in case you didn't notice, we're not any closer than we were when Jessica Wright was found murdered."

"That's all true, but tell me this. How is walking away going to help? You walk away and he wins. He's beaten you."

Garrett let out a low laugh. "Have we ever not been beaten in this case? Six girls are dead or missing now. Six. We never had a chance. He's always had the upper hand. We have no solid evidence of who this guy is. Every lead takes us in the wrong direction. He's playing games with us, and I'm tired of losing."

He watched as Philips rolled a body bag on a stretcher toward the van. Someone would go to Marissa's parents and tell them that their little girl wasn't coming home. That they'd never watch her walk across the stage at graduation or walk down the aisle. There would be no grandbabies. No happily ever after.

But it wasn't going to be him this time.

22

Jordan sat on a padded barstool in her sister's kitchen and stared at the retro pink backsplash. Only Clara could add a pink stove and refrigerator to baby-blue cabinets and make it look like the design came straight off HGTV. If she tried the combination herself, it would end up looking like a buttercream cupcake threw up. She took a sip of the strong coffee she'd just brewed, trying to ignore the numbness that had spread through her over the past twelve hours. She hadn't been able to sleep last night. Instead, she'd stared at the sliver of moonlight coming through the curtains of the guest room, until she'd finally gotten up, needing to search for her own answers. She'd started digging through the case files of each girl, looking for that one evasive clue she missed, but there was nothing there she hadn't seen before. Which was why she completely understood Garrett's anger and frustration. She felt it herself. TBI had brought her in to solve the mystery, but so far, nothing they'd done was getting them closer to finding whoever was behind it. And now it was too late for Marissa and her family.

Clara bounced into the kitchen, her normal perky self, interrupting Jordan's thoughts. "Morning. Did you find something to eat? I've got every frozen breakfast item you can think of. Waffles, sausage biscuits, pancakes, breakfast burritos—"

"Thanks, but I'm not particularly hungry." Jordan glanced at the clock. "And anyway, I'm going to have to leave in about fifteen minutes. I just needed to get some caffeine into my system and try and wake up."

Clara braced her hands on the counter across from Jordan. "You're working too many hours. You don't look like you slept much last night."

"I didn't, actually. Last night was rough."

Her sister's smile disappeared. "I saw the news about that girl and the Angel Abductor. That's why you're back in town, isn't it?"

Jordan nodded.

Clara poured herself a cup of coffee, then took a sip. "I don't know how you handle things like that. If I had to deal with a whacked-out serial killer after seeing firsthand what he'd done . . . I don't know. I'd be a basket case. I'd never make it. Being a nurse comes close to pushing me over the edge every now and then as it is."

"To be honest?" Jordan said. "Sometimes I don't handle things very well. And this . . . this case has affected everyone involved."

"I don't blame you." Clara grabbed a banana out of the fruit basket and started peeling it. "Do you want one?"

"I'm fine, Sis. Seriously. Garrett called a little while ago and asked me to meet him for breakfast. I promise I'll eat something there if that will make you stop worrying about me."

"I don't think anything will make me stop worrying about you." Clara tossed the peel into the trash under the sink. "How is he, by the way?"

"Blaming himself."

"Why?"

"He followed a lead that turned out to be another dead end. And while there was really no way to know, he's taking it hard. This case has gotten under his skin, and I'm not sure how to help him."

"You can't really blame him. I mean, six girls are dead, which is terrifying. When even the FBI can't solve a case like this, it makes me wonder what kind of genius this guy must be."

"Thanks a lot," Jordan said.

"I didn't mean it personally," Clara said, taking a bite of her banana.

"I know. I'm just extra-sensitive right now." Jordan scooted around the counter, washed out her cup, then stuck it into the dishwasher.

"You know I'm here," Clara said. "I don't know how I can help, but if there's anything you need, please let me know."

"You've already done more than enough putting up with me the past few months when I'm in and out."

"Just so you know, Alex and I love having you here. It's nice to have all of us—including Dad—under one roof. But it does make me miss Mom more."

"Me too." Jordan eyed the pink ceramic frog that had been a part of her mom's collection and smiled. Memories of Mom were everywhere.

"Have you and Garrett ever talked about getting back together?" Her sister's question took Jordan by surprise.

"I'm just saying that while you might not admit it, I see something in your face every time his name comes up." Clara leaned forward. "You're still in love with him, aren't you?"

"I would hardly say 'love' is the word that describes what I feel for Garrett."

"Then what do you feel?"

Jordan blew out a huff of air. It wasn't exactly a question she felt like dealing with. Not today. "We're just friends, Clara. Nothing more."

"I've heard that one before, but you don't sound very convincing. And if you ask me—which I know you're not—the two of you are perfect together. You both understand the tough world of law enforcement, something I certainly can't relate to."

Jordan grabbed a dishcloth and started wiping down the kitchen counter. "Things between us have always been complicated. And yeah, maybe I can't shake some of the feelings I used to have when I'm with him, but I'm only here temporarily. I'll go back to Memphis, back to my job, and there won't be any reason for me to see him anymore."

"Maybe that's your problem. The two of you have danced this same dance for long enough. The man's still single, and if you ask me, it's because he's never found anyone who lived up to you. He's in love with you and has been as long as I've known him. You know that, don't you?"

"It's not love, Clara. For either of us."

"Really? I saw the way he looked at you when he came over right before Mom died and later at the funeral. Did you know he comes over at least once a month to play chess with Dad and watch whatever ball game is on TV?"

"No." Jordan dropped the cloth onto the counter. "He never told me that."

"I'm telling you, the man's still in love with you, but until both of you decide that having a relationship is more important than having a career, you'll continue going home at night to an empty house."

"There's nothing wrong with being single, Clara. I'm free to do what I want, when I want. I can eat what I want. Go where I want."

"I never said there was anything wrong with being single. But when you're in love with someone, and they're in love with you, it's crazy not to make some sort of compromise to be together."

Jordan frowned. "Like I said, it's complicated. I'm not sure either of us is in a place to go forward with a relationship. And honestly I'm not sure we ever will be."

"Please. Performing a septal myectomy is complicated. What

you and Garrett need is a kick in the pants. A wake-up call. Because one day it's going to be too late and you're going to look back on what you gave up, for what? Long hours and a half-decent paycheck?"

Jordan wrung out the cloth and hung it on the sink. "Then what do you think I should do?"

"Tell him you love him."

"I never said I loved him."

"You don't have to. It's written all over your face. Every time he calls. Whenever you mention his name. I'm not a relationship expert, but even I can see it. Seriously."

"I don't know. Maybe you're right and I've never stopped loving him, but I'm not sure if loving him is going to be enough in our situation."

———

Thirty-five minutes later, Jordan hurried across the parking lot to the café where Garrett had asked her to meet him. The sun was out, leaving a trail of warmth in its path. What if Clara was right? Was love enough to hold their relationship together? And what was she supposed to do? Just sit down across from him and tell him she loved him? She wasn't even sure if she still did. If she told him that, he'd probably think she'd gone nuts.

Garrett sat in the back of the restaurant, staring across the open space as customers ate their breakfast and fueled up for the day with mugs of coffee. She could see the fatigue in his eyes as she approached the table. He probably hadn't slept last night either. It was crazy to even think they could be a normal couple. An FBI agent and a criminal investigator didn't exactly have a lot of free time on their hands. And on top of that, they didn't even live in the same city.

"Hey . . ." She slid into the booth across from Garrett, pushing aside her sister's crazy thinking that had only ended up messing with her mind this morning. "Sorry I'm late."

"It's fine." He was nursing a cup of black coffee, looking as if he hadn't slept for days.

"You don't look fine. What's going on?"

He stared straight ahead, avoiding her gaze. "I handed in my resignation, Jordan. I wanted you to hear it from me and not someone else."

"Wait a minute." She felt as if she'd been slapped across the face. "You couldn't have just eased into this news?"

"There isn't a way to ease into this." He looked up at her. "I'm serious, Jordan. I'm walking away from all of this."

"Wait a minute." A streak of anger washed over her. "I heard what you said to Sam, but I didn't think you really meant it. We were all upset."

"I meant it. I'm done."

"You can't simply quit and walk away."

She regretted the harshness in her voice, but he'd taken her completely by surprise. She'd expected to show up and discuss the case with him. She'd even considered risking it all and telling him that despite everything that had happened, she did have one regret. Walking away from him all those years ago. But now?

"I can walk away and I am." He leaned forward, gripping the edge of the table. "Marissa is dead because I made the wrong decision. You were right. We should have been out there spending every second searching for that car."

"There was no way for you to know that."

"Yeah, well, my decision cost a girl her life."

"Don't turn this into a martyr case. No one else is."

"What about the family? What happens to them now? I lost a case, but they lost a daughter."

"This is about more than this case, just like it's about more than the decision you made to leave your father's firm."

"You know my father."

Jordan frowned. She'd never exactly been fond of his father. The man she'd met while they were dating had made it crystal clear she wasn't good enough for his son. She didn't have the right bank account, and she didn't have blue blood flowing through her veins. Garrett had always stood up to him, but somehow she'd ended up feeling like she was in the middle of a battle she didn't want to fight when he was around.

"What about your father?"

"When I was ten, my father told me I was destined to be a lawyer," Garrett said. "He told me how I could make a difference in the lives of people, and that was what I wanted. Not the money or my name on the building. I never cared about any of that. I wanted to study law and practice, because I could be a part of the system that made sure justice was being done. That's what I wanted."

"And that's what you've done. Both as a lawyer and now with TBI."

"That's where you're wrong. It started out that way. But then I found myself defending guilty clients who were happy to pay for loopholes. Maybe that's not how my father started off, but it became less about the clients and more about billing as many hours as possible. He forgot why he did what he did, and he wanted me to be like him."

"You were never like him. You aren't like him."

"It doesn't matter. I'm going back, Jordan."

"Wait a minute. Back to your father's firm?"

"No. Back to ensuring that justice gets done. Or at least that it has a better shot of winning."

"I don't understand."

"There was a case I read about a few years ago. A young, single mom. She needed a lawyer for her son, but she didn't have the money to pay for a decent one. Her son ended up going to prison. Four years later, new evidence turned up and he was exonerated. If he'd had a decent lawyer, he never would have gone to prison in the first place. I haven't been able to stop thinking about him, even after all these years."

"You can't blame yourself for every case gone wrong, Garrett."

"You don't get it. I couldn't save Marissa or the other girls, but I can save families like hers. I don't need billable hours. I have my trust fund. I can work pro bono on cases I want to take and actually make a difference."

"You already do make a difference. Can't you see that? I've seen you interact with Sarah Boyd's family, and with the families of the other girls. You have a way of relating to them on a personal level that gives them hope that the person who shattered their lives will pay for what he did. They know you're out there, determined to find the truth and make certain justice is served and this guy is caught. Not every cop can do that, but you can. They need hope. Something to give them a reason to wake up in the morning."

"They need whoever is behind this found. But it's not going to be me that finds him."

"They need you."

"No, they don't." He shook his head. "I'm sorry, I really am, but I've made up my mind. This isn't the first time I've thought about this. It's been niggling in the back of my mind for months. I need to do this. I want to do this."

"What about us?" She asked the question before she realized what she was saying.

Garrett frowned. "I didn't think there was an us."

"I just meant . . . I meant I'll miss working with you."

"I'm going to be busy getting this practice up and going. You'll be back in Memphis."

He was right, wasn't he? Her sister had filled her mind with nonsense, making her question everything she'd put behind her. But it was time to admit that their relationship was never going to move forward. It was never going back to what it used to be.

She scooted toward the end of the bench. "I probably should go. I've got a ton of work I need to finish up. I'm heading back to Memphis in the morning, where we'll be monitoring things on our end, but I guess that doesn't matter anymore to you, does it?"

He watched her leave the restaurant. He knew he was a fool to let her walk out of his life again, but he also knew he wasn't going back. He couldn't do it. She'd once asked him if he ever asked questions like where was God when Julia was abducted. Julia, Becky, Jessica, Bailey, Sarah, Marissa. He'd asked that question every time a new girl had gone missing. He still wasn't sure, but he knew God hadn't done anything to save Marissa the night she'd breathed her last breath. And neither had he. And that was something he was going to have to live with the rest of his life.

PRESENT
DAY

23

Garrett tossed the empty takeout box into the trash next to his desk, then glanced at the clock. He should be home by now. He'd already worked over forty hours this week, and it was only Thursday. But he really didn't feel like going home to an empty house. He'd spend a couple more hours working on his notes for tomorrow's meeting, then more than likely end up crashing on the couch in his office. It wasn't the most comfortable place to sleep, but it beat driving home just to turn around and be back again in the morning.

He glanced at the doorway that led into the small reception area of his office space. If Libby knew what he was planning, she'd tell him he needed a life, or a girlfriend, or at the least a good night's sleep. And sleeping on the couch wasn't exactly restful.

He picked up the file he'd been working on before dinner, then studied the framed photo of Sarah Boyd he kept on his desk. He tapped his fingers against the folder. Not a day went by that he didn't think about them. Marissa Dillinger, Sarah Boyd, and the other four girls. Their cases had changed him. Forced him to question his faith. Reminded him that while he didn't want to be like his father, neither could he simply walk away from trying to bring justice to the world. The photo of Sarah had become a constant reminder of what he'd left behind, but also of what he had no intention of going back to.

His secretary popped her head in the doorway. "Anything else you need me to do before I leave?"

"Not tonight. Go home, Libby. I'll be done here in a couple of hours."

She nodded at the like-new leather piece of furniture he'd picked up at a secondhand store. "You work too hard. Make sure you go home and get a good night's sleep. And sleeping on the couch doesn't count."

He shot her a sheepish smile at her predictable words. "It's not so bad."

She shook her head and smiled back. "See you tomorrow, boss."

He dove back into the file as she locked the front door behind her. It was a familiar scenario. A child custody battle turned violent. It was a situation where no one ever completely won. Especially the children who were caught in the middle, along with the mom who was working three jobs just to keep food on the table while she feared for her and her children's lives.

His cell phone buzzed on the edge of his desk. He picked it up, glanced at the screen, then hesitated. Unknown caller. He wasn't in the mood to talk to whoever was on the other end of the line, so he put the phone on silent and ignored the call.

Ten minutes later, a knock on the front door pulled him out of his thoughts. He frowned and pushed back his chair. This wasn't the kind of neighborhood where girl scouts made the rounds selling cookies. Still, he walked into the tiny reception room. The day after Thanksgiving, Libby had strung up lights on the barred window, and set up a tabletop tree with fiber optic lights and red and gold ornaments in an attempt to add a bit of festivity to the tired office space. A couple weeks after that she'd started playing Christmas music, leaving him with "I'll Be Home for Christmas" constantly running through his head.

Garrett checked the security camera on the desk, then stopped short.

Sam Bradford?

He hurried to the front door and unlocked it. "Sam?"

"I heard you were working in the neighborhood. Thought I should check it out for myself."

"It's good to see you, but wow . . . I'm speechless." Garrett gave the man a bear hug, then took a step back. A decade-plus had filled in the gray hairs that had once peppered his hairline, but other than that, he hadn't changed much.

"Speechless isn't exactly the reaction I was expecting," Sam said.

"Sorry, it's just that you're about the last person I expected to see today."

"I should have come sooner. I've been hearing good things about you and this place."

"Then it wasn't from my father." Garrett laughed.

"I always hoped that relationship would turn around."

"Me too. Instead, he just gets more cantankerous as the years pass, if that's possible. But I stopped letting it bother me years ago. I had to."

Sam took off his jacket and hung it on the coatrack Libby had picked up at a flea market last summer. "I hear congratulations are in order for a public service award you've now won for the second year in a row. I guess you turned out to be quite a lawyer after all."

"Thanks, but all I know is that I'm lucky to do what I love and not have to worry about money."

"What does your father think about your throwing away your trust fund?"

"He keeps reminding me that one day the money will run out, and he won't be there to bail me out."

"I can see his concern. You're not exactly working in one of those posh downtown offices like he is."

"Never cared much for the view," Garrett said as he ushered Sam into his office.

He glanced around the room, trying to see it from Sam's eyes. The paint was beginning to chip on the ceiling. He'd bought the majority of the furniture secondhand. A couple of the pieces of art on the wall were drawings from kids whose families he'd worked with.

"Besides," Garrett said, "rent is cheap here, and clients are plentiful. And I'm doing what I love, so I can't complain."

"Is that why you're sleeping here on the couch most nights?"

Garrett chuckled "You always were a top-notch investigator."

"Just a good guess actually," Sam said. "So what exactly do you do?"

"I work primarily with nonprofit organizations to make sure they're complying with state and federal laws, along with local childcare centers and volunteer centers. I also take on individual cases depending on the need." He walked up to the coffeepot behind his desk. "Can I get you some coffee? It's probably lukewarm and stale."

"Just how I like it," Sam said, making himself at home on the couch. "I always felt like it was partly my fault that you left. I should have tried harder to talk you out of it."

"Forget it, because you couldn't have. And besides, that was over a decade ago. I've moved on. No regrets."

"Even with Jordan?"

Garrett heated up the coffee in the microwave for thirty seconds, then handed Sam the mug before leaning against the edge of the desk across from him. "That's a subject I'd rather not delve into."

He kept up with her through other people. She'd stayed on with the FBI and had slowly climbed the ranks. Which didn't surprise him one bit. She'd always been good at what she did.

"Have you seen her lately?" Sam asked.

"You never could take a hint that a topic was off-limits, could you?"

Sam just smiled.

Garrett sighed. "Not for a long time. I ran into her once . . . four . . . maybe five years ago. She seemed to be doing well."

He'd been invited to a fundraiser in Memphis, and she'd been there. Even after all this time he could remember exactly what she looked like that night. That silky, light brown skin, curly hair, wearing a dress that made his jaw drop. She'd come with a date, but he noticed there was no ring on her finger. He'd walked up to her like a school kid and said hi. They'd spent the next few minutes talking about nothing at all, while he remembered everything that had ever happened between them. Somehow forgetting her had become impossible, even after all this time.

"You let a good one get away," Sam said. "You should have married her."

"Maybe, but it turned out she didn't exactly think the same about me. She wanted a career more than a family."

"That might be up for debate. I have a feeling she might have stuck around if you'd run after her."

It wasn't the first time he'd questioned his decision to walk away, or thought about picking up the phone and calling her. But after everything that happened, it was time to move on. Besides, his job kept him busy and that was the way he liked it. There was always someone who needed his help.

"So you haven't found someone else?" Sam asked.

Garrett frowned at Sam's persistence. Like Jordan, his love life—or lack thereof—was a subject he'd prefer to avoid. Especially when his mother was around. On his fortieth birthday he'd stepped into a room full of her influential friends and a dozen single women—all daughters of wealthy families, most a decade or more younger than him, and all very interested in the only bachelor in the room. He wondered what his mother had told them to get them to come.

Available: Handsome, single man with large trust fund.

But he hadn't connected with any of them. For some reason—even after all these years—he still found himself comparing every woman he met to Jordan. And so far no one had lived up to his expectations. Or at least what he felt toward her. Which wasn't fair, but tell that to his heart.

"And what about you?" he said, changing the subject. "Heard you have a second career."

If Sam noticed Garrett's shifting the conversation away from himself, he didn't say anything. "I started a private investigation agency. It keeps me out of trouble after retirement, since I'm not sure I'll ever be able to walk away completely from that life. The cases that refuse to let go. Especially those that went cold."

"How's Irene?" Garrett asked.

"Still keeping me in line. She talked me into going somewhere warm for our fortieth."

"I was always jealous of the two of you. You made marriage look so easy."

"Ha!" Sam sipped his coffee. "Forty years of marriage is hardly easy. Three miscarriages, two boys, and a handful of bumps along the way. But I'll admit it was completely worth it."

It was what Garrett had once wanted, but instead, he'd managed to build a life here. And while he might not have the name of his father's firm behind him, he didn't need that either. He was doing what he'd always wanted. Making a difference. He'd made his choice and was happy with it.

"As good as it is to see you," Sam said, "I'm not here just for personal reasons."

"I'm all ears."

"Another girl's dead." Sam pulled a folder from his briefcase and dropped it onto Garrett's desk. "We think the Angel Abductor is back."

"What?" Over ten years had passed, and Garrett had heard the rumors that the man who'd killed the girls was dead. "Who is she?"

Sam laid a Polaroid photo of a girl on Garrett's desk. "Her name is Chloe Middleton, and she was sixteen years old. She loved volleyball, music, and photography."

Garrett shook his head. He didn't want to see this. Didn't want to see her. "I'm really, really sorry to hear that, but I don't know what I have to do with this."

"My agency's been working with some of the victims' families, but so far we still haven't been able to discover the identity of their abductor and murderer. Another girl is dead. We need this to end."

"We tried that before. Remember? And in case you happened to forget, I blew it big time. Marissa Dillinger is dead because of what I missed back then."

He'd never been able to completely put Marissa's death behind him. He still had nightmares every once in a while about finding her warm body buried in a deserted grove of trees.

"Marissa's death was never your fault. You made a call with the evidence we had. You couldn't have known what was going to happen."

"Tell that to her parents."

Sam shook his head. "Is that why you're stuck in this shoddy neighborhood? Atoning for what you think you did wrong a decade ago?"

"Of course not." Garrett couldn't hide the flash of anger that ripped through him.

"Then hear me out. I think you might have been on the right track way back then," Sam said.

"What does that mean?" Garrett sat down on the arm of the couch.

"Think of that as your incentive to show up tomorrow morning, but here's the bottom line. I'm bringing the team back together, and I want you to come work this case with us."

Garrett stared at his old colleague. "You can't be serious."

"Why wouldn't I be?"

"Because you don't need me. You've closed dozens of cases without me, and you can certainly close this case without me."

"I want the entire team. Including Jordan."

Garrett's jaw tensed at the mention of her name.

"The FBI is sending her in. She knows this case as well as any of us do."

Garrett pressed his hands against his thighs, then stood up. "I'm not sure I want to come back, Sam."

"Because of Jordan?"

"No. It's because I don't want to go back there."

"Just think about it then. I won't need an answer until tomorrow."

"Tomorrow?" Garrett started pacing the worn carpet in front of the couch. "I've got clients in the morning, and a court date in the afternoon. I don't have time off."

"You see things uniquely. The details that often get swept over. And besides that, we make a good team. We might not have solved this case, but we did solve dozens, if not hundreds, of other cases. But if this is happening again—with the Angel Abductor—we need to put an end to this once and for all, Garrett. Before someone else dies."

Garrett turned toward the window that overlooked the parking lot. Some of the blind slats were broken, letting in too much light from the streetlamp. The bars on the windows were rusty, and three of the glass panels needed to be replaced. Most people thought he was crazy to have stuck it out in this neighborhood for so many years, but he *had* found purpose again. The only hole in his life—if there even was one—was that he didn't have someone to share it with. But most days he got home too late and too tired to care that no one was waiting for him.

He glanced at Sarah's photo. He'd never forgotten. Never forgotten that Marissa's family had counted on him to find her, and he'd made a mistake. A mistake that had cost her her life. Sam had to understand why he couldn't go back.

"Meet us at seven tomorrow morning at the bureau. We'll be working with their Missing Persons Task Force."

"I'm in the middle of a case, Sam."

Sam caught his gaze before heading for the door. "Just give us an hour. And see if that doesn't change your mind."

24

Garrett strode across the parking lot of the TBI headquarters for the first time in years, hoping he wasn't going to regret his decision to show up. Sam had always been persuasive, and in many ways while Garrett had been on the force, Sam was the father figure he'd never really had. But even that hadn't been enough to get him here. What had clinched the decision to come was the possibility of a second chance to right a wrong.

For years he'd gone over different scenarios in his head. If he'd followed the lead Sam had given him, if he hadn't put as much manpower into investigating Fisher, maybe things would have turned out differently. On the other hand, maybe it hadn't mattered which lead he'd decided to follow. Maybe the outcome would have still been the same. But all of that was something they'd never know. Marissa was dead, and in real life that ending would never change.

He stepped through the glass doors of the bureau and into the open atrium nestled between the two wings. A sense of familiarity

218

washed over him as he paused in the lobby in front of the central security checkpoint. But it wasn't the familiar building or even the sunlight streaming through the long row of windows above him that held his attention.

She was standing in front of the security checkpoint, looking even more beautiful than he remembered, if that was possible, in her black jeans, boots, and a dark-red scarf to ward off the chill of the holiday season.

I should be over you by now, Jordan Lambert, but I'm not sure I ever will be.

"Jordan." He walked up to her, trying to ignore the intense feelings sweeping through him that seeing her again brought on. "I guess you weren't expecting a trip here today either, were you?"

"No, but I was hoping I'd run into you before you went in." She shoved a wayward curl behind her ear and shot him a smile. "I thought it would be less awkward to see each other for the first time out here before we met with everyone else and dove into the case."

"That wasn't a bad idea, though I hope there isn't any reason for there to be anything awkward between us."

"I hope not too, it's just that it's been so long."

She looked relieved, but all he could think about was the last time he'd seen her. The last time he'd kissed her. And how he couldn't for the life of him remember at that moment why he'd said goodbye without telling her how he'd always felt.

He shoved back the memories. "When did you get into Nashville?"

"I drove in last night and am staying with my sister. What about you? You're still working as a lawyer?"

"Yeah." They took the passes from the uniformed officer and headed into the secured building. "I think I'm far better suited for what I'm doing now."

"I can't help but wonder what your parents think," she said.

He let out a low laugh. "Nothing's changed there. They still

219

think I've gone off the deep end. It's pretty much a topic that is completely avoided. I bet your dad, on the other hand, is thrilled you're in town."

"He is." She stopped in the middle of the atrium. "And I understand you probably see him more than I do. You never told me the two of you took up chess and watch ball games together once a month."

"After your mom died, I told you I'd look in on him. Turns out, we enjoy hanging out. There's nothing like a close ball game on the big screen with him and a couple of his old army buddies."

"I'm not even going to ask what the two of you talk about." She laughed as they started walking through the open office space. "But thank you."

And he wasn't going to tell her that her dad had been his source of updates on how she was doing. Her father had tried over the years to get him to come over when Jordan was home visiting, but he'd always managed to find an excuse. At the time it seemed enough knowing she was okay. But seeing her now made him wonder if he'd been wrong.

"I just can't believe how long it's been since I've seen you," Garrett said. "It's as if time has stood still for you. You look exactly the same."

Beautiful.

She avoided his gaze. "I don't think you've aged much either."

"A few gray hairs maybe."

"Are you still running?" she asked.

"I ran the Nashville Marathon a couple weeks ago. Trying to stay fit."

"Congratulations. Maybe I'll see you one day in Boston."

"Maybe."

He smiled as they approached the conference room, but he wasn't interested in shallow pleasantries. Instead, he had this sudden urge to push aside the past decade, along with any regrets, and pick up where they'd left off.

But that wasn't going to happen.

He glanced at his watch. "I suppose we should go in. They're waiting for us."

She nodded, then slipped inside the room ahead of him.

The rest of the team was already sitting at the long table in the room, and the sight brought with it a surge of memories. While Jordan might have barely aged in the past decade, that wasn't true for everyone. Michaels had gone completely bald and put on a pound or two. Sam, as he'd noted last night, had a headful of gray hairs, but still seemed as fit as he'd been a decade ago. Nikki Boyd, Sarah Boyd's sister, stood in the back of the room talking with Sam. She looked completely at ease in her law enforcement role.

"It's good to see you, Agent Boyd," Garrett said, shaking her hand.

"It's Agent Grant now, actually," she said, holding up her left hand. "I got married eight months ago. But I'm Nikki to you, Garrett."

"Well, congratulations, Nikki. It's nice to hear some good news in the middle of all this."

"I appreciate your agreeing to come," she said, turning to Jordan. "Both of you."

"Me too," Sam said.

Garrett didn't tell them he had yet to make up his mind whether he was in or not.

"We'll go ahead and get started now that everyone's here," Nikki said.

Garrett greeted Michaels, then took a seat next to Jordan at the table as Nikki moved to the front of the room and sat down next to a man he didn't recognize.

"It's good to see you all here, though as we know, the circumstances could be better," Nikki said, scooting her chair forward. "For the past two years, I've been a part of TBI's Missing Persons Task Force along with my partner, Agent Jack Spencer." Nikki nodded toward the man sitting next to Garrett. "Two days ago, we received a call from the sheriff in Rutherford County. They found the body of a young girl, half buried in a grave. Her name is Chloe Middleton, and everything about the case points to our Angel Abductor being back, including the Polaroid photo taken right before she was killed. Which is why we've asked to bring the four of you on board. We need to close this case."

"I understand you might have discovered the identity of the Angel Abductor?" Jordan asked.

Nikki nodded. "We thought we might have. About a year and a half ago, I was involved in a missing persons case involving a teenage girl. Long story short, our suspect, Randall Cooper, didn't end up being the Angel Abductor like I thought he might be, but he claimed to know the man behind the abductions."

"Who is he?" Garrett asked.

"Cooper told me they met in prison and that the other inmates called the man the Coyote. He kept Polaroid photos of the girls hidden away—photos that Cooper said he saw. He also said that the Coyote confessed that he had been the one behind the abductions. Then Cooper was transferred to another prison and lost track of the man. But it gave us a direction to go in.

"I spent weeks trying to track town the Coyote, until a friend of mine who works in the prison system came up with something. He researched the dates that the Coyote was in prison, talked to other inmates who knew him, and was finally able to come up with a name. Robert Wilcox."

"What was he in prison for?" Jordan asked.

"Surprisingly enough, he was in prison for fraud. Not murder." Nikki handed out the files sitting next to her. "I'll give you the highlights now, but these files have everything we currently know about this man."

Garrett opened up the file, then froze at the familiar photo staring up at him. His muscles tensed. Heart raced. How was this even possible?

"Wait a minute. This is Jason Fisher. I interviewed him a decade ago in connection to Marissa Dillinger's disappearance."

"That's why we wanted you here, Garrett," Jordan said. "When Nikki came to me about the case, I made the connection to Fisher from the photo of Wilcox."

How had it taken all these years to make that connection? Now another girl was dead.

Garrett shook his head. "We decided he couldn't be involved. In fact, he was at the police station when she was shot and when her body was found. With the medical examiner's time-of-death, he had the perfect alibi."

He stared at the familiar face on the photo. None of this made any sense. Unless . . .

"You think he was working with someone else?" he asked.

"It's one of the things we're exploring." Jack Spencer tapped on the folder in front of him. "Here's what we do know. Robert Wilcox—we believe that's his real name—was wanted on a felony embezzlement charge in another state. He moved to Nashville back in 2002 and got a job at Raynott International Group, using the alias Jason Fisher. For almost a decade he somehow managed to get away with it."

Anger simmered inside Garrett. "And during his free time he abducted and killed young girls."

Jordan nodded. "When he was arrested in 2010, he was booked for federal mail and wire fraud crimes as Robert Wilcox, and for some reason, his alias was never discovered. We did recently find a missing persons report filed by an executive at Raynott for one of their employees—"

"Jason Fisher." Garrett combed his hands through his hair. How had no one caught this?

"The file we have on him—for both names—is actually pretty sparse," Nikki said. "Most of the information comes from the sister of a previous girlfriend, and a couple people he worked with. We know that his parents are deceased and that he had a stepbrother named Gregory Jennings, who's also dead. He was hired by Raynott, as we know, where he worked as a financial analyst helping clients know when to buy and sell investments."

"We looked into that being his connection with the girls' families back when Marissa was murdered," Garrett said.

"We were able to find connections with Raynott to four of the victims," Jordan said.

Nikki nodded. "We've started interviewing his coworkers at Raynott, and we're discovering that while everyone liked him, no one really knew him. He had a master's in finance and was described as smart and funny, but most of the time he stayed to himself. In fact, so far we can't find anyone who says they were close to him."

"But here's where things get interesting," Jack said. "Just over two years ago, Wilcox escaped from prison during a transfer and disappeared."

"So we don't even know where he is?" Garrett asked.

"Here's the clincher," Nikki said. "The Coyote—Wilcox—Fisher—whatever you want to call him, is dead."

"Dead?" Michaels said.

"His body was found in a back alley in Memphis just over a year ago. He was murdered—stabbed multiple times. His killer was never found."

Garrett's head spun at the implications. None of this made sense.

"So what are you implying?" he asked, trying to sort through the details. "That Cooper lied? Or maybe this Coyote, who turned out to be Wilcox, was simply spinning his own lies?"

"Both are possibilities," Jack said. "Even though we don't have a confession from Wilcox—just a statement from another convicted criminal—we believe both were telling the truth. In going through the timeline and the information you found on Fisher back then, Garrett, everything about him fits."

"On top of that," Nikki added, "Cooper had a Polaroid photo

of my sister, which means that it's almost certain he really had been in contact with our abductor."

"But the piece that doesn't fit is Marissa's death," Jordan said. "Hers doesn't, and Chloe's doesn't. Who killed them?"

"That's what we have to figure out," Jack said. "Because either Fisher is our man, and he was working with someone, or we're looking at a copycat. It's always possible that after all these years, the specific details of our killer's MO, like the Polaroid, leaked."

Garrett stared at Fisher's photo, hating even the possibility that the Angel Abductor had been in this building, and they'd let him walk out.

"If I decide that I'm in, what happens next?" he asked.

"We dig up everything we can to find out who he might have been working with," Nikki said. "Thankfully, Garrett, your investigation into Fisher a decade ago has already given us a head start."

Jordan reached out and squeezed his arm. "What do you say, Garrett? Are you in?"

25

Jordan kneaded the back of her neck with her fingertips, trying to stave off a headache that had been coming on the past couple hours despite the pain medicine she'd taken earlier. She glanced at the photo of Chloe—victim number seven—hanging on the whiteboard they set up in the front of the room. She still couldn't believe they were back working on this case after all these years.

But they were.

We need to find whoever's behind this, God.

She grabbed two more ibuprofen from her purse, wishing she had her stronger prescription ones. She'd started getting migraines about two years ago. The doctor had assured her they were due to hormonal changes, but that didn't take away the frustration of having to deal with them when she needed to be concentrating on work.

Garrett tossed the wrapper from the sub he'd just eaten into the wastebasket, then stopped next to her desk. "You okay? I know it's been an intense day so far."

"It's nothing. Just a headache." She looked up at him, grateful

226

he'd decided to officially join them on this one last case. "Listen. I've been going through the information you were able to dig up on Jason Fisher when you originally thought he was a suspect. The man was a genius when it came to covering up his financial trail. That explains why he was able to use an alias and disappear for so many years. But I might have found a piece of property he owned."

"Here in Nashville?"

Jordan nodded. "The owner's name is listed as a trust, but there is a link to Fisher."

"Why list the owner as a trust?"

"Most people do it to provide anonymity, which would make sense in his case." Jordan scanned her notes. "The house is paid off, and the woman living there is Rose Winters. I haven't been able to find out much about her except that she has a Tennessee driver's license and no police record. She doesn't even have a social media presence."

"Maybe that's not her real name," Garrett said, leaning against the edge of the desk.

"At this point, anything is possible." She leaned back in her chair. "I haven't been able to find any other connection between the two of them, but they obviously knew each other."

"Maybe she's a relative we missed, or an old girlfriend?"

"It's definitely possible, though the only girlfriend we know of died a couple years before Wilcox did. In the meantime, I'm going to send everything I've got to research so they can analyze it themselves. It's going to take quite a bit more digging."

"You've got an address?"

"Yes." Jordan tapped her pen on the computer screen. "The house is east of here, about thirty minutes or so."

"Good. I think we need to go pay Rose Winters a visit."

Twenty-five minutes later, Jordan undid her seat belt as Garrett parked the same Toyota Camry he'd driven a decade ago in front of Rose Winter's home. She wasn't surprised he was still driving his old car. Little, it seemed, about him had changed. That must be why she felt just as comfortable around him as she always had. She glanced at his familiar profile that still managed to stir up her emotions. But while her sister might have been right about how they'd always danced around the edges of a relationship, she knew that seeing him again after all these years wasn't going to change anything between them. Not anymore.

Instead, they walked together up to the two-story, sage-green house that sat back a couple dozen yards from the road. The front yard was neatly trimmed, with a few shrubs and trees and a brick walkway. The porch was old and had been repaired with a couple new boards that were a slightly different color. A wooden swing hung next to two Adirondack chairs with gray cushions, and closer to the door was a set of empty planters and a mailbox hanging askew on the wall. All the place needed was a bit of TLC.

Jordan rang the doorbell, hoping they were going to find someone at home.

A dog started barking, then a few seconds later an older woman answered the door. She kept the screen door shut while the brown-and-white basset hound continued barking at her feet.

"Daisy . . . quiet." Her eyes narrowed as the dog settled down. "I'm sorry. Can I help you?"

Jordan held up her badge, wondering if this was the woman they were looking for. "I'm Special Agent Jordan Lambert with the FBI and this is Garrett Addison, a consultant with TBI. We're looking for Rose Winters."

The woman looked behind her, then shook her head. "I'm sorry. Rose isn't well and can't be disturbed."

"It's very important that we see her," Jordan said, glancing into the house. The entryway held a small decorative table and a large piece of abstract art hanging on the wall above it. "I promise it won't take long."

"Like I said, I'm sorry, but because of her health, she rarely sees people. And today she's feeling particularly poorly."

Jordan glanced at Garrett and let out a sharp huff of air. At the moment, Rose Winters was the closest thing they had to a lead. They needed to speak with her.

"If we can't see Ms. Winters, then maybe you can help us." Garrett held up his phone and showed the woman a photo of Robert Wilcox. "Do you know this man?"

She stared at the photo, then shook her head. "I'm sorry. No. Now if you'll excuse me—"

"We understand Ms. Winters knows him," Jordan rushed on. "She's not in any trouble. All we need is information about him."

"Like I said, I don't know him, and I'm sure Rose doesn't either. Now if you'll excuse me," the woman said before slamming the door shut.

"That went well," Jordan said, shivering as she shoved her hands into her coat pockets.

"We could insist she come in for questioning. We did that with Fisher."

Jordan had just started down the porch stairs when the front door opened again.

"Excuse me . . . I couldn't help but overhear you asking for me."

"Rose Winters?" Jordan asked as she headed back toward the door.

"Yes."

"I'm Special Agent Jordan Lambert with the FBI, and this is Garrett Addison."

Rose stepped out of the house onto the porch, closing the screen again so the dog wouldn't get out. Jordan studied the woman. She was somewhere in her mid to late thirties, she had fair, almost sallow skin, and long brown hair that was pulled to the side in a braid.

She tugged her thick maroon sweater tighter around herself. "Maggie works for me and can be a bit overprotective sometimes, but she means well. What can I do for you?"

Jordan looked behind Rose and saw Maggie still standing in the doorway. "Would you mind if we spoke to you for a few minutes?"

"Of course not." Rose turned back to Maggie. "Why don't you make some coffee for us, Maggie? We can drink it here on the porch. I could use some fresh air. The weatherman said that another cold front is on its way, but the sun's out for now."

Jordan waved her hand at the offer. "We don't need anything, thank you. We just need to ask you a few questions."

"Okay, but it really is no trouble, trust me. It gets so boring here some days. I don't get many visitors."

Maggie frowned at Rose's response. "You don't have to speak to them, Rose, and besides that, you're going to get chilled out there."

"I'm fine, Maggie. It's just a few questions, and if you don't mind, I'd still like some coffee." Rose sat down on the swing and motioned for them to sit down on the chairs. "You'll have to excuse her. She tends to worry about me."

"She said you were sick," Garrett said.

"It's nothing serious for the most part. Just some minor heart issues that make me tire quickly. I stay cooped up in the house most of the time. Today happens to be one of my good days."

"It's a nice house," Jordan said. "How long have you lived here?"

"About ten years, I guess."

"Do you live alone?"

"Maggie has a bedroom and bathroom downstairs. She takes care of me. My parents were killed when I was young, and I spent most of my life in foster care. But I'm not sure what your questions have to do with Daisy."

Jordan eyed the front door. "The dog?"

"She's a great little guard dog, but I know that my neighbor's always complaining about how much she barks."

"Actually, we don't respond to complaints about barking dogs."

"Oh . . . I guess I assumed that's why you're here." She shifted her gaze to the neighbor's house. "And why I thought I should talk to you. I don't want things getting out of hand over a dog,

230

but a couple days ago, Mickey—my neighbor—threatened to go to the police."

"This is what we're here for, actually." Garrett held out his phone so she could see the screen. "We need to know if you know this man."

"Of course. That's my brother, Bobby Wilcox. Wait . . ." She looked up from the photo. "Is he in some kind of trouble?"

Jordan glanced at Garrett. "He's your brother?"

"Half brother, actually. We have different last names and grew up in separate foster homes. We've never been extremely close, but I do hear from him every once in a while."

Maggie stepped out onto the porch and handed Rose a mug of coffee.

"That's all for now, Maggie. Thank you."

"But, Rose . . ."

"I'm fine, Maggie."

"So you knew he was in prison?" Jordan asked.

"Of course. He told me he'd been arrested for embezzlement, but that he was innocent. The last time I spoke with him, he was working with a lawyer on an appeal, but far as I know, nothing he's done has worked. Though I don't remember the last time I heard from him. I know it's been a year . . . maybe two."

"Did you know he escaped from prison?" Jordan asked. She caught the surprise on Rose's face as she asked the question.

"What?"

"About two years ago," Garrett said.

"Like I said, we weren't particularly close, but no. I had no idea." Rose took another sip of her coffee and set it on the armrest. "Though maybe that makes sense."

"What do you mean?" Jordan asked.

"The last time I spoke with him, his words were so . . . cryptic."

"What did he say?"

"He told me not to worry. That I might not hear from him for a while. When I asked him why, he just said that it was better I didn't know. That I'd be safer not knowing." She caught Jordan's gaze. "But there's something else, isn't there? Something you're not telling me."

"I'm sorry to have to tell you this," Jordan said. "But about a year ago, your brother was found murdered in a back alley in Memphis."

Rose's hand shook, spilling the drink across the side of the swing and onto the floor.

Jordan leaned forward. "Rose?"

Rose shook her head. "I shouldn't be that upset. I mean, we weren't really close, but still. He was always nice to me. How did he die?"

"He was stabbed," Garrett said.

"And did they catch his murderer?"

"Not yet. I'm sorry."

Her hands gripped the handle of the cup. "I wondered why I hadn't heard from him, but I never expected something like this."

"Do you know if he had friends in Memphis?" Garrett asked.

"No," she said. "I can't say that I know any of his friends."

"We appreciate your time." Jordan glanced at Garrett, then stood up. "Though there is one more question. Do you think your brother was capable of murder?"

"Murder? Why would you ask that?" Rose frowned. "Bobby went to prison for stealing money, not for killing someone."

Jordan studied the woman's reaction and caught genuine surprise on her face.

"Why would you ask that?" Rose asked again.

"He confessed some additional crimes to a fellow prisoner," Jordan said.

"What kind of crimes?"

"There are rumors that he abducted and killed a number of girls before he went to prison," Garrett said.

"Bobby? No way." Rose stood up. "He made some mistakes, but he'd never hurt anyone."

"Thank you again for talking to us, and again, we're sorry for your loss." Jordan started down the steps with Garrett, then stopped. "By the way. Do you own this house?"

Rose shook her head. "It belongs to Bobby. Or at least it did when he was alive. He wanted someone living in it while he was in prison, and I needed a place to stay, so he let me live here."

"Well, thank you for speaking with us." Jordan handed her a business card. "Will you call me if you think of anything else that might help?"

Rose nodded as she took the card. "Of course."

As soon as they got into the car, Garrett asked, "What do you think?"

"I don't know. On the surface, she seemed open and genuine. She even told us the truth about the house. And the news about her half brother seemed to come truly as a surprise, though I can't help but wonder if she was lying about her relationship with Bobby. Part of me felt as if she knew more than she was telling us, or at the very least that she had a closer relationship with him than she implied."

"What about Maggie?" he asked as he pulled away from the curb and headed out of the neighborhood.

"I think we should look into her a bit more as well."

"I agree," he said. "She might be nothing more than an overly concerned caregiver, but on the other hand, she certainly didn't seem happy about us being there. At all."

She glanced at him. "I'm glad you decided to come on board with this case."

"Honestly, I came pretty close to not showing up this morning."

"I know it couldn't have been an easy decision, but no one blames you for what happened with Marissa. They never did."

"That didn't stop me from blaming myself." He drew in a sharp breath. "There's something I never told you before that might help you understand my decision."

"What's that?"

Garrett's fingers tightened around the steering wheel. "When my grandfather became senator, he owned a huge piece of land over in Lawrence County. There was over a hundred acres of forests for hunting, a spring-fed creek, and even a stocked pond for fishing."

"Sounds like a young man's dream. You must have loved it."

"I did. Growing up, I spent as much time there as possible. Between my grandmother's homemade sweet potato pie and a pond full of bass and bluegill up for grabs, you can imagine how much I hated it when it was time to go back to school."

She sat quiet beside him. Giving him the time he needed to continue.

"It was a Saturday morning, and I had a brand-new St. Croix rod my grandfather had gotten me for my twelfth birthday. I decided to head out to the pond and do some fishing."

He paused for a minute as he got onto the freeway and merged into traffic. "I was about a hundred yards from the pond, when I heard someone screaming. I ran toward the clearing. And that's when I saw her. She was lying at the edge of the pond, her feet in the water. Someone had slit her throat."

She heard the pain in his voice as he spoke. "Oh, Garrett. It's one thing having to deal with death as law enforcement, but as a twelve-year-old?"

"I dropped my rod and bent down over her. She was still breathing, just rattling gasps of air." Garrett stared straight ahead. "I've never been so terrified in my life. I started to run for help, but she must've known she wasn't going to make it. She grabbed on to my hand and wouldn't let go. I had no idea what to do. I'd never known anyone close to me who'd died, let alone watched someone die. I told her it was going to be okay. That I'd call for help and get her to a hospital. That she wasn't going to die. But she did. Right there in front of me."

Jordan studied his profile. "And you blamed yourself."

"I forgot my bait that morning and had to run back to the house to get it. I spent the following weeks and months wondering what might have happened if I'd gotten there sooner. Would I have been able to help her?"

"There's no way you could know. You might have been killed as well."

"That never mattered. What mattered was that she died and I didn't save her. And maybe it's crazy, but those feelings of guilt have never completely gone away."

"Did you ever find out who she was?"

"Amy Phelps. She was a local girl. They eventually found the man who killed her. An ex-boyfriend named Jimmie Prime."

"Why didn't you ever tell me this before?"

"I haven't talked about that day to anyone since that summer."

"After we found Marissa's body—if I'd have known what was driving your anger . . . things might have ended differently." *Maybe things would have ended differently between us as well.*

"Sometimes I think I live my life wondering," he said.

"What do you mean?"

"I always wonder what might have happened. If I'd never heard that girl scream in the woods that morning. If I'd never walked away from my father's law firm. If I had dug deeper on Jason Fisher instead of quitting the force."

Jordan couldn't help but add another what-if . . . *If you'd never let me walk away. If you'd have asked me to stay instead of joining the FBI.* She sighed. "Sometimes you have to stop looking back and simply look forward."

She studied his face. The familiar curve of his jawline . . . his chocolate-brown eyes . . . his cleft chin. She'd never forgotten the details. Not even after all these years. Suddenly she realized how much she'd missed him. A decade had flown by, and he still looked just as appealing as the first day she'd met him.

Her phone rang, and she grabbed it out of her pocket.

"Sam? What's up?"

"Where are you?" he asked.

"On our way back from Rose Winter's house. What's wrong?"

"I need you to head downtown now. I'm sending you the location. 911 just got a frantic call about an attempted kidnapping and a missing girl they believe is connected with the Angel Abductor. We need to find this girl now."

26

Jordan punched the GPS coordinates into her phone as Garrett took a sharp right and headed south toward downtown.

"Sam also patched the audio file of the 911 call through to my phone," she said, pulling up the file and pushing play after making sure it was on speaker.

"Nine-one-one operator. What is your emergency?"

"I—I need help. Someone grabbed me. He shoved me into a car . . . took my picture . . . he was crazy. Kept going on and on about how I looked like an angel. I managed to get out of the car and run, but now I'm lost and afraid he's going to find me again."

"Can you tell me where you are?"

"I'm somewhere in downtown Nashville. There are so many people. I think I lost him, but I'm not sure."

"What is your name?"

"Zoe . . . Zoe Granger."

"Zoe, I'm tracking the GPS on your phone and sending officers to help you. I'm hearing a lot of noise. Can you tell me where you are?"

237

"There are a bunch of restaurants, and live music outside. It's so loud I'm having trouble hearing you."

"Zoe, I need you to listen carefully. I want you to go into the closest restaurant right now. Tell the manager what happened and wait there. I'm going to send an officer to get you, but stop worrying—you'll be safe."

"Okay . . . There's a restaurant ahead . . . Kade's Bar & Grill. I guess I could go in there, but how long until they get here? I'm afraid he's still following me."

"I'm going to stay on the line with you until the officers arrive. It will just be a few minutes."

"Okay."

"Can you describe the person who was after you?"

"He was wearing a dark-blue hoodie."

"And what about you, Zoe? Can you tell me what you're wearing, so the officers know who to look for?"

"Yeah . . . jeans and a . . . a gray bomber jacket and a gray-and-pink backpack, but—"

The audio went dead.

"Sounds like she got cut off," Jordan said, switching back to her call with Sam. "Sam, what happened to the audio?"

"We're not sure. The 911 operator lost her and hasn't been able to get her back."

"How long ago since the call went through?" she asked.

"About fifteen minutes. They patched it through to Missing Persons as soon as they got the call."

"Someone was on their toes." Though she wasn't surprised. The recent murder of yet another girl had the city on high alert again.

"How long before you can be there?" Sam asked.

"We're on the freeway now," she said, glancing out the window at the heavy traffic. "I'm hoping five . . . ten minutes tops, unless we get stuck in traffic."

"Metro police has been called in as well, but the streets are crowded and so far they haven't been able to find her."

"I thought she went into a restaurant?" Jordan asked.

"They're checking now, but they're afraid she might have panicked and run."

"So what's your theory at this point?" Garrett asked, as soon as she'd hung up. "Copycat or accomplice?"

"I don't know." She moved her head in a slow circle, trying to release some of the tension in her neck. "There are so many variables entering the equation, it's hard to come up with a legitimate behavioral pattern."

Over a decade between the last two murders.

Their only suspect had been murdered.

And now two more abductions in less than forty-eight hours.

"All I know is that whoever's out there doing this has to be stopped," she said.

Leave it to bad luck to have them hit downtown Nashville when the one-block section they needed to get to was closed to traffic due to some kind of open-air concert. Jordan let out a huff as they exited Garrett's car and started walking the extra blocks to get to the location the victim had last been heard from. Not that she believed in luck, but still. The streets were crowded with hundreds of people, listening to the music and eating.

It was the perfect place to hide. Right in the middle of a crowd.

Maybe that's what Zoe wanted. A place where she felt safe, lost in the crowd. A band played on a stage in the midst of countless bars, restaurants, and a large crowd of people. The smell of BBQ wafted through the air. On any other day, Jordan wouldn't have minded indulging in the festive atmosphere the city was known for.

"Just got a text from Michaels," Garrett said. "He and Sam are almost here."

Jordan searched the crowd for a sign of Zoe and her pink backpack. The sidewalks were filled with families with their children, older couples, and groups of teens. How in the world were they supposed to find her?

"What are you thinking?" Garrett asked.

"Something seems . . . off. I just can't put my finger on it."

"What do you mean?"

She slipped her hands into her pockets, wishing she'd brought her scarf. Now that the sun had dropped, so had the temperature. "This isn't how he works. Even if she did escape, what in the world was he doing here in the middle of downtown? Would he really be confident enough to grab her out here? In the middle of all these people?"

"Then you're thinking this is looking more like the work of a copycat."

"Yes. And I'm thinking that the rules have changed, and there's no way we can know what his next step is."

Which was exactly what had her worried.

Cars were parked along the crowded streets until the point where the road was blocked off. Then the road swelled with people. The music was getting louder as they got closer to the stage.

"There's Kade's Bar & Grill," Jordan said. "Let's try there first."

A perky hostess approached them inside. "Table for two?"

"No." Jordan held up her badge. "We're looking for a young woman wearing a bomber jacket and carrying a gray-and-pink backpack."

"Sorry," the hostess said above the noise. "I already told the other officers that came in here that I haven't noticed anyone like that. But as you can see, it's crazy busy."

"We'd still like to look around."

"Fine," she said, stepping aside.

Jordan and Garrett split up and started through the crowded floor that was packed with tables and customers and waiters delivering food. She studied the crowd, searching for the girl. Nothing.

She headed back to the bathrooms, then stepped inside the women's and searched the stalls, but the room was empty.

Zoe wasn't here.

"Anything?" Garrett asked as she exited the restroom.

Jordan shook her head. "The hostess was right. Either she left, or she never made it here."

Jordan's phone rang as they stepped out of the restaurant into the busy crowd. "What have you got, Sam?"

"The dispatcher is working with the cell service provider and has been able to track the phone. I'm sending you her GPS coordinates now."

Jordan brought the coordinates up on her phone, then quickened her pace next to Garrett through the crowd. She looked for a flash of pink from Zoe's backpack and wished they had more to go by than simply what she was wearing.

"Do you have a photo of the girl yet?" she asked Sam.

"No, but I'll make sure you get one as soon as I do," he said. "How close are you?"

"She's got to be right here."

Jordan searched the face of every person they passed. Every young girl walking down the sidewalk. But none of them fit the description. No one seemed upset.

"Jordan . . ."

Garrett was picking up a cell phone from under the lit-up window of a shop. He clicked on the screen, and a shot of a blonde girl stared up at her.

"This has got to be her phone, but what's it doing here?" she asked.

He checked the call log. "I don't know, but the last call was made to 911."

Jordan scanned the crowd. "She has to be nearby, but she wouldn't have just ditched her phone on purpose."

"What if he found her again?"

It was the only explanation that fit the scenario. Whoever was after her had managed to track her down before they had. But surely out of all these people, someone would have noticed.

Jordan called Sam back. "Where are you?"

"We're walking your way. I can see the two of you now," Sam said.

"We've got a problem. We found the phone, but no sign of Zoe."

"I'll call it in, but keep looking. We need to find her."

But what were their options now that there was no way to trace her?

Jordan caught sight of Michaels and Sam a few seconds later as they approached them on the crowded sidewalk.

"She's not here," Jordan said, holding up her phone. "We need a plan."

"An AMBER Alert was just activated, and we finally got a photo of the girl. We're sending it out to the officers searching the area—"

The crack of a gunshot ripped through the air. A woman behind Jordan screamed, followed by a dozen more screams that echoed around her while people scattered for cover in doorways and behind planters. Some ducked for cover behind trash cans while others ran into shops. Jordan pulled out her service weapon and scanned the street. They needed to find the source of the gunshot, but with all the noise on the street, she had no idea where it had come from. She turned back around, then froze.

Michaels lay on the ground, with blood pooling on the sidewalk beneath him.

"Michaels . . ."

Sam crouched down beside him, trying to stop the blood. "Did anyone see who did this? Garrett—call 911!"

Jordan studied the fleeing crowd and listened for the sound of more shots. With the surge in mass shootings across the country, officers were now trained to take immediate action and neutralize the shooter. The goal of an active shooter was to inflict as many casualties as quickly as possible. But so far she'd only heard the one shot.

Sam shouted at an officer who'd come running to help, "We need this area cordoned off, then see if you can come up with a witness who saw the shooter."

"There!" Someone shouted on the other side of the street. "Up ahead. That's him."

Jordan caught sight of a fleeing figure in a rust-colored sweatshirt and ball cap.

"Sam . . ." Jordan grabbed Garrett's arm. "Stay with Michaels. We'll go after the suspect."

More officers were already arriving at the scene as Jordan and Garrett sprinted down the street to where she'd seen the suspect turn and run. Not everyone had heard the gunshot, which meant there were still dozens of people milling around the streets, oblivious to what had happened. All she'd seen was the man's hooded figure; she hadn't seen a face. But there was one thing that was becoming apparent to her. This felt less like a random shooting in downtown Nashville, and more like a hit on Michaels.

Whoever shot him had planned this.

This was personal.

They kept running down the sidewalk, dodging startled pedestrians. Neon lights flashed above her, vying for her attention, but they were gaining on him. They followed him through a crowd coming out of a restaurant, then stopped on the other side.

Jordan struggled to catch her breath. "Where is he?" she asked Garrett.

"I don't know. He was just here."

In the busy streets he could escape anywhere. Down one of the darkened alleys, into one of the bars or restaurants. It was like looking for a needle in a haystack.

"I'll call in the description we have," Garrett said. "We'll get every officer in the vicinity searching for him."

She stopped on the sidewalk and tried to catch her breath. Her phone rang and she pulled it out of her pocket.

"Jordan, it's Nikki. We've got a problem."

"You know about Michaels?"

"I just heard," Nikki said, "but there's something else. A woman just showed up at headquarters with her daughter, upset

243

because she received an AMBER Alert that her daughter was missing."

"What?"

"Zoe Granger's standing right in front of me. She never made a 911 call, and she's fine except for the fact that she lost her phone this afternoon. We need to find out what's going on."

Jordan felt her stomach drop, followed by a wave of nausea as she relayed the news to Garrett, then started back down the street toward Sam and Michaels. "It was a trap," she said to Nikki. "The whole thing. The 911 call . . . the phone they knew we'd be able to track . . ."

Zoe had never been on that phone. There had been no missing girl.

"What do you mean?" Nikki asked.

"Someone wanted us here at the same place at the same time. Shooting Michaels was planned."

The ambulance had just arrived by the time they got back. Paramedics were already working on Michaels.

"Sam?" Jordan said, stepping up beside him. "Please tell me he's going to be okay."

"I don't know. I just don't know."

More sirens screamed in the distance.

"I still don't understand what's going on," Garrett said. "If this is someone who wants us to think they're the Angel Abductor, why kill Michaels? That's completely outside his pattern."

Jordan struggled to make sense of the puzzle. "Maybe this isn't related. Maybe all of this was simply a ruse to get him here."

"He's got a list a mile long of people he's put away. It could be any one of them," Garrett said.

"What we do know is if this is someone who worked with Wilcox, then he's escalating," Jordan said.

"So now he has a bone to pick with the police? Chloe's murder and this whole debacle has to be related somehow, and yet I'm not seeing anything. Why lure us here? And why Michaels?"

Jordan felt a shiver run through her. "He could have taken out all of us. We were all right there. But maybe that's exactly what he wants us to know."

"If this is our abductor, he played games in the past. Framing Matthew Banks, shattering your car window and leaving a note . . ." Like her, Garrett was struggling to make sense of this. "So do we take Fisher out of the equation?"

"Fisher's dead and whoever shot Michaels is clearly alive. And as for Fisher, all we really have is the confession of a fellow prisoner who's also dead, and a few facts that line up."

Sam looked toward the blinking blue light from one of the metro police cameras that could be found on most street corners downtown. "I'll coordinate here from the scene. I want the two of you to return to the bureau. Work with Nikki and Jack to tap into the city's security cameras and do whatever you need to do to figure out who's behind this."

27

Michaels was dead.

Garrett's vision blurred as he stared at the computer screen where he'd been searching through video footage from metro police security cameras, trying to track down their shooter. He blinked a couple times, then rubbed his eyes. Several analysts were going over the video, but he'd hoped since he'd been at the scene when Michaels was shot, he might have an advantage in knowing what to look for. So far his attempts to find their shooter had failed.

Garrett let out a sharp sigh. An APB had been sent out to all law enforcement with a vague description they'd been able to compile from a couple of witnesses on their shooter. They were questioning potential witnesses and conducting an extensive canvassing of restaurants and stores around the location of the shooting. But so far they hadn't been able to come up with anything solid.

Outside the bureau, a flag hung at half-mast, but there was no time to mourn at the moment. They needed to find out who had done this. He glanced up at the live press conference playing on the TV mounted in the corner of the room. They'd released a statement that had described Michaels as a hardworking, honest agent who had been dedicated both to his work and to his family. But that wasn't going to bring Michaels back or help his wife and daughter move on without him.

"How's it going?"

Garrett looked at Jordan, who'd been working with Nikki. "So far, nothing, but he's got to be here somewhere. The preliminary investigation projects that Michaels was shot at fairly close range, but with the crowds, it makes it hard to see anything."

Jordan sat down on the edge of the desk. "I just got a call from Rose Winters."

"Really?" He leaned back in his chair. "Did she think of something that might help us?"

"I'm not sure. She seemed pretty shook up, actually," Jordan said. "She received a threatening phone call that accused her brother of being involved in the abductions."

"Any specifics?" Garrett asked, trying to put the pieces together.

"That's all I know. She was too upset to talk on the phone, and asked us to come back by."

"We could send an officer to take her statement," he said, feeling as if they were already spread too thin.

"We could, but if there's a possibility that someone's out there with proof of what Fisher did, I'd like to talk with her in person."

"Okay, then." He grabbed his coat off the back of his chair. "Let's go."

Garrett walked up to Rose's house with Jordan as a light snow began to fall. Now that the cold front had arrived, most people were bundled up indoors with their heaters turned up. Beyond the wind whipping through his coat and the occasional car rumbling past, the neighborhood was eerily quiet.

Jordan rang the doorbell. When no one had answered thirty seconds later, she rang it again.

"She should be home," Jordan said. "I told her we were going to come by."

Garrett felt an unwelcome shiver as he looked inside the front window, but the blinds were shut and he couldn't see anything. Something felt wrong. This entire case seemed like one big game of smoke and mirrors. A game where their abductor had managed to stay in control of the situation by dropping false trails and fabricating evidence. Sorting through what was real and what wasn't real had become a nightmare, and at this point, they didn't even know for sure if their latest victims—Chloe Middleton and Abram Michaels—had died by the hand of the abductor who had originally killed Jessica Wright, or if they were looking at a copycat.

"Maybe I should try knocking," Jordan said.

She reached for the screen door handle, and a split second too late, he saw the wire.

"Jordan!"

Garrett grabbed her hand and pulled her off the porch. They hit the dirt a second before the explosion shook the ground like an earthquake. Glass from the front window shattered, falling like rain, and the sky turned black from the smoke.

He pulled her against himself, covering their faces from the heat.

Twenty seconds later his ears were ringing as he stared at the burning house. Adrenaline pumped through him. If he hadn't seen that wire, they'd both be dead.

"Jordan . . ." He reached out and wiped a streak of blood smeared across her cheek where something had scraped her. "Are you okay?"

"I think so." She managed to sit up next to him, but he could tell she was shaking. "If you hadn't pulled me away . . ."

It was something he'd rather not think about at the moment. Michaels was dead, and now he and Jordan had almost been killed. Whatever was going on, this was no coincidence.

"Let's get up, but we need to move slowly. There's glass everywhere."

She stood up beside him, pulled out her phone, and called 911. He studied the burning house, quickly dismissing the urge to go inside. The heat from the fire was far too intense. If Rose or Maggie had been home, they would have answered the door. Unless for some reason they'd been unable to answer.

Jordan hung up the call. "Where'd you learn to look for something like that?"

"When I was on the police force, we had bomb technicians train us on explosive recognition and response. I was always glad I never had to use what I learned."

"Until now." She took his hand and frowned. "The fire department is on its way, but you've got a piece of glass in your hand. If you hold still . . ."

She slowly pulled out the thin shard.

"Ouch," he said.

She held up the glass, then wrapped her scarf around the wound. "You're going to need stitches."

"I'm fine," he countered.

"Don't be stubborn. You're not fine."

"And you are?" he asked, closing his fingers around her hands that were still shaking. "Because someone just tried to kill us."

"I know."

"You think it was Rose?"

"It makes sense," she said. "Rose is the one who asked us to come."

Sirens wailed in the background. The snow had begun to fall harder, but he could still feel the heat from the house.

"So we have two options," he said. "Rose wanted us dead and lured us here, or someone else used Rose to lure us here."

"Which means if she's innocent, she could be inside," Jordan said. "Maybe someone didn't want her to tell us what she figured out."

"Like who's been murdering young girls? But we still don't have enough information."

Garrett glanced back at the house as a fire engine pulled up along the curb, its sirens competing with the crackling of the fire. The firefighters moved into position to extinguish the orange flames eating at the structure. Smoke billowed above the roof. A pair of patrol cars pulled in behind the large truck, and a couple of neighbors who'd decided to brave the cold stood at the end of their drives trying to figure out what had just happened. He still had no idea.

Thirty minutes later, the house—now cordoned off with yellow crime scene tape—smoldered beneath the still-falling snow. While they'd waited for the firefighters to put out the fire and secure the house, Garrett had directed several of the officers to help them canvass the neighborhood, but so far no one knew much about Rose Winters.

The fire chief called to them as they were finishing up an interview with one of the neighbors. "You told us to let you know if we found anything."

"Did you?" Garrett asked.

"Oh, yeah. We'll still need to do a thorough investigation, but I think you're going to want to look inside."

Garrett and Jordan headed back toward the house with the chief. "Can you tell what caused the explosion?"

"The house was wired with an IED and set to explode as soon as someone opened the screen door," the chief said. "We found wiring inside along with a trigger, so when the door was opened, a surge detonated an accelerant, which in turn caused the explosion."

"What kind of person is knowledgeable enough to rig a house to explode?" Jordan asked.

"That's hard to answer," the chief said. "But what I do know is that with the internet, information that wouldn't have been possible for most people to even imagine a few years ago is now readily available." He nodded toward the house. "I'll take you inside, but you'll have to be careful. Thankfully, the fire ended up being pretty localized, but the place is full of broken glass and some of the metal is still hot."

"Was there anyone inside?" Garrett asked as they headed through the front door of the house.

"We've got one body in the living room, though my guess is they didn't die in the explosion. They were shot."

Five seconds later, they were standing over the charred body.

"We don't have an ID yet—"

"Her name's Maggie," Jordan said, glancing at the fire chief. "She worked for the homeowner as a caregiver and housekeeper. Are you sure there isn't another body?"

"We've done a thorough check and didn't find anyone else, but there's something else we found that you're going to want to see."

Garrett and Jordan followed the chief down the hallway to a room at the far end, then stepped inside. He felt his blood run cold.

This was *his* room.

The Angel Abductor.

Rose's statement that she wasn't close to her half brother had clearly been a lie. The room had been damaged by both smoke and water, but most of the contents hadn't burned.

"Garrett . . ." Jordan stepped up next to him, clearly as shocked as he was. "She—and Maggie—had to have known about all of this."

A soggy bulletin board taking up a large portion of the back wall was covered with dozens of surveillance photos, lined up in neat rows against it. Garrett felt a shiver run down his spine. All the abducted girls were there. Jessica Wright . . . Becky Collier . . . Julia Kerrigan . . . Bailey McKnight . . . Sarah Boyd . . .

"Amanda Love is here," Jordan said. "He took her as well."

And that wasn't all. A second board held random black-and-white surveillance shots of each officer who had been involved in working the case. Jordan, Michaels, Sam, Nikki, Jack, and himself.

He stepped up to the board and stared at the photo of him leaving his dingy law office. Sam kissing his wife goodbye in front of their house. Michaels buying lunch at a local deli. There was even one of Jordan in the parking garage when her back window had been shattered . . .

How had they not seen this coming?

"Garrett . . . look at this."

Newspaper articles had been precisely cut out and pasted in a scrapbook. The edges of some of them were charred, but not enough that they couldn't tell what they were. Dozens of articles about the abductions, starting back in 2002 when Jessica Wright had been killed, then later when the media had begun to call him the Angel Abductor. Article after article from each case, through the most recent, the kidnapping and murder of Chloe Middleton.

But that wasn't all. There were half a dozen different identities, driver's licenses, passports, credit cards—all with Fisher's photo.

"Robert Wilcox . . . Jason Fisher . . . ," she said. "It *was* him."

"He could become whoever he wanted to." Garrett pointed to a police badge with his gloved hand and caught the horror in Jordan's eyes. "Nikki was right. This is how he did it. He lured them into his car with some kind of story they bought."

The one person those girls had believed they could trust was the person who'd betrayed them.

"What have you got here?" Sam asked, walking into the room. He stopped midstep in the doorway.

"We found him," Garrett said.

"But we've still got a problem." Jordan stepped over a broken lamp. "Wilcox or Fisher—whatever you want to call him—is dead. He might be the one responsible for the earlier murders, but what about Chloe Middleton? What about Michaels and what just happened here?"

"Someone else was involved. Maybe someone who blames us for Wilcox's death?" Garrett threw out.

He read aloud from an article hanging on one of the boards.

"'Memphis police responded to a call that a man had been stabbed in an alley outside a bar early this morning. The unidentified man was pronounced dead at the scene. Eyewitnesses said that the man had been involved in an argument the night before.'"

"It has to be Rose," Garrett said. "It's the only thing that makes sense."

Jordan stepped up next to him. "And Fisher's death was the trigger."

"Even though it's been over a year since his death?" Sam asked.

"What she's done—bring us all back together—would've taken months of planning," Jordan said.

"So what's her end goal?" Sam asked. "Why blame us for her brother's death?"

"On the surface it might not make sense," Jordan said, "but we did some digging back at the bureau into Rose's history that makes things fit together a bit more. She was adopted when she was two, but her parents were killed in a fire that destroyed the home three years later. After that, she was put in the system. Off and on for the next decade. According to a couple sources, Robert became her protector of sorts."

"Two kids lost in the system," Garrett said. "But while I feel sorry for what they went through, that doesn't explain why they did what they did. A lot of people go through a lot worse and don't end up killing innocent children."

"Agreed. According to her medical history, though, she had an IQ off the charts. She'd been under psychiatric care for years and had never been stable. And now she's looking for revenge for her brother's death."

"Even if we had nothing to do with it?"

"Yes, because it makes sense to her. We were the ones chasing down the Angel Abductor—her brother—all these years. She sat across from us drinking coffee and lied to us about her relationship with her half brother. She had to have known exactly what he had done and had obviously already planned what she was going to do next." Jordan planted her hands on her hips. "She had to have been the one who killed Marissa as well."

"While her brother sat talking with us," Garrett said. "But why would she agree to talk with us?"

"Maybe she was looking for information. An attempt to see if she could find anything out."

"So what are you saying?" Sam said. "That she killed Chloe Middleton in order to reopen the case, and bring our team back together?"

"That's exactly what I'm saying."

Sam's phone rang and he stepped to the other side of the room to answer it.

"We've got to find her," Garrett said.

"She might not just be after us," Sam said a moment later, hanging up his phone. "I need you to call for back up."

Jordan and Garrett hurried after him as he rushed toward the front door. "Sam . . . what's going on?"

"I'm not sure," he said, "but I've got to go. That was Irene. She's at the house alone and someone's trying to break in. We got cut off, and now I can't get ahold of her again."

28

Jordan jumped into the passenger seat of Garrett's car while trying to call her sister, but after a dozen rings there was still no answer.

"Who are you trying to call?" Garrett asked, as he quickly followed Sam toward his house.

"My sister and her husband," Jordan said, this time trying her brother-in-law's number.

Nothing.

"Is she at work?" Garrett asked.

"I think she went in at three, but the boys should be at home or on their way home with their dad."

"I'm sure they're fine. If Rose is the one behind this, she can't be everywhere at once, though we can't even be a hundred percent certain that Irene's her target."

"Do you really believe that?"

His hands gripped the steering wheel. "Honestly, I'm not sure what to believe at this point."

Jordan felt a shiver of fear rush through her as she tried calling her sister again. Michaels was dead. Sam's wife was in danger. It seemed pretty clear that Rose wanted the rest of the team dead, but what if she was planning to go after their families?

Clara finally picked up on the sixth ring.

"Jordan?"

"Clara, where are you?"

"At work, why? You sound upset."

"I just need you to listen before you say anything." Jordan paused, hoping she wasn't blowing things out of proportion. "I need you to do something for me. I need you and Alex and the boys to go get Dad and leave town for a day or two. Maybe go to Memphis or Chattanooga. I don't care where you go, just leave the city until I tell you it's safe."

"Wait a minute, Jordan. Slow down. What are you talking about? I'm in the middle of a shift. I can't just leave."

"I can't give you details, but you know I wouldn't do this if it wasn't serious."

"I knew this day would come," Clara said. "This is some kind of terrorist attack, isn't it? You're with the FBI, so you know these things in advance."

"No . . . it's not a terrorist attack. Just a case we're working on where there's the possibility that they're targeting my team's families."

There was a long pause on the line. "Wow . . . you're serious, aren't you?"

"I wouldn't be making this call if I wasn't."

"Okay . . . I'll leave now and go get the boys and Dad."

"Clara, call me when you're out of town. And try not to scare the boys, or Dad, for that matter. Make it an adventure somehow for them. I'll let you know as soon as the threat is over." Jordan set down the phone. "Am I overreacting?"

"I don't think so," he said. "We've seen what she's capable of."

"You're right."

"What's your analysis of her at this point?" Garrett asked, pulling onto the freeway behind Sam. The snow had stopped, but not before leaving a light dusting of white on the edges of the roads.

"In many ways, she has to be a lot like her brother. She's precise, smart, and not afraid to take risks."

"You think she's working with someone else?"

"She might be, but I don't think so. This is very personal to her. There didn't appear to be any signs of anyone in the house besides her and Maggie. It also doesn't seem to me that she's the kind of person who would trust someone. She didn't even trust Maggie enough to keep her alive."

Ten minutes later, they pulled into the driveway of the two-story house that was located just outside the city limits. Two patrol cars were in the driveway, but while streetlights had already come on, Sam's house was completely dark.

Jordan jumped out of the car with Garrett. Sam was just a few seconds ahead of them.

"The power's off," he shouted. "Something's wrong."

"Sam, wait."

"I'm not waiting. My wife is in there."

"Rose Winters just blew up her house," Jordan said. "Let Garrett check to make sure the house isn't rigged, and this isn't another trap."

"Hold it right there." One of the responding officers shone a flashlight at them.

Sam held up his badge and introduced them.

"Sorry about that," the officer said. "We just got here, but it doesn't look like anyone's inside."

"Search the property," Sam said to the officers. "We'll go inside."

They walked up onto the front steps. The only light came from a distant streetlight and their flashlights.

"Give me a second," Garrett said, studying the door. "It looks clear, but we need to be careful. Watch where you're walking and stop if you see anything that doesn't look right."

Jordan and Garrett waited for Sam to unlock the front door,

then stepped behind him into the dark house. Sam tried turning on a light, to no avail. Jordan shone her light around the living room. The beam caught the recliner and a framed mountain scene hanging above the couch. But no sign of Sam's wife.

"Irene?" Panic filled Sam's voice as he began searching the house. "Irene, are you here?"

Over forty years of marriage . . . God, don't let it end like this. Please.

They cleared the house, room by room, then met up in the kitchen.

"Her car's still in the garage," Sam said. "But she's not here."

"The back door's not completely shut," Garrett said, pulling the door open and stepping out onto the back porch. "There's a chance she got away."

"Or that she was taken," Sam said.

"We don't know that," Garrett said.

"If Irene was safe, she'd have already called me."

"Maybe not." Jordan's flashlight beam caught the edge of a cell phone lying in the shadows. "Is this hers?"

"Yes." He took it from Jordan and scrolled through her call log. "Her last call was to 911."

"Have the officers outside see if they can get the power back on, then search for any signs of a struggle," Garrett said. "We'll start canvassing the neighborhood to see if anyone saw something."

"Where would she go if she escaped?" Jordan asked Sam.

"Considering she doesn't have the car or her phone, I'm guessing to one of the neighbors'." Sam's cell phone rang as they headed out the door. "Irene? Irene, where are you?"

Jordan hurried next to Sam down the driveway as he spoke to his wife.

"She's at the neighbors'. Three doors down."

Despite being a man on the north side of sixty, Sam was hard to keep up with as they sprinted across the yards.

Sam burst into the house ahead of Garrett and Jordan and pulled his wife into his arms. "Are you okay?" he panted.

"I'm still shaking, but I'm okay," she said, looking up at her husband.

He reached a hand to the neighbor woman. "Thank you so much for helping."

He turned back to Irene, led her to the couch, and sat down beside her. "Tell me exactly what happened."

"I'm not sure. I was in the back room, painting, when the power went out. I checked my phone to see if there was a storm coming through that might have messed up the power, but the neighbors' lights were on. That's when I heard glass breaking in the front of the house. I grabbed the gun out of our bedroom, called 911, then you. I lost my phone trying to escape."

"Did you see the person who broke in?"

"No. I'm sorry."

"That's okay, sweetheart. The only thing that matters is you're safe."

Jordan's phone rang and she stepped into the entryway to take the call. "Nikki?"

"Did you find Irene?"

"Yeah. She was at a neighbor's, and she's okay. No sign, though, of the intruder so far."

"So you don't have proof that the break-in was connected to our abductor?"

"No, but I think we're safe in going along with that assumption."

"I agree, but we've got another problem. There's another girl missing. Her name's Kelsey Jacobi. She's seventeen years old, blonde, and went missing just after Chloe Middleton, but so far there's been no sign of her."

"Is there a connection between the two girls?" Jordan asked.

"Not that we can find."

So now, Rose had very likely taken another girl? One girl was dead. The second they still might be able to save.

"Why are we just finding out about it now?" Jordan asked.

"That's what I'm trying to figure out. Apparently her parents were out of town on an anniversary trip, so no one noticed she was missing until they returned today. Jack and I will run things from here, but I need someone to go speak with Kelsey Jacobi's family. We need to make finding her a priority. I'm sending each of you the address now."

A minute later, Jordan hung up the call, trying to process the news, but all she could think about was another girl was missing.

"What's going on?" Garrett asked, stepping into the entryway beside her.

"There's another girl missing they believe is connected to Rose," Jordan said, filling him in on the details.

"This has got to end."

She reached up to rub her neck. "I know."

"Is your head hurting?"

She nodded. "And the explosion didn't help."

"You should have let the paramedics check you out."

"I get migraines occasionally, but my doctor has assured me it's nothing serious. I just need to grab my prescription at my sister's house. I'll be fine after that."

"Sam and I can meet with the family," Garrett said.

"Doesn't he need to stay with Irene?"

"He's just arranged for a friend of his to pick her up. She'll stay with him and his wife until this is over. He's retired law enforcement, so she should be safe there," Garrett said. "I'll talk to one of the patrol officers about taking you by your sister's, then you can go on to the bureau. We'll plan to meet you there."

"Garrett, I don't need an escort—"

"Forget it. You're not going by yourself. Not after what's happened today."

Jordan didn't miss the determination in Garrett's eyes and decided it wasn't a battle she wanted to fight. "Fine. I'll meet you back at the bureau."

Twenty minutes later, she asked the officer to wait for her in the car while she ran inside her sister's house. Clara and her family had already left, having decided to spend the weekend in Gatlinburg. The house was unnaturally quiet, considering it was normally filled with two rambunctious boys. Toys lay scattered around the living room, along with a pile of Wii games and books, and a couple of empty pizza boxes sat on the counter. All signs that they'd left in a hurry.

But at least she knew they'd be safe until this was over.

We so need this to end, God.

She headed down the hall toward the guest room, fighting both the pain of the migraine and the fear of what they were facing. An ever-widening threat with a girl's life on the line. Michaels dead, and his killer wanting her dead as well. The thought sent an unwanted chill through her.

She stepped into the guest room, then jumped at a loud screech. Her heart raced as she took a step back and slammed her elbow into the doorframe. She flipped on the bedroom light and looked down at the orange chicken dog chew she'd just stepped on.

Seriously?

She was clearly too high-strung. She'd been annoyed at Garrett's overprotectiveness, and yet here she was jumping out of her skin because of a stupid chew toy. Grabbing the bottle of pills from the nightstand, she turned off the lights and hurried out of the house.

It was snowing again when Jordan slipped back into the squad car, thankful the heater was running full blast.

"Did you get what you needed?" the officer asked.

"I did. And thanks. I appreciate the ride."

"No problem."

She downed the pill with a gulp from her water bottle, then settled in the seat while the officer headed out of the neighborhood, back toward the bureau. Maybe Garrett's overprotection wasn't really what had annoyed her. It was this dance they were playing. The one they'd played for well over a decade. This constant hello ... goodbye. They'd been flirting with a relationship since they were rookies. And over the years, whether she'd meant to or not, she'd always ended up comparing other guys to him.

Because I love him.

She stared out the window at the passing traffic and the falling snow, surprised by the thought. Seeing Garrett again made her wonder if she should let go of the stubborn pride she'd held on to all these years, call a truce, forge ahead, and give the relationship a try. She wasn't sure if she could go another decade without resolving the unanswered questions between them.

But she had no idea how he felt. No idea if he was in a relationship or single. Just because he didn't have a ring on his finger didn't mean he hadn't lost his heart to someone else.

She'd thought she was finally at a point where she felt satisfied with her life—being single, her relationship with friends and family, her relationship with God. But seeing Garrett made the perfect world she'd created seem incomplete and left her longing for something more. Why was the thought of leaving as soon as this case was over suddenly not an option she wanted to think about?

The headlights of another vehicle coming at them from the side way too fast jerked her back to the present. The officer laid on the horn, but it was too late. She felt the impact of the other vehicle, heard the grinding crush of metal hitting metal, and then everything went black.

29

Garrett checked the time as he walked into the bureau. He could smell takeout—Chinese, if he wasn't mistaken—making him realize he'd missed dinner, but food was the last thing on his mind at the moment.

The photos of two girls hung next to the timeline they were constructing. Chloe Middleton and Kelsey Jacobi, both tied to this terrifying string of abductions that had spanned well over a decade. The reality of what it must be like for the two girls' families right now was crushing.

"What did you find out from Kelsey Jacobi's family?" Nikki asked.

"Besides being another grieving family," Garrett said, "they're also feeling an enormous amount of guilt because they were out of town and didn't even realize she was missing until today."

"From what they've been able to put together," Sam continued, "she went over to a friend's house last night about eight, stayed till just after midnight, and never made it back home."

"We were given the case because it has all the markings of our abductor, so I think we need to continue to run on the assumption that we're dealing with another Angel Abductor case, even though we still don't have a body or a Polaroid."

Garrett looked around the open office space. "Where's Jordan?"

"I thought she was with you," Nikki said, stepping back from the board.

"No. I arranged for a patrol officer to take her to her sister's house to pick something up, then she was supposed to come straight here."

Nikki shook her head. "I haven't seen her since the two of you left to go talk to Rose Winters."

"Something's wrong." Garrett pushed Jordan's number on his cell phone and waited for her to pick up. No answer. He felt the familiar twist of his gut he'd been experiencing the past few hours.

God, please tell me nothing's happened to Jordan.

"What time did you leave to talk to the Jacobi family?" Jack asked.

"About six o'clock." Garrett checked his watch. That would have been over an hour and a half ago."

"Who was the officer she went with?" Nikki asked, picking up her phone.

"Roberts . . . Robertson. With metro police."

"Give me a second."

Garrett's pulse raced as he stood in the middle of the room waiting for Nikki. He'd made Jordan go with a police escort so she'd be safe. Had he made the right call?

A minute later, Nikki hung up the call and turned back to Garrett. "They found Robertson's patrol car a few minutes ago. It was T-boned near the corner of Russell Street and South 15th."

"That's not far from Jordan's sister's house." Garrett grabbed his coat and keys. "Tell me she's okay."

"That's the problem," Nikki said. "The first eyewitness to the scene said there was no one else in the car. In fact, there's no sign of her at all."

"Wait a minute. How is that possible?" he asked. "What about the officer she was with?"

"He's going to be okay, but he was found unconscious. He doesn't remember anything that happened today."

Maybe Robertson didn't remember, but Garrett did. Michaels was dead, he and Jordan had barely escaped an explosion, Sam's house had been broken into, and now Jordan was missing. Rose was trying to take them out one by one. And if anything happened to Jordan . . .

He pushed back the panic. They'd find her. More than likely a motorist had decided to drive her to the hospital instead of calling 911. He blew out a sharp sigh. She was fine. She had to be. She was good at what she did. She might not typically spend her time out in the field, but she had been thoroughly trained with the best agents.

Please, God, let her be okay.

"Agent Addison?"

Garrett turned around.

"Sorry to interrupt, sir, but this envelope was just delivered with your name on it."

Garrett grabbed the envelope and ripped it open. Inside was a black-and-white Polaroid photo of Jordan. He let the photo fall onto his desk as a shot of fear rushed through him. "This can't be happening. Jordan's dead. She's killed her."

Nikki put on a glove and picked up the envelope. "We don't know that. Not yet."

"We know who's behind this and what she wants," he said. "She wants everyone she believes responsible for her brother's death, dead. She killed Michaels, and now Jordan's gone. We don't know if Kelsey is still alive. Rose Winters isn't going to stop until she takes down all of us."

"Then we have to be the ones to stop her," Sam said.

Garrett turned to leave. He should have been there with Jordan, making sure she was safe. He never should have let her go to her sister's without him. Rose clearly had a detailed plan. Like her brother, she saw it as a game. She'd been watching them. Planning to pick them off one by one in a final act of revenge for her brother's death.

Outside the snow had turned into rain. He'd been too late to save Marissa, but this time . . . this time he couldn't lose again.

But it was more than that. He'd been so foolish. He'd let more than a decade go by without telling Jordan how he really felt. Without admitting to himself that he was still in love with her. That he'd always been in love with her. How could he have wasted all these years? Pride. Stubbornness. He could think of a dozen words. The truth was, he loved her and needed to be with her. Wanted to spend the rest of his life with her.

He stepped in a puddle, soaking his shoes. He looked up at the sky.

I need to know where you are, God. Right now. Maybe it's the one question I shouldn't ask. Maybe I should know the answer. Maybe I'm just supposed to trust you, but sometimes . . . sometimes everything around me seems so dark.

"Garrett? Where are you going?"

He turned to Sam, trying to choke back the emotion. This wasn't going to help Jordan or Kelsey if they were still alive. He needed to think. To figure out where they were. "I need to find them."

"We're already doing everything we can by canvassing the area, checking surveillance footage, searching for Kelsey's car—"

"And if that's not enough?"

"We will find them, but we can't just go charging out of here. We need a plan."

"A plan? Do you have one that will save them? They need us."

"I know you're angry, but running out there without a plan isn't going to help anyone. You know that. We're a team. We have to work as a team. That's the only way we're going to find them."

"Fine, but I can't just sit at my desk. That Polaroid is proof that Rose is going to kill Jordan, if she hasn't already."

"Jordan's smart, Garrett. If anyone can get out of this situation, she can."

"And Rose Winters is smart as well. She's been planning this for months and now we've got another dead girl because of her."

"We're going to find both Kelsey and Jordan. Alive."

Garrett shook his head. Sam couldn't promise him that. No one could promise him that.

"You're in love with her, aren't you?" Sam asked.

Garrett's shoulders slumped as a heavy wave of fatigue sliced through him. He was so tired. Emotionally, spiritually, physically. He'd tried for so many years to forget the way Jordan made him feel.

"I think I loved her from the first time I saw her." He shoved his hands into his pockets. "She sat down next to me with those crazy curls of hers and smiled. She was so smart and funny, and yet somewhere along the line—thinking I was doing what was best for her—I lost her."

"Then let's go find her."

"How do we get her back?" Garrett asked.

"We have to figure out where Rose would take Jordan, and the only way I know to do that is to go back through the evidence. We found one property. Maybe we can find another."

"Fisher buried his girls on public land, including Marissa, if we assume Rose was behind her death. I have no idea how to narrow things down. It could take days . . . weeks. We don't have time."

"Then start thinking like Jordan. What would she do? Where would Rose Winters take her captives?"

Garrett thought for a moment. "Jordan gave me a rough profile of the woman. She was afraid to leave her own environment because it was the only place she felt safe. We know she rarely left the house. Jordan said that more than likely her fear was irrational, but she didn't know how to deal with it."

"Good. What else?"

"If she was the one who killed Marissa, she probably went where

Vanishing Point

Fisher instructed her to go. Without him, she'll go someplace familiar, because she doesn't do well outside her comfort zone. She doesn't like changes or situations where she feels out of control. Fisher gave her that stability. He bought her a house and kept her comfortable. That was how she could deal with life. But now the house isn't an option for her."

"So what do you suggest?" Sam asked.

"We need to go back through the evidence from her house. The photos, news clippings, anything that might hold the answer."

Five minutes later, they were systematically going through the piles of evidence they'd been able to salvage from Rose's house, including surveillance photos of their team and photos of the girls Fisher had stalked and killed. Garrett had no idea if the endeavor was anything more than a waste of time, but he also had no idea where else to look.

And he wasn't going to show up at Mr. Jacobi's house and tell him that his daughter wasn't coming home. He couldn't do that. Just like he couldn't do that to Jordan's father.

He searched in silence for an hour alongside Sam and Nikki, then ran across something that sent a shock through him. It was a photograph of a landscape. He'd seen this location before. The picture was one of the few that didn't have someone in it. Instead there was a large open green space with trees in the background. A narrow dirt road leading to a small barn. To the left was an abandoned red tractor.

"Did you find something?" Nikki asked.

"Maybe. I've seen this place before."

"Wait a minute . . . I think I saw this as well." Sam picked up the photo and nodded. "Definitely the same location, just from a different angle."

"Is there any way to get a location on a physical copy?" Garrett asked as he held up the photo.

"We can try to get a match in the lab. There's been a lot of advancement in the past few years by searching through GPS-tagged images online, and while the results aren't 100 percent accurate, at least it will be a starting place."

Nikki took the photo from Sam. "I'll get this to the lab. In the meantime, keep searching."

Nikki returned an hour later, just as Garrett was about to admit his idea was a waste of time.

"I've got a location, and the title of the property is under the same trust as the house where Rose was living. I'm printing out the aerial photos and topographical maps as we speak. The property is seventeen acres of land located east of here."

Garrett grabbed his coat. "Let's go."

The scene as they drove up onto the property was exactly as the photo had portrayed, except that it had been taken in a different season. The land was made up of open grassland and woods. Thirty minutes from the city and the perfect place to hide.

And the perfect place to bury a body.

Help us find them, Jesus.

They approached the house from the east. Darkness had long since settled in, and the night was darker still, with a thick layer of cloud cover blocking any light from the moon. The rain had stopped temporarily, but Garrett barely noticed.

The SWAT team opened the door of the house, then swept the house in front of him.

"Clear."

"Clear."

Garrett walked through the house and down a narrow hallway, before stepping into a room in the back. Curtains flapped in the wind from an open window that brought a chill into the room.

He ran the beam of his flashlight across the floor. If they weren't in the house, they would search the entire property.

Something moved in the shadows.

Garrett swung his flashlight to the far side of the room. "Jordan?"

He found her tied to the bedpost. He knelt down beside her and pulled the gag out of her mouth.

"Garrett?" Her voice was weak and raspy, but she was alive. A thin line of blood trickled down the side of her face.

He cupped his hand against her cheek and stared into her eyes. "Jordan, please . . . tell me you're okay."

She drew in a ragged breath as she looked up at him. "I didn't think you were going to find me."

He wiped away the trail of blood with the back of his hand. "I never would have stopped looking, but I thought I'd lost you."

She gasped again for air, the pain evident in her eyes.

He glanced down to see if she'd been hurt, then stopped at her abdomen. Blood had soaked through the shirt she wore.

"Jordan . . ." He ripped off his coat and pressed it against the wound, trying to stop the bleeding. "Jordan, what did she do to you?"

"She shot me when I tried to run away. Garrett, you have to find Kelsey."

"Sam!" Garrett shouted. "Sam, I've got her. Get the paramedics in here now."

He could tell she'd already lost too much blood. It was soaking the carpet where she lay.

"You're going to be fine, Jordan," he said, suppressing the panic that was rising in him. "And you have nothing to worry about. I'm going to make sure you're okay. I promise."

He couldn't lose her. There were so many things he wanted to say to her. Things he should have already told her. Like how much he loved her. How he wanted to spend the rest of his life with her. Start a family with her.

I can't lose her, God. Not now.

"Do you know where Kelsey is?" he asked.

"I don't know, but you need to find her." Jordan pulled on his hand. "Rose took her. She's planning to kill her just like the other girls. She said . . ."

"Jordan, stay with me. I need you to focus." Garrett pushed away the panic. "What did Rose say? There are acres and acres of land and it's dark. Did you see something . . . anything that might help us narrow down where she might be?"

"She said . . . I heard her say that they were going for a short drive into the woods."

"Garrett?" Sam entered the room, his weapon raised. "You found her?"

"She's been shot," Garrett said.

"We've got an ambulance on standby." Sam shouted at one of the officers to get the paramedics.

"Rose is here with Kelsey," Garrett said, keeping the pressure on her wound. "Somewhere on the property. Jordan thinks they drove into the woods."

Sam pulled out a map of the area. "There's a road that winds through the property and just east of us is a thick grove of trees."

We can't be too late, God. Not this time.

"I'll contact local law enforcement," Sam said, "and have them meet our team here with the dogs. We'll find her."

"Did you notice any car tracks out there?" Garrett asked.

"Yeah," Sam said. "They were headed toward that grove."

"That's where she's taking her." Garrett looked back at Jordan as a pair of paramedics entered the room. Her face had paled. She was going into shock.

"I'm coming with you—" he said, squeezing her hand.

"No. Go find Kelsey. Make sure this is over once and for all."

"Jordan—"

"Sir, I need you to step back."

Garrett moved out of the way of the paramedics as they put her on a gurney, then put an oxygen mask over her face. Seconds later, the ambulance sped away into the darkness. Garrett's chest heaved.

He needed to focus. He needed to find Kelsey.

30

Kelsey could hear dogs barking in the background. She'd always been afraid of them. When she was five, one had bit her on the back of her leg, leaving a nasty scar behind. But she wasn't as afraid of the dogs as she was of the person coming toward her.

She pulled her coat tighter around herself, wishing she didn't feel so cold. Wondering how she'd trusted the wrong person. She'd always tried to be nice. Always tried to follow the rules. But now she wouldn't be going to prom or her brother's birthday party this weekend. She wouldn't be helping her mom with decorations . . .

The dogs were getting closer. The terror that had settled in the pit of her stomach welled up in her throat like a vise, slowly tightening with every second that passed. She wanted to vomit. But instead she stood, frozen. Waiting for the next move. She had no idea if it was police dogs looking for her or if it was simply a pack of strays.

She studied the dark figure. Rose had heard the dogs as well. The frantic barking in the distance. Maybe someone *was* looking for her. Was it even possible? No one knew where she was except the woman with the dark curly hair, and for all she knew, that woman was dead. She'd seen Rose shoot her. But the dogs . . . maybe someone did know she was here.

"They're out there, and they're coming for you." Her heart pounded in her chest as she spoke, hoping to make her captor feel at least a fraction of the fear she was feeling. "Can you hear the dogs? Someone knows I'm out here," she said, forcing confidence into her voice. "Someone sent the dogs to find me."

"Shut up."

Rose dropped the camera onto the ground but still held on to the photo. Maybe Kelsey wasn't the only one afraid. She could tell that Rose was trying to decide what to do next. Kelsey could see the panic in her eyes. If Rose shot her, if someone was looking for her, they would hear the shot and find her.

Please, God. Please show me what to do.

She heard the voice a second later.

Run, Kelsey.

She hesitated. Maybe it was God, maybe it was just her own mind, but either way the command was clear. If she wanted to live, she had to run. She didn't care anymore about the gun or getting shot.

Before she could second-guess her decision, she swung around and started running. Rose shouted at her. Demanded that she stop. She heard the gun go off and waited for the searing pain to hit her, but nothing happened. Rose had missed. So Kelsey kept running across the hard ground that was covered with fallen leaves and branches. There was no way to maneuver in a straight line. No way to know where she was or where she should go. But maybe it didn't matter. As long as she ran. She tried to move quietly so she couldn't be followed, but layers of shrubs, dead leaves, and broken branches made it impossible.

A limb scraped against her face. The dogs' barking grew more frantic, and she didn't know whether to run to the noise or away from it.

She had no idea where she was, but God had to be here some-where. Wasn't he? Wasn't he the one who'd told her to run?

The cloud cover had broken, allowing the moonlight to filter through the trees, but it still wasn't enough for her to see more than a few feet ahead. Everything began to look the same as she skirted a fallen tree. Was she just going in circles?

Her ankle twisted when she stepped into a hole. Searing pain shot up her leg. She stumbled to the ground, twisting and falling flat on her tailbone. The panic engulfing her turned into terror. It was as if she were in some sort of nightmare and couldn't wake up. She lay still for a moment, listening to see if Rose was still fol-lowing her. A branch snapped. Leaves crackled. Rose was behind her, not even trying to mask the noise. Which meant she had to keep running. She tried to push herself up, but the pain in her ankle was excruciating. She had run out of options.

The only thing she could do now was hide.

She could still hear the dogs, but their barks seemed fainter. Had they lost her scent?

No, the dogs would find her. And so would her abductor. She squeezed her eyes shut, praying the dogs were search dogs. If they were, she wondered what her parents would have given the police so the dogs could track her. Maybe her favorite baseball shirt, or the Keep Calm one she'd worn yesterday.

But what if Rose found her first and killed her? The wind blew across her face. She wished she had the coat her mom had bought her for her birthday. The one with the furry hood and zipper. She shivered as she lay as still as she could, biting her lip against the pain in her ankle.

Her mom never would have let her go to Trina's house last night. If she hadn't been out, her car wouldn't have broken down, and Rose wouldn't have offered to help her.

She held her breath and tried not to cry. Strange noises sur-rounded her. Some she recognized, like crickets and the wind blowing through the trees. Other sounds were foreign, upping her fear level.

"I know you're out here."

She froze. Rose was getting closer. It was almost over. She couldn't run anymore. Couldn't fight.

"You won't be able to hide from me, can't you see that? No one is coming for you. No one."

Rose was almost there. Kelsey could see the woman's shadow in the moonlight as she passed Kelsey's hiding place. She hadn't found her. Not yet.

"I told you not to run, but you wouldn't listen to me."

Something crawled across Kelsey's face. She fought to stay still. Wind blew through the treetops above her.

Someone shouted. The dogs' barking was getting louder again. They were coming for her. But who would find her first?

31

They were running out of time. Garrett followed the grid line he'd been assigned to in the wooded area of the property. His lungs were burning from the cold, and yet he couldn't stop. Kelsey was out here somewhere. Neither could he think about Jordan. Not now. They needed to find Kelsey, for himself as much as Jordan.

The darkened forest whispered around him. Shadows danced as he moved forward, his bright light catching the uneven terrain around him. Tree limbs swayed and creaked in the darkness. He could hear the search dogs barking periodically to his left. Their eerie howls pierced through the cold. The underbrush crunched under his feet.

I know you're here, God. In spite of everything that's happened. That has never changed. Even when I don't understand.

Over the past decade, Garrett had come to realize more and more that his faith couldn't rely on what was happening around him, or whether or not he understood how God worked. His faith had to rely on God himself—who never changed—even when he didn't understand what God was doing.

But faith sure was easier when miracles happened. And tonight they were going to need a miracle if he was going to bring Kelsey home.

His radio crackled. "We found a grave. No body."

Garrett let out a sigh of relief. Maybe there was still a chance to bring her home alive.

He caught something moving to his right out of the corner of his eye.

He swung his light around.

The beam pierced the darkness, catching something red. Kelsey cowered beneath the heavy limbs of a tree. She was crying. Shaking, he was sure, both from fear and the cold. He glanced around as he called in the news, but so far there was no sign of Rose.

Garrett knelt down beside her. "My name's Garrett Addison, and I've been working with law enforcement to find you. You're going to be okay now. You're safe."

She looked up at him as if she wanted to disappear. He could see the lingering terror in her eyes, unsure if she should trust him or not.

"Are you hurt?" he asked.

She pressed her lips together and nodded. "It's not bad, but I twisted my ankle."

"Okay. Can you tell me who took you?"

"It was a woman. Her name is Rose. She took my picture and told me she was going to kill me, but I ran."

"She can't hurt you now." He pulled off his jacket and wrapped it around her shoulders. "Do you think you can walk if I help you?"

"I think so."

"Then let's get you out of here so you can go home."

Garrett wrapped his arm around Kelsey's waist and started walking her back toward the house. He kept his flashlight trained on the terrain in front of him, his senses on high alert. This wasn't over yet. They still had to find Rose and put an end to this once and for all.

A branch snapped behind them as he grabbed his radio. Garrett turned around. Rose Winter stood in the middle of the trail with a gun pointed at them.

"Garrett Addison. Thanks for finding her for me. She turned out to be a feisty one."

He felt for the distress button on his radio and pushed it, while motioning Kelsey behind him, thankful when she quickly complied. "It's over, Rose. I need you to put the gun down."

"Why would I do that? You killed my brother, and now it's up to me to make things right again."

"By targeting more girls and my team? By killing more people?" Garrett wondered if it were even possible to reason with someone like her. "We had nothing to do with his death. Your brother died because he was drunk and got killed fighting someone in a back alley."

"No." She shook her head. "You don't understand. I promised Bobby I'd keep him safe. That I'd help him."

"Is that why you killed Marissa?"

She frowned. "I killed Marissa because he needed an alibi so he could stay out of prison. I had to give him that."

Once they got the distress signal, it wouldn't take Sam and the others long to figure out what was going on, but he needed them to proceed with caution. The last thing they needed was more bloodshed.

"Keep your hands where I can see them," Rose said, "and toss that radio over here."

"Okay." Garrett lobbed the radio to the ground about two feet from Rose. "But this is over, Rose. There are over a dozen officers in these woods looking for you, and they're on their way here right now. There's nowhere for you to run anymore."

Her demeanor had changed from the first time they'd met her. No longer was she the sweet, sickly woman she'd portrayed at her house. Instead, she possessed an air of confidence and a deep bitterness edged her tone. Everything they'd seen had been nothing but an act.

"You're wrong. It's not over. Not yet. You put Bobby in prison. Made him go into hiding." She shook her head. "No one understood him except for me. Bobby was special, and I owed him so much. He took care of me all these years with the money he made. Bought me a house and gave me someone to take care of me. I would have liked to see him more often, but I always knew he had important things to take care of. He was so smart."

"He killed innocent girls."

"He didn't mean to. He couldn't help himself. It was like a game he had to win."

"It was never a game," Garrett said, "It was people's lives. Those girls had families. Mothers and fathers. Brothers and sisters. They all lost someone just like you lost Bobby."

"You don't understand." Her hands were starting to shake. "He told me that I owed him. Told me exactly what I needed to do to help him, and I did. I did everything he told me to do."

Garrett stopped talking. There was no use arguing with her. Somehow she'd rationalized what Bobby had done and put the blame on his team. Michaels was dead, Chloe Middleton was dead, and Jordan was fighting for her life. All because of some sort of twisted sense of revenge.

He saw them before he realized how close they were. Six armed members of the search and rescue team quickly moved into position, making a semicircle that flanked both sides of him and Kelsey, with their weapons pointed at Rose.

"I need you to put your gun down now, Rose," Garrett said. "It's over, and I don't think you want to die this way."

She looked around at the half-dozen weapons aimed at her.

"Rose, put your gun down and drop to your knees," he repeated.

She hesitated another few seconds before finally complying. Seconds later, they were disarming her and cuffing her hands behind her back.

"Kelsey?" Garrett turned around. "Are you okay?"

She nodded, still shaking, but it was finally over.

Thank you, Jesus. He wrapped his arm around her shoulders. "Let's get you out of here."

Someone had called Kelsey's parents. They were waiting next to a patrol car near the house when Garrett and Kelsey stepped into the clearing. The moment they saw their daughter, they started running toward her.

"Mom . . . Dad . . ."

Garrett felt a swell of emotion rise in his chest as they pulled her into their arms, all three of them crying. They might not have been able to save the other girls, but this family wouldn't have to go through the nightmare the others had.

"What about you?" Sam asked, walking up to him. "You okay?"

Garrett nodded. "Just relieved this is finally over."

"So am I. We found two more graves on the property during the search," Sam said. "They matched photos found at Winter's house. We're pretty sure they'll turn out to hold Becky and Sarah's bodies."

It wasn't going to be the ending those families had wanted, but at least they'd finally have the closure they'd searched for all these years.

"What about Jordan?" Garrett asked. "Have you heard anything about her?"

"Not yet."

Garrett pulled out his phone. There was a voice message from Jordan's dad he'd missed.

"Garrett, this is Daniel Lambert. I was told you were out searching for another girl. I wanted to let you know that Jordan has just gone into surgery. I promise I'll call as soon as I know something, but we need to pray." There was a long pause on the line. "The doctors aren't sure she's going to make it."

32

Garrett stepped off the elevator and walked up to the nurses' station, his adrenaline still pumping. He hadn't slept in over twenty-four hours, but he didn't care. He'd just gotten the message that Jordan was out of recovery and could see visitors. And he knew that until he saw her in person, he wouldn't be able to sleep.

"I'm looking for Jordan Lambert?" he said to the dark-haired nurse behind the desk.

The woman looked at her computer screen. "She's in room 417."

"Thanks."

A moment later, Garrett stepped inside the room. Jordan was lying on the bed, hooked up to an IV and a couple monitors, while her father sat next to her in a metal-framed chair.

"Garrett . . . hey." Jordan shot him a sleepy smile.

"Hey, yourself," he said. A wave of relief washed over him. This could have ended so differently.

"It's good to see you." Daniel Lambert stood up and shook Garrett's hand. "My girl's been asking about you."

281

"I had to come see for myself that she was going to make it."
He turned back to Jordan. "How are you feeling?"

"Better, now that I know you're okay, though you look terrible.
Have you slept at all?"

"Forget about me," he said, shaking his head. "I'm not the one
everyone's worried about."

Daniel looked at his daughter. "We got our miracle, but now
that you're here, I'm going to grab some coffee."

"Please, don't leave on my account."

"Don't worry. I could use a few minutes to stretch my legs."

Her father leaned over and kissed her on her forehead. "I'll be
back."

Garrett waited until her father left the room before sitting down
beside her in the chair. "How are you really feeling?"

"Like I never want to get shot again." She gave him a weak
smile. "But the doctor told me that despite a scare early on, the
surgery went well. They're expecting a full recovery."

"You've got bragging rights now, you know, with your first
gunshot."

"Don't even try to make me laugh." She grinned, but her smile
quickly faded. "Please tell me you found Kelsey."

"We did. She's shaken up, but already back with her family."

"It almost happened again, Garrett. If you hadn't been able to
stop Rose, another girl would have died."

"It's finally over. The Angel Abductor is dead, and Rose can't
ever hurt anyone again."

"I thought I was going to die, Garrett." The fear she must
have felt still lingered in her eyes. "I've faced death before, but
this time . . . there was no light in Rose's eyes when she shot me.
And at that moment, I knew I was going to die. Just like the girls
she'd killed."

"But you didn't. You're safe. And so is Kelsey."

He took her hand and laced their fingers together. There was
so much he'd realized about her—about himself—over the past

twenty-four hours. So much he needed to tell her. He'd come so close to losing her for good. It had put his own life into perspective and made him realize how much he needed her in his life.

"Do you remember when Dana Kerrigan asked me where God was when her daughter was killed?" she asked, breaking into his thoughts.

"Yes." That day seemed like forever ago.

"I've never completely stopped struggling with that question. If I close my eyes, I can still see the heartbreak on her face and hear the desperation in her voice. But do you know what still bothers me the most about that situation?"

Garrett shook his head.

"I didn't know how to answer her. It made me realize that I had my own questions about God. Like how he could have let someone get away with killing all those girls. And more personal questions, like why didn't he heal my mother?"

He understood the questions completely. He'd met with grieving parents desperate to find their daughters. And later, he'd watched those same parents forced to come to grips with the horrifying reality that their daughters weren't coming home. Those encounters had left him with his own battle deep within his soul. To question God's presence somehow seemed sacrilegious, but at the same time, how could he not?

"Every time a tragic case came across my desk," Jordan continued, "it left me with unanswered questions. Julia's mom spoke out loud what I'd always been afraid to ask."

"And have you found any answers?" he asked.

"Maybe. I think I've found that asking where God is when something bad happened is the wrong question."

Her statement surprised him. "What do you mean?"

"We ask that question as if we're surprised when evil surfaces. But in reality, I think we've forgotten we live in a fallen world. We've forgotten that God gives us the freedom to make choices And while he gives us free will, that freedom doesn't mean he stands over us and fixes everything. There are consequences that too often hit innocent people. Does that make sense?"

"It does," Garrett said.

"And what I'm realizing is that when he doesn't intervene, it doesn't mean he isn't there. I think it means just the opposite. He decided not to just sweep down and fix our problems every time something goes wrong. Instead he chose to redeem us eternally by sending his Son."

Tragedies like the Oklahoma City bombing, 9/11, Hurricane Katrina, and Sandy Hook flipped through Garrett's mind. The reality of a fallen world was clear. And yet like Jordan said, wasn't God's plan really a plan of redemption? Yes, he believed that God was capable of fixing our problems, but he chose instead to rescue and redeem humankind permanently.

"Maybe," he said, trying to put his thoughts into words, "there isn't necessarily a particular 'reason' for something to happen. Maybe the truth is that things happen because we live in a world where pain, death, and loss are all naturally a part of life. No one is immune."

Jordan nodded. "Jesus told us that in this world we'd have many troubles. Sometimes we do experience God's blessings, but he never promised us that everything would be perfect in this world."

"Only in the redeemed world to come," Garrett agreed.

"What he does promise is to walk with us through the bad times. As crazy as it seems, somehow, when bad things happen, we start to see God's grace. We start to dig deeper. Sometimes it takes trauma to get someone searching for God. And hard times give us compassion toward others, deeper love, and more courage."

He looked down at their entwined fingers. Everything she was saying reminded him of one of the reasons he'd fallen in love with her. She never gave up searching for God and his truth, even in a career where she was surrounded by so much evil.

"So what happens next?" Jordan asked. "Even though we can finally put this case behind us, I can't forget that the families who lost their daughters will always be surrounded by reminders of what happened to them."

"I've thought a lot about that as well, but there is something you need to know." He took a deep breath, still reveling in the fact that he was here with her and that she was going to be okay. "I've never been so scared I was going to lose you, Jordan, and I can't let you walk away again without telling you how I feel."

"Garrett, you don't have to do this. This wasn't your fault."

"This has nothing to do with guilt. Trust me." He pushed a loose curl back behind her ear. "When you moved to Quantico all those years ago, I should have run after you. I don't want to make the same mistake today. I'm not a rookie cop anymore, trying to prove something to myself. What's happened to these families has taught me what's really important in life and how quickly it can all be taken away. I just can't believe that it's taken me this long to figure it out."

"What are you saying?"

"What I'm saying is that my biggest regret is letting you go. I fell in love with you the first time I saw you. You were so beautiful and funny and smart. I don't think I've ever stopped loving you. You don't have to answer right now, but the bottom line is . . . I want to marry you, Jordan."

"Wait a minute." Her eyes widened. "Is this a proposal?"

He glanced up at the monitor beeping quietly above her bed and grinned. "I guess this isn't exactly the most romantic place for a proposal, and I don't even have a ring, but yeah . . . I want to marry you, Jordan. I can work in Memphis just as well as I can here. As long as I'm with you, that's all I really care about."

He felt his heart rate speed up as he waited for her to respond. Maybe he should have waited until he had a ring and the perfect proposal planned, but he felt he couldn't wait even one minute longer.

"Yes," she said.

He studied her face and caught a hint of amusement. "You just said yes?"

"I did." Jordan laughed, then touched her side at the pain. "You sound surprised. What were you expecting me to say?"

"I don't know." He really had no idea what he'd expected. Only that he had no plans to walk out the door until he knew exactly how she felt. "At best, I thought you'd need time to think about it."

"I already have. Because you're not the only one questioning our past and wondering how we managed to keep sidestepping a relationship all these years," she said, rubbing her thumb across the back of his hand. "I feel the same way. You've always been my one regret, Garrett. The one person I never should have walked away from."

"There are going to be a lot of details to work out—"

"I'm not worried about any of that," she said. "In fact, there's only one thing I really am worried about."

"And what's that?" he asked.

"Promise me that I'm not going to wake up tomorrow and discover I dreamed all of this. I'm pretty pumped up with pain meds."

Garrett laughed. "As long as you promise me you won't wake up tomorrow and regret anything you've just told me."

"Never."

"Then I can think of a way to absolve your fears by making it as clear as possible how I feel."

"How do you feel, Mr. Addison?"

He smiled as he leaned forward, stopping briefly to brush aside one of her curls before brushing his lips against hers. Then he cupped the back of her head and slowly kissed her again. She pressed her hand against his chest as she responded to his touch, sending a current of electricity running through him.

"Does that clarify things a bit?" he asked, moving back and catching her gaze.

"Oh yeah," she said, reaching up to touch his unshaven jawline. "Though you don't mind if I suggest a very short engagement, do you?"

"Are you kidding me?" He leaned over and kissed her again. "I agree completely."

Epilogue

December 20
3:48 p.m.
Bridgewood Cemetery

"We are gathered here together to celebrate the life of Sarah Marie Boyd. As we grieve, we acknowledge our human loss and pray that God will grant us grace and peace. We pray that in our pain and hurt, we might find a measure of comfort and hope in our sorrow, knowing that our lives don't end with death."

Garrett stood beside Jordan and Sam at the back of the crowd while the minister spoke at the graveside memorial. Dozens of white markers decorated with flowers and crosses were spread out across the green lawns. He'd seen firsthand how death was as much a part of life as birth, but its reality still came coupled with a profound loss. And that loss, whether expected or unexpected, always left behind scars.

The pastor said his closing remarks as the sun began to set, then ended with a prayer to which everyone responded with a heartfelt *amen*.

Garrett looked down at Jordan and laced their fingers together. "It feels surreal that all of this is finally over."

"I'm just relieved that they can't hurt anyone else."

"How are you feeling?" he asked. She'd insisted on coming to Abram Michaels's funeral this morning as well as Sarah's funeral this afternoon, even though the doctor had only released her from the hospital twenty-four hours ago.

"I'm okay, just tired."

"We need to get you home." Garrett turned to Sam. "Would you mind walking Jordan to my car? I'll catch up in a minute, but I'd like to speak to Nikki first." He turned back to Jordan. "If that's okay?"

Jordan squeezed his hand, then took Sam's arm. "Go on. I'll be fine."

Garrett walked across the lawn to where Nikki and her husband stood a few yards away from Sarah's grave. He hoped he wasn't intruding. A thick row of clouds hovered along the horizon, but the sun had partially broken through the cloudy cover. Somehow the bright rays from heaven seemed fitting. Like a reminder that God was truly a part of today's proceedings.

"Garrett." She gave him a hug, then took a step back. "I appreciate you and the team being here. I don't believe you've met my husband. This is Tyler Grant. Tyler, this is Garrett Addison. I've told you about him."

Garrett shook Tyler's hand. "It's nice to meet you."

"It's nice to meet you as well. I'm grateful for all you did to help bring closure to Nikki and her family. I know it's been a hard-fought battle for all of you."

Garrett nodded at the acknowledgment. Because while his struggle could never compare to the Boyd family's, they weren't the only ones needing closure. His grief might have manifested differently, but it was a grief all the same. A grief that had made him realize that saying "I love you" should never wait until tomorrow. And that love—no matter how brief—was worth it.

Tyler squeezed his wife's hand. "I'll let the two of you talk while I go find Liam and check on your parents."

"Tyler lost his first wife a couple years ago," Nikki said, as her husband walked away. "Liam's his son. It's been an adjustment for the three of us, but absolutely wonderful at the same time."

"I'm glad to hear that."

Nikki turned back to him. "Thank you for coming today. It means a lot to my family."

"How are your parents doing?"

"They're strong. They've learned to rely on each other. And I think, in a way, knowing Sarah hasn't been suffering all these years has actually helped. Having the chance to give Sarah a proper burial helps as well. Not that this is how I wanted it to end, but maybe now my family will have some closure."

"Your sister's disappearance changed your life."

"If you would have told me a decade ago that I'd end up working on a TBI task force, i probably would have laughed at you. I was pretty happy being a schoolteacher."

"I heard rumors you had some good news in the middle of all of this?" he asked, hoping he wasn't asking too personal a question.

Her broadening smile assured him that it wasn't a taboo topic. "I'm still trying convince myself it's real, but yes, we're expecting."

"When's the baby due?"

"May."

"Congratulations!"

"Thanks." Nikki smiled and laid her hand across her stomach. "The baby was a bit of a surprise, but a good surprise. Though I heard you have your own good news."

"I asked Jordan to marry me, and she actually said yes."

Nikki laughed. "Somehow I'm not surprised at all."

"Let's just say it's been a long time in coming." He put his hands in his pockets. "Listen, I won't keep you any longer, but I thought you might want to know that Sam and I went to visit Kelsey Jacobi."

"How is she?"

"Physically she's okay. It's going to take her time to heal emotionally, but I think she'll get through this."

"I can't tell you how glad I am to hear that. Even though my heart breaks for the families of the other girls who never came home, knowing Kelsey is back with her family takes away some of the sting of today."

"I agree. Sarah's disappearance was the one case that almost derailed me. The case that forced me to look at life differently."

"I owe you a lot for helping my family find resolution. I guess, in a way, I always knew she was gone, but that doesn't mean it doesn't still hurt. But at least we finally got the closure we needed."

A minute later, Garrett headed back across the grass to his car where Jordan waited for him.

"Thanks, Sam," he said.

"No problem. I'll see the two of you later."

"It's beautiful, isn't it?" she said, taking in the splash of color across the sky in the sunset as Sam walked to his car.

"Very," Garrett said.

"How is Nikki?" she asked.

"It's been hard for her and her family, but at least they finally have the closure they've needed for so long. Maybe now they can begin to heal."

Garrett stared a few moments longer at the sunset before turning back to Jordan.

"This might not be the most romantic setting, but I thought it might be time to make things official between us." He shot her a smile. "That is, unless you've changed your mind about marrying me now that the pain medicine's wearing off."

She let out a soft laugh. "Never."

"Good." He pulled out a single diamond ring with a vintage ornate silver band. "This was my grandmother's. She left it to me when she died."

"Garrett . . . It's beautiful."

"We can look for something together when you're feeling better—"

"No." She smiled up at him. "This is perfect. You are perfect for me."

1

Northeast Tennessee near the Obed River

The initial step off the sheer face of a three-hundred-plus-foot drop was always the most terrifying. Nikki Boyd leaned back into her harness as far as she could, locked her knees, then peered over the edge of the sandstone cliff that dropped into the ravine below. The terror faded, followed by a shot of pure adrenaline as she kicked off and plunged over the edge.

Legs horizontal to the rock face, Nikki shimmied down the side of the cliff, kicking loose a few rocks along the way. The stress of the past few weeks began to dissipate into the crisp morning air. A day climbing and rappelling with Tyler Grant had definitely been the right thing to do. They'd come, not to dismiss memories of Katie's death, but to celebrate her life. Which was exactly what they were doing.

Halfway down, Nikki glanced up, then slowed to a stop. The rope had shifted and now ran over a sharp edge of the cliff wall. She caught her toes against a narrow ledge and fought to catch her balance. While perhaps not common, it was possible to sever a weighted rope on a descent.

"You okay?" Tyler hollered down at her.

"The rope moved and it's running over a sharp edge."

She'd been told by more than one experienced climber that they hated rappelling because it was the most dangerous part of the day. And this was why. No matter how much training and preparation, no matter how many times she checked her equipment, things could still go wrong. And it just took one mistake. But all she needed to do was unweight the rope and move it to a safer place.

"Can you move it?" Tyler asked.

"I'm trying."

"You're going to have to take some of your weight off the rope."

"Like I said, I'm trying."

Her gloved fingers held on to a crack in the rock face while she searched for another crack for her feet. Her fingers cramped. A trail of blood dripped down her arm. She didn't even remember scraping it. Her feet finally found a narrow crevice, alleviating her weight on the rope enough to give it some slack. All she needed to do now was redirect the rope's path.

Simple.

But she couldn't get enough leverage to unweight the rope.

"Nikki?"

"Just a minute . . ." Sweat beaded across her forehead as she stood on her tiptoes, her fingertips pressed back into the crack, heart pounding against her chest.

She'd heard plenty of stories about things like this happening. Freak accidents against the side of a sheer cliff. Climbers plunging to their deaths.

You know this isn't how I want to die, Jesus . . .

And certainly not today. Not on the anniversary of Katie's death. She glanced at the ground below, then felt her breath catch. If she couldn't move the rope to a safer spot, it could snap above her.

"Nikki?" Tyler shouted from the top of the cliff. "What's happening?"

She drew in another breath. "I'm okay, but I'm having trouble moving the rope."

She hung balanced on the ledge, trying to figure out what to do. Accidents like this weren't all that common, but as with any sport, there were always variables you couldn't count on. She shifted her gaze to the ground. Two months ago, a college student had plunged to his death near here. The steep, rocky terrain made it a popular spot for risk takers.

She pushed the thought aside. What she needed to do was focus on solving the problem. Theoretically she knew what to do, but she was going to need both hands. Which was a problem. Currently, with her right hand holding the rope behind her to keep her from sliding down, she'd need to run the end around her legs a few times in order to secure it. But that was a move even an experienced rappeller would hesitate performing. Unless—

"Stay put, Nikki, I'm coming to you."

"I can figure this out."

"Stay put," he ordered. "I'm coming down."

"Okay, just be careful."

A handful of small rocks bounced off her helmet as Tyler descended toward her on a separate rope.

"How was your date last night with Ryan?" he called down to her.

Her date? Was he serious?

She never should have told Tyler about Ryan. Now he was simply trying to distract her. Trying to get her to focus her thoughts away from the fear and panic. Panic because she was stuck on a narrow ledge a hundred-plus feet off the ground with the potential of a severed rope. And with it the reminder of how quickly life could spiral out of control.

"The date went fine," she finally answered.

She could hear him making his way down the sheer cliff above her. His feet scattered another volley of pebbles.

"Fine doesn't tell me anything," he countered. "Give me some details. Last night was your third date with Mr. Perfect. You've got to have something interesting to share."

Details? He really wanted details while she was hanging off the side of a cliff praying she wasn't about to plunge to her death?

A cramp gripped her calf as her fingers dug deeper into the rock crevice above her. She tried to wiggle her leg without losing her footing on the ledge. There honestly wasn't much to tell. Ryan was six foot three and looked like a model straight off a Banana Republic ad. On top of that, he made a great living, owned his own house, and was completely debt free.

None of those things, though, was the real reason she'd agreed to a second and third date. She'd half expected him to be a snob, but surprisingly, he wasn't. At all. Instead, he was down-to-earth, complimented her without making her feel he wanted something in return, and treated her like she was the only one in the room when they were together. She'd never met another guy quite like him—except perhaps Tyler.

Which was why Tyler had dubbed him "Mr. Perfect" the first time she'd told him she'd gone out with a guy set up by one of her mother's friends at church. Making it to the third date was something of a record for her—as of late anyway. But despite Ryan's "perfection," she still wasn't completely convinced he was perfect for *her*. Everyone—including her mother—had already made the decision she'd finally found Mr. Right in Mr. Perfect. But making that decision for herself felt a lot like taking that first step off the cliff. A shot of terror along with a huge rush of adrenaline.

A sharp pain jetted through her head, and Nikki realized she was clenching her jaw. She took in a deep breath and forced herself to relax. "He's not perfect, and there's nothing new I want to share with you."

Tyler laughed as he dropped next to where she hung and stopped. "The guy owns his own company, runs half marathons for fun, and supports orphans in Africa."

"So he's a good guy. That doesn't mean I'm planning on—I don't know—*marrying* him."

"Yet."

Nikki frowned. No, those were her mother's plans. Besides, talking with Tyler about her date was . . . well . . . awkward.

"One of us needs a bit of a boost in the romance department, and since I'm not going there, that leaves you," he said.

She caught a flicker of pain in his voice. How did you start dating again after losing the love of your life? She wasn't even going to ask that question.

"There's a slightly deeper ledge six inches to your right for your feet. It will give you some extra support, but I think the simplest solution at this point is to transfer you to my rope."

Nikki drew in a deep breath as she felt for the ledge, then managed to shove her toes into the crack.

"What did the two of you do?" he asked.

She watched while he locked off his belay device and ran the bottom of his rope through hers, grateful for his special ops training.

"We went to dinner and the symphony."

"And . . ."

"That was it. Dinner, good food, and interesting conversation."

"Do you like him?"

She hesitated. "He's nice. A gentleman."

"Like I said. Mr. Perfect, though I'm not sure that *nice* is what a guy wants to hear."

"Then what does he want to hear?" Nikki wiggled her toes while still trying to keep her balance. The cramp had spread from her calf to the arch of her foot.

"That he's intriguing . . . intelligent . . . funny . . . a bit romantic."

"He brought me flowers," she said. Somehow he'd found out she loved wildflowers and had brought her a bouquet.

"But no fireworks yet?" Tyler asked.

"I'm just getting to know him."

For Tyler and Katie, it had been love at first sight. She'd never believed in the notion until the day they'd met. But that wasn't exactly her own experience. Her longest relationship—two and a half years—had ended in a nasty breakup. Not exactly a scenario she wanted to repeat.

Like the scenario she was dealing with right now.

"You're good to go," Tyler said finally. "Ease down slowly."

Nikki tightened her fingers on the rope as she made her way down the rest of the cliff with Tyler following. She skidded down the slight incline at the bottom of the rock, then disconnected from the rope.

"Let's not try that again," she said, thankful her feet were finally once again on solid ground.

"You're telling me. You okay?"

She brushed the dust from her pants, then peeled off her gloves. "I think my ego's more bruised than I am. I anchored the rope in the wrong spot."

"Sometimes you do everything right and it still isn't enough."

She caught the sadness in his eyes as they began collecting the equipment. Why was that statement always so hard to accept?

"You're sure you're okay?" he asked again.

She held out her hands, unable to stop them from shaking. "I'll admit, that was a bit sobering."

He pulled her against his chest while she tried to let go of the fear that had surrounded her only moments before. She snuggled into his shoulder. His heart was beating as fast as hers. She looked up at his familiar brown eyes and short, military cut hair and felt his day-old beard brush lightly against her cheek. His arms tightened around her shoulders, making her feel safe and protected.

He knew as well as she did that sometimes doing everything right simply wasn't enough.

But thankfully, today hadn't ended in tragedy.

"As long as you're okay," he said, "that's all that matters."

She let out a soft swoosh of air. She didn't want today to hold another reminder of what could go wrong. How in one fragile moment life could suddenly slip away and be gone forever. But that fact wasn't something either of them could ever forget.

"Thank you." Her heart rate was beginning to slow to normal. "You saved my life, you know."

He brushed away a strand of her shoulder-length blond hair that had fallen across her cheek, then took a step backward. "Being here with you today has made me realize—not for the first time—that I'm the one who needs to thank you."

"For what?"

"For coming with me today." He squeezed her hand before pulling off his helmet. "For everything you've done for Liam and me. I'm honestly not sure I would have gotten through the last year without you."

"I miss her too. Maybe that's why I'm feeling so distracted today."

Nikki felt the tears well in her eyes and tried to blink them back. She'd promised herself she'd be strong for Tyler. Blubbering like a baby wasn't keeping that promise. But while the pain had dulled even a year later, sometimes the loss still felt like it had happened yesterday. Sometimes she still heard Katie's voice. Heard the phone ring and expected it to be her, until she remembered that Katie would never call again. But as much as she missed her best friend, her grief was nothing compared to what Tyler and Liam had gone through.

"You ready to call it quits for the day?" he asked.

"Are you kidding?" Nikki blinked back the rest of her tears and smiled. "We've barely started. I didn't wake up before dawn to give up and go back home again before breakfast."

They'd planned this day for months. A day out of the city, near the place where they'd sprinkled Katie's ashes. A day to celebrate Katie's life. She would have wanted them to be here today.

"How about a break then?" he asked. "Your hands are still shaking."

Nikki pressed her palms against her sides. "I could use some coffee. And if you're hungry, my mom packed breakfast to go along with the thermos she sent with us."

"I love your mom." Tyler smiled as he started for the trail

leading away from the cliffs. "But the smell drove me crazy the entire trip here."

"Me too, and there's plenty."

There always was. Boyds' BBQ in downtown Nashville had been in the family for three generations, and Nikki's mom never missed an opportunity to ensure her daughter stayed well fed.

"How about we take care of that scrape on your arm first," Tyler said. "Then we can eat some of your mom's breakfast and get at this again."

Nikki nodded, then glanced at the gash where she'd noticed the blood earlier. "You know you don't have to baby me."

He smiled at her and shook his head. "You've always been there for me, Nikki. Just let me do the same thing for you."

Five minutes later, she sat on the tailgate of Tyler's pickup truck in the parking lot while he pulled out the first-aid kit and started cleaning her wound. He washed away the trail of blood caked with dirt from the mountainside, then covered it with an antibacterial spray.

Nikki winced.

"You're worse than Liam," he teased.

"Funny, but that stuff—whatever it is—stings. Remember you're going to school to be a psychologist, not a doctor, Mr. Grant."

"I think I can handle this assignment, Special Agent Boyd."

She laughed, thankful that most of the panic was finally wearing off, because she still had her eye on conquering a couple of climbing routes that had gotten the best of her the last time she was here. Today, she was determined to stay focused and make it to the top of at least one of them.

Her phone rang, and she pulled it out of her back pocket.

She glanced at the caller ID. Unknown. "I should ignore it, but it could be my sister-in-law trying to get ahold of me. She was supposed to go see her obstetrician this morning."

"Anything wrong?"

"Maybe. She's only got a couple weeks before her due date, but she started bleeding last night."

Which had Nikki worried. She'd watched Matt and Jamie navigate an emotional roller coaster through eight years of infertility and three miscarriages. This pregnancy finally promised the first grandbaby of the family, and just last week they'd finished the nursery. If anything went wrong now . . .

"Go ahead." Tyler pressed a butterfly Band-Aid over her cut. "I've got my phone on in case Liam needs me. You'd better answer."

Nikki nodded and took the call.

"Agent Boyd." The voice of her boss, Tom Carter, took Nikki by surprise. "How is the great outdoors treating you?"

She glanced at Tyler, who'd started putting the first-aid supplies back into the plastic case. "I'm fine, sir, thanks."

"Good. Listen, I hate to put a wrinkle in your day, but I have a favor to ask of you."

Nikki frowned. Saying no to her boss was somehow harder than saying no to her mother. "I'm here with Tyler Grant, sir, we're—"

"I remember you mentioned you were going climbing." He paused. "Today's the anniversary of his wife's death, right?"

"Yeah."

"How's he doing?"

Tyler had met her boss during a joint military training exercise designed to increase the military's ability to function in an urban setting. According to Carter, he'd been highly impressed with Tyler's skills and instincts.

"He's okay. We're having a good time. The weather's perfect." There was no use mentioning she'd been clinging to the side of a cliff a few minutes ago, afraid for her life. "What's the favor, sir?"

"I just got a call from a friend. Actually, I went to university with his father, and we stayed close until he died. The son's name is Kyle Ellison. He's not far from where you are with his sixteen-year-old sister, celebrating her birthday over the weekend. Problem is, she went out for a walk this morning and didn't return."

Nikki glanced at her watch. It was just past eight. "Has he called the local authorities?"

"Not yet. He's convinced she probably just wandered off the path to get a closer look at some wildlife and sprained her ankle, something like that. He called me for advice."

"How long has she been gone?"

"He's not sure. She was gone when he got up, around seven."

Which meant they were already looking at a minimum of two hours ago, and maybe longer.

There was another pause on the line before her boss spoke again. "Listen, all I'm asking is for you to look into it for me. I'll text you the address of the private cabin where they're staying. Interview the brother and the girl's friends, then pass it on to the local law enforcement if you need to. The boy's scared."

"Okay. I'll see what I can do."

Nikki hung up the phone and glanced down at her climbing clothes. With her tan lightweight climbing pants, orange T-shirt, and hiking shoes, she wasn't exactly dressed for the job, but it would have to do for now.

She jumped down from the tailgate. "That was my boss."

"What did he want?" Tyler asked.

She hesitated. "A favor."

"He wants you to work a case."

Nikki nodded, trying to read Tyler's expression. "It shouldn't take long. A quick interview about a missing girl who's probably just lost out here somewhere."

"I don't mind." He shot her a smile. "As long as I get some of your mama's cooking as soon as we're done."

Nikki laughed, hoping he truly didn't mind. She'd already begun sorting through the limited information she had. Because with missing persons cases, time was never on their side. If the girl *had* been abducted, at a mile a minute she could easily be across the state border by now. But hopefully the girl's brother was right. She'd simply gone out walking and gotten lost or turned her ankle. Most kids who went missing were found.

Nikki tossed Tyler the truck keys that he'd laid on the tailgate.

"They're staying in a private cabin not far from here. I'll pull up the directions on my phone while you drive."

The familiar feeling of guilt swirled through her as she slid into the truck and fastened her seat belt. Because not knowing what's happening to someone you love can be the hardest thing in the world to handle. And something she understood far too well.

Acknowledgments

I'm always so grateful to those who come alongside me to help bring the ideas in my head to life. To my fabulous team at Revell, thank you for all of the hard work you do in order to get my stories into print and into my readers' hands. To my wonderful agent, Joyce Hart, your support throughout the past decade-plus has been such a blessing. Thank you to Ellen Tarver for helping me see and fix the flaws in my story from the beginning; and to my family who continues to encourage me to keep writing. And I'm thankful to my heavenly Father for giving me both the desire and opportunities to continue writing for him.

Lisa Harris is a Christy Award finalist for *Blood Ransom* and *Vendetta*, a Christy Award winner for *Dangerous Passage*, and the winner of the Best Inspirational Suspense Novel for 2011 (*Blood Covenant*) and 2015 (*Vendetta*) from *Romantic Times*. She has over thirty novels and novella collections in print. She and her family have spent almost fourteen years as missionaries in Africa.

When she's not working, she loves hanging out with her family, cooking different ethnic dishes, photography, and heading into the African bush on safari. For more information about her books and life in Africa, visit her website at www.lisaharriswrites.com or her blog at http://myblogintheheartofafrica.blogspot.com.

RIDE ALONG ON
NIKKI BOYD'S OTHER ADVENTURES . . .

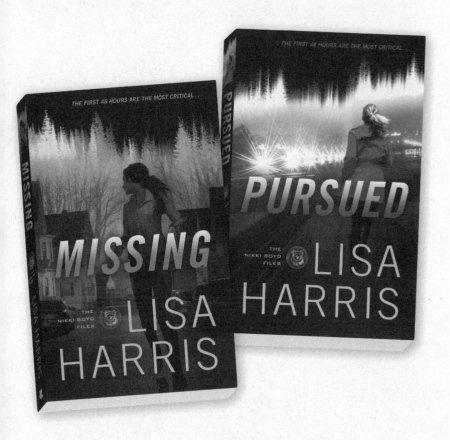

Christy Award–winning and bestselling author
Lisa Harris puts you right into the action in
these fast-paced thrillers.

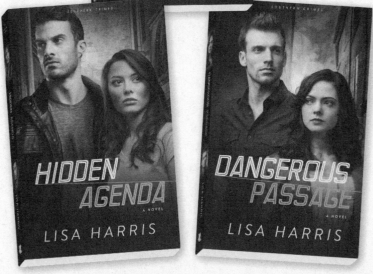

meet

LISA HARRIS

---

lisaharriswrites.com

AuthorLisaHarris

@heartofafrica